SHAYAN VIRANI

Silent Ties

Tangled Fates

First edition

ISBN: 979-8-218-86321-0

This book was professionally typeset on Reedsy.
Find out more at reedsy.com

Chapter 1

It's a busy Friday evening, and the popular burger place down the street buzzes with conversations, the clatter of trays, and the steady hum of machinery. Every table is claimed, filled with laughter, quiet murmurs, or the occasional outburst from a restless group. Amid the noise, a figure steps in, his mid-length messy hair settling down from the wind outside, his skateboard tucked under one arm, eyes scanning the room like he's searching for more than just a seat.

He orders his usual, a spicy chicken sandwich, with everything but pickles, and a cookie. He looks around for a place to sit. All the usual spots are taken, except for one. A girl sits alone at a corner table, idly picking at her fries, her expression distant, as if she's somewhere far from the chaos around her.

The figure hesitates, then makes his way over. He stops by her table, casting a long shadow over her tray. "Hey," he says, voice steady but unreadable. "Mind if I sit here? No other spots."

The girl looks up, startled from her thoughts. For a moment, she seems ready to refuse, but something shifts in her gaze of dark colored eyes. "Sure," she says, almost reluctantly, gesturing with a quick nod towards the seat across from her.

He sits, the sound of wrappers crinkling breaking the silence between them. At first, they don't speak, two strangers sharing a table by necessity. But then, almost imperceptibly, the air shifts. A fleeting glance, a passing comment about the noise or the crowd, something small cracks the silence, and a conversation begins.

There's a strange weight in the air, like the world outside has just taken a breath, waiting. Shawn settles into the seat, unwrapping his sandwich while Valerie quietly continues eating her fries. The noise in the restaurant is almost deafening: half the guys' football team is crammed at a long table near the back, laughing and shouting over each other, while the girls' volleyball team chats animatedly at the tables nearby. It's as if each team was celebrating a victory.

Shawn glances toward the chaos, then back at Valerie, noticing her distant expression as she absentmindedly pokes at her fries. She had straight hair, a darker shade of black than normal, but not jet black. The ends reach down to her mid torso. Her hair wasn't long, but it certainly was beautiful.

"You okay?" Shawn asks suddenly, his voice cutting through the awkward silence. Valerie looks up, startled. "Yeah, I'm fine," she replies quickly, but her voice wavers just enough to betray her. A smile emerged out of her pink lips, seemingly forced, her fingers fidgeting with the fry in her hand.

Shawn raises an eyebrow, unconvinced but not wanting to push. "You sure? You look like... I dunno, you've had a rough week or something."

Valerie stammers, "It's– it's nothing, really. Just one of those days." She averts her eyes, clearly trying to deflect, but the crack in her demeanor is evident.

Shawn doesn't press further. "Alright," he says simply, taking a bite of his sandwich and leaning back into the chair, "If you say so." The conversation dies down after that, but something about the interaction lingers. Valerie steals a glance at him, grateful he didn't pry too much, while Shawn senses there's more to her story than she's letting on.

As Shawn finishes his meal, he crumples the wrapper into a ball and tosses it onto his tray. Standing up, he looks down at Valerie and gives a small nod. "Thanks for the seat, and the company," he says casually, a faint grin tugging at the corner of his mouth.

Valerie looks up, caught off guard for a moment. "Oh, yeah. No problem," she replies, her voice softer than before.

Shawn walks toward the exit, his skateboard tucked under one arm, the cool night air visible through the glass doors. As he pushes them open, Valerie steals a quick glance his way, watching as he disappears into the night. A flicker of something crosses her mind, gratitude, curiosity, or maybe just relief that he didn't pry too much.

She sighs, leaning back in her seat for a moment before gathering her things. A few fries remain uneaten on her tray, but she doesn't feel like finishing them. As she stands, she notices the football and volleyball teams still in the back, their laughter and antics filling the air. She gives them a passing glance but doesn't linger, slipping out of the restaurant and into the quiet of the evening. The night ends as uneventfully as it began, but something about it feels different, like the faintest spark of change had been ignited.

Chapter 2

The morning sun pours through Shawn's window, casting streaks of light across his room as his cat stretches lazily at the foot of his bed. Shawn groggily rolls out of bed, shaking off sleep, and drops to the floor to exercise and stretch, his cat observing him with mild curiosity. The faint chill in the air from his open window invigorates him as he finishes, standing to gaze briefly at the sun rising from his window.

After a quick shower, Shawn throws on his baggy gray sweats, a hoodie, and his varsity-style jacket. With his headphones in, he shakes his head to the beat of a song, grabs his backpack, and locks the door behind him, munching on a protein bar.

Outside, the world feels alive, and Shawn takes in the fresh air as he waits for the bus. A group of familiar kids stands nearby, their chatter filling the quiet street. Aaron, his friend and occasional seatmate, gives him a nod as the bus pulls up. Once onboard, Shawn slouches into his usual spot by the window, zoning out as the city passes by in a blur.

At school, the day trudges on. First-period math is a challenge, not because it's hard, but because staying awake is. Shawn's head dips to the desk more than once, the monotony of the teacher's voice lulling him into brief moments of rest. Between classes, he keeps to himself,

4

blending into the crowd while observing more than interacting.

The afternoon hallways buzz with the usual energy. Shawn weaves through the crowd, headphones in, heading toward his locker. His mind is elsewhere, thinking about homework, his next gaming session, or maybe skateboarding later that evening.

As he turns the corner, someone barrels straight into him, sending Shawn stumbling back a step. "Hey, my bad man," Shawn says, pulling his backpack back up and glancing up.

The guy: tall, broad-shouldered, and clearly in a bad mood, glares at him like Shawn just insulted his entire family. His jaw tightens, and he steps closer, his voice dripping with hostility. "The hell is your problem?"

Shawn frowns, confused. "Dude, I literally just said sorry. Chill."

But the guy doesn't chill. Without warning, he swings a fist towards Shawn's face. Instinct takes over. Shawn ducks, the punch grazing just over his head, and he steps back to create distance. The hallway grows quieter as nearby students notice the tension.

Shawn straightens, his stance shifting slightly, "You really wanna do this here?" he asks, his voice calm but carrying a warning.

The guy doesn't answer, he's already charging again. This time, Shawn sidesteps, planting a quick jab to the guy's ribs that sends him stumbling. When the guy turns, Shawn doesn't give him the chance to swing again. In one smooth motion, he raises his backpack like a shield, blocking another sloppy punch, then shoves the guy backward with enough force to make him lose his balance.

The crowd now fully surrounds them, phones out, voices shouting out encouragement. The guy tries one last time, rushing Shawn like a bull. Shawn shifts his weight, hooks a leg around his opponent's, and sends him crashing to the floor with a thud.

"Enough," Shawn says, his voice low and controlled. He steps back, picking up his backpack. The guy groans on the floor, clutching his side. The students erupt into murmurs as Shawn walks away without a backward glance, his headphones already back in place.

For him, it's just another distraction in an already long day. But for the students, it's a scene they won't stop talking about anytime soon, something all the walls around the school will soon hear.

Lunch offers a slight reprieve. Shawn finds his usual quiet corner in the cafeteria, munching on a sandwich while scrolling through his phone. Occasionally, a passing friend or classmate stops to say hello, but Shawn keeps these interactions brief.

By the time the final bell rings, Shawn feels a mix of relief and fatigue. He boards the bus home, headphones in again, drowning out the day's noise.

Back at home, he kicks off his shoes and tosses his bag aside. After grabbing a snack, he opens his laptop and a bag of chips to unwind, immersed in the familiar escape of virtual reality and video games. He takes a break to finish some homework, zoning out but finishing it.

As the evening rolls in, Shawn grabs his skateboard and heads out. The crisp night air clears his mind as he carves through the streets toward the burger place down the street, his usual go-to spot for a late meal. Little does he know, tonight's trip will lead to more than just food, it will bring the start of something he never saw coming.

He joyfully swings the door open while humming to a song playing in his headphones, holding his skateboard in one hand and the familiar smell of burgers and fries filling the air as he steps inside. It was quieter this time, no noisy sports teams crowding the tables, just the hum of low conversations and the occasional ding of the kitchen bell, along with murmurs in the kitchen behind the counter.

As he scanned the half-empty place for a seat, his eyes landed on a familiar figure. The girl was there again, sitting at the same table, quietly eating her fries. She had the same distant look in her eyes as before, her fingers lightly drumming on the edge of the table as if lost in thought.

Shawn hesitated for a moment. He hadn't really thought much about their interaction last time, but now, seeing her in the exact same spot, looking just as withdrawn, he felt a small pull to approach.

He walked up to the counter, ordered his food, and glanced her way again as he waited. The place wasn't full, but he wondered if she'd mind if he joined her again, or if she even remembered him.

When Shawn's order was ready, he grabbed his tray and made his way over. He noticed Valerie hadn't looked up once, too engrossed in whatever thoughts were swirling in her head.

"Mind if I sit here again?" Shawn asked, his tone casual, almost the same as last time.

Valerie looked up, surprised, just like before. She blinked, recognizing him after a second. "Oh, uh, yeah, sure. Go ahead," she said, motioning to the empty seat across from her.

Shawn sat down, setting his tray on the table. For a moment, they were quiet, the sound of wrappers crinkling and fries crunching filling the space between them. Shawn wasn't the type to push a conversation, but something about Valerie's silence felt heavier this time.

"You always sit here alone?" Shawn finally asked, breaking the silence.

Valerie glanced up, her expression softening into something between a smile and a sigh. "I guess it's my go-to spot," she said. "Quiet, away from everyone."

Shawn nodded. "Yeah, I get that. Sometimes it's better to just… have your own space."

Valerie nodded, picking at a fry. "What about you? You always come here alone?"

"Pretty much," Shawn said with a small shrug. "Not really a people person, I guess. Plus, the food's good."

That earned a tiny laugh from Valerie, small, but genuine. It surprised even her.

The conversation stayed light, just like before, but it lingered a little longer this time. Shawn didn't push, and Valerie didn't offer much, but there was an unspoken understanding between them: a quiet acknowledgment that maybe, sitting together wasn't so bad.

When Shawn finished his food, he stood up and nodded to her again. "Thanks for the seat."

"Yeah," Valerie replied softly, glancing up at him. "See you around."

As Shawn left, Valerie found herself watching him again, just for a moment. She didn't know why, but something about him made her feel… not so alone.

Chapter 3

Val's mornings start with the soft glow of sunlight streaming into her cozy, aesthetic room as she opens the curtains, letting the day begin with warmth. She washes her face, brushes her teeth, and turns on a light, cheerful morning song, its melody filling the air while she stretches by her bedside. Her first task of the day is feeding her pets. She showers some fish food into the tank near her bed, watching the fish dart around their tank.

She yawns and with a small, peaceful smile, moves on to get dressed in a stylish yet comfy outfit that suits her mood. With the quiet house all to herself, Val spends the next few hours immersed in her studies. She logs into online meetings and courses, her focus unwavering as she works through her assignments. When lunchtime rolls around, she steps away from her screen to make herself something simple, eating alone in the quiet kitchen, she's used to being home alone often.

After lunch, the afternoon slows down as Val takes a break to enjoy her favorite drama shows, curled up in her hanging chair, her mind lost in the stories she loves. It's her way of escaping the solitude that sometimes feels overwhelming. By the time evening approaches, she refreshes herself, fixing her hair and adding a subtle touch of makeup before heading out.

The burger place is her escape, a place to break free from the monotony, to be surrounded by noise, and to reclaim a little piece of the world outside her quiet home.

Wow it's loud today, she wonders, walking into the restaurant. She stands nearby the order kiosk, waiting for her order and glances around. A little girl catches her eye. The girl smiles at her while ignoring her dad, who tries to get the girl's attention to feed her. Val waves at her and she laughs and finally turns around. Val watches her be handfed by her father, and smiles as the little girl gives her father a hard time, not eating anything and playing with her dolls. She turns around to the announcement of her order number, thanks the cashier and walks to her little comfort spot to eat and lose herself in her thoughts.

In one of the corner booths sat two people she vaguely recognized from her time in middle school. Natalia and Alex. Two of the most popular people in the school ever since elementary. They weren't hard to spot, Alex's focused expression as he gestured at something on his phone, and Natalia's signature vibrant energy as she leaned forward, teasing him about whatever he was showing her.

Val looked out the window and bit into a fry. She thought about what she would do tomorrow, considering it was Friday and she wouldn't have much work to do.

From the corner of her eye, she notices a figure walk up to her.

"Hey," he said, "Mind if I join you again?"

Valerie looked up, slightly surprised.

"Oh hey again," she says, her eyes flicking around for a moment, as if deciding, before she gave a small nod. "Yes."

Shawn sat down across from her, both of them quiet for a few moments. There was something different about the atmosphere today, still that same unspoken understanding from last time, but something else too. Neither of them seemed eager to fill the silence, and somehow, that was just fine.

After a few moments, Valerie broke the silence, her voice softer than usual. "So, how's the skateboarding going?" she asked, gesturing towards his skateboard, trying to keep it light.

Shawn glanced up, surprised at her question. "It's chill," he replied, a small smile tugging at his lips. "I like it... it's kind of like my escape, my way of having fun, y'know?"

Valerie nodded. "I get that."

The conversation didn't go much deeper than that, but somehow, it didn't feel forced either. They just... existed in the same space for a while, the kind of quiet understanding that didn't require constant words to fill the gaps.

When Shawn finished his food, he stood up, offering a nod of gratitude. "Thanks for letting me sit with you, again."

Valerie gave him a small smile. "Yeah. Catch you around."

As he walked out, Valerie found herself reflecting on these little interactions with him, they were always the same, but something about them made her feel a certain way.

Valerie got up and walked past the table of the other two.

She noticed them watching Shawn skateboard away.

Natalia noticed him first. She nudged Alex with her elbow, nodding toward Shawn.

"Hey, isn't that the guy from last week?" Natalia whispered. "The guy who won that fight?"

Alex glanced up, "Yeah, I think so. Didn't he sit with that girl? What's her name... Valerie?"

"Valerie," Natalia confirmed, her tone curious. "She's always alone, huh?"

Chapter 4

The school bell rings, signaling the end of the first period. Shawn walks out of the classroom, running his hand through his messy hair, already thinking about what to do next. He spent the entire class zoning out, the lesson barely catching his attention. He doesn't care much for English, not the way others do. He doesn't have the patience for novels and essays. his mind always gravitates toward more physical outlets, like skateboarding or gaming. But today, the teacher announces a new group project, and Shawn's name gets paired with someone he hasn't spoken to much before: Alex.

Shawn's seen Alex around, of course. The guy's smart, known for his academic achievements, always with his nose in a book or tapping away on his phone, typing out some assignment or message. Not the type of guy Shawn usually hangs out with, but this assignment is mandatory, and the two have to work together.

Alex meets Shawn by the lockers, looking a little out of place but trying to mask it with a calm expression. He adjusts his glasses as he sees Shawn approach, running a hand through his messy brown hair.

"Hey," Alex says, his voice a bit hesitant. "We're paired for the project, right?"

Shawn nods, leaning against the lockers and folding his arms. "Yeah, looks like it." He eyes Alex, noticing the lack of assurance in his tone. "What's the project about?"

"It's about symbolism in literature," Alex replies, a slight frown creasing his forehead. "We need to pick a book and discuss the deeper meanings. I was thinking of something like The Great Gatsby, but I guess we could go with whatever."

Shawn grins, already half-distracted. "You're probably way ahead on this, huh?" He knows Alex's reputation for being the "smart guy" around school, always on top of assignments and acing everything. Shawn's more of a wing-it kind of guy. "I'm just here for the grade," he adds with a chuckle.

Alex's lips twitch into a faint smile, the corner of his mouth lifting just a little. "I don't mind helping out. But we should at least make it interesting, right?"

Shawn shrugs, pushing himself off the lockers. "Sure, whatever. As long as we're not bored to death, I'm good."

As they walk toward the cafeteria, Shawn and Alex fall into a natural rhythm, exchanging thoughts about the project.

"I've never been great with symbolism," Shawn admits, his tone casual. "It's like reading between the lines, but sometimes I'm just trying to get through the lines first."

Alex snorts lightly, the sound soft but genuine. "I get that. But symbolism isn't as complicated as people make it sound. It's just understanding what's not being said. Like, Gatsby's whole thing with the green light, it's about desire, yearning for something impossible. It's pretty straightforward if you think about it."

Shawn glances over at Alex, his brow furrowed in thought. "Huh, guess I never looked at it like that." He pauses for a moment, the wheels turning. "You really like this stuff, huh? English, literature, all of it."

Alex shrugs, pushing his glasses back up the bridge of his nose. "Yeah, it's… it's kind of like a game for me. Decoding things, finding patterns. Not that it always makes sense, but it's a challenge."

Shawn nods, eyes half-glancing at the lunchroom doors ahead.

13

"Sounds like my kind of thing. Just a little less complicated."

They reach the cafeteria doors, and Alex holds one open for Shawn, stepping through first. The noise of students eating, talking, and laughing fills the air. They scan the room for a place to sit, and Alex spots a table by the windows where he usually sits with Natalia.

"There's a spot," Alex says, gesturing toward the table. "Come sit with us."

Shawn follows his gaze and spots Natalia sitting alone, her phone in hand, quietly absorbed in whatever she's reading. He nods, more out of curiosity than anything else. "You two always sit there?"

Alex shrugs, a small smile tugging at his lips. "Yeah, pretty much. I mean, she's my best friend, so…"

Shawn glances at Alex, surprised by the easy admission. "Best friend, huh?"

Alex nods again, his gaze softening as he looks over at Natalia. "Yeah. She's one of the few people who gets me, you know? She's not like the others."

Shawn processes this, still unsure about the dynamic between them but not wanting to pry too much. "Alright, lead the way."

As they approach the table, Natalia looks up from her phone, her gaze steady, but she doesn't seem startled, just like she expected them to come over. There's an air of quiet confidence about her.

"Hey, Nat," Alex greets her with a small nod. "Mind if we sit here?"

Natalia doesn't immediately answer, her eyes briefly flicking between Shawn and Alex before she gives a small nod. "Sure. You guys are a bit late, though."

Shawn slides into the seat across from her, his usual laid-back demeanor settling in. He watches her for a moment, noting how calm and collected she seems. There's something about her presence that draws him in, but he doesn't say anything.

14

For a few minutes, they all sit quietly, the background chatter filling in the silence naturally. Shawn's attention drifts, watching a group of younger students spill out of the cafeteria doors, laughing and jostling one another as they head outside. He can't help but notice the subtle patterns of people's interactions, the way Natalia gestures with her hands slightly when she talks, or how Alex taps his pen absentmindedly against his notebook.

Eventually, Alex breaks the quiet. "So, about the project," he says, opening his notebook and tapping at the pages. "I think we should choose a scene from Gatsby that really sticks out. Something with obvious imagery but a deeper meaning at the same time."

Shawn leans back in his chair, trying to keep up but mostly letting his eyes wander across the cafeteria. "Okay, okay… I think I can do that. Just tell me what to look for."

Natalia chuckles softly, watching them. "You'll do fine. Just don't make it more complicated than it is."

Shawn glances at her, raising a brow. "I'll try. No promises."

Chapter 5

The crisp autumn air is refreshing as Natalia walks down the tree-lined street, the faint sound of rustling leaves accompanying each step. She can hear the steady rhythm of her sneakers hitting the pavement, her strides purposeful and confident. She's used to this quiet solitude, even if the reason for today's walk is a bit unusual.

In the back of her mind, she can still hear Mrs. Carter's praise from earlier that morning, and a smile pulls at her lips.

"You're one of the brightest students I've ever had, Natalia.
Always reliable, always on top of things. You'll go far."
It's not the first time she's heard such words from teachers, and certainly not the first time from Mrs. Carter. But somehow, hearing them today feels different. She's always been the type to get things done, whether it's academic achievements, athletic triumphs, or maintaining a solid social circle. People like her are often expected to be perfect, balancing everything effortlessly. And that's what she does, or at least makes it look easy. But to be truly acknowledged, for someone to pause and genuinely appreciate her for who she is, that feels... rare.

Her thoughts drift as she steps onto the familiar sidewalk leading up to the student's house. She adjusts the envelope in her hand, carefully holding the papers inside. Mrs. Carter had entrusted her with delivering these documents to a student who's been home schooled for a while.

Most of the time, Natalia wouldn't think twice about it, but there's something different about today. Maybe it's the fact that she's used to being in the spotlight, captain of the track team, a standout in classes, always surrounded by friends, she's rarely given a task that's so personal. She's used to performing for crowds, leading teams, being the one everyone else looks to. But here, at this moment, she's just doing something quietly on behalf of someone else. It's a different kind of responsibility. A chance for her to do something good without fanfare.

As she walks up the front steps of the apartment, she feels the cool metal of the door handle under her fingertips, and she pauses for just a moment. She's always been a little hesitant with situations like this. But that feeling doesn't last long. She's never one to doubt herself for too long. If there's one thing Natalia knows, it's that she's capable of handling whatever comes her way.

The door in front of her is simple, an apartment just like any other in the complex. Modestly decorated, but with an inviting charm.

She knocks three times, the sound sharp and clear in the quiet street, and then takes a step back, casually crossing her arms.

She doesn't look around, doesn't feel the need to. She knows people are everywhere, but it's never bothered her. She's used to people noticing her, whether it's for her athleticism, her smarts, or just her presence in any room. She's comfortable with it now, and she's learned how to carry that kind of attention without letting it get to her head. Confidence comes naturally when you've spent years perfecting the balance of school, sports, and social life.

The house is silent after her knock. She checks her phone briefly, nothing urgent, and looks back toward the door, waiting for someone to answer.

The world feels like it's on pause, her mind still buzzing with the events of the day, the expectations of others, and the weight of this responsibility. A simple delivery. Nothing too extraordinary. But it's just another moment that shapes the person she's becoming.

The door creaks open slowly, breaking the stillness of the moment. Natalia sees Valerie standing there, her casual style, comfy hoodie and jeans, giving her an approachable, laid-back vibe. Her expression softens as she meets Natalia's eyes, and for a split second, there's a flash of recognition.

"You're Natalia, right?" Valerie says, her tone warm but with that quiet energy Natalia recognizes. "I'm Val. You must be the one the counselor mentioned. Come on in."

Natalia nods, her smile returning. "Yeah, that's me. I've got your papers from the school," she says, holding up the envelope.

Valerie steps aside, gesturing for her to come in. As Natalia walks through the doorway, she catches a glimpse of the living room. It's cozy, but there's an undeniable sense of lived-in chaos, like someone's always moving around here. A couple of books on the coffee table, a backpack tossed near the couch, some sneakers abandoned in the corner.

Valerie takes the envelope with a grateful smile. "Thanks so much for doing that. It's very kind of you." She looks at Natalia, sizing her up a little more carefully now that they're standing face-to-face. "I'm sure you're used to this kind of thing, huh? Always being the one people count on."

Natalia laughs softly, slightly uncomfortable with the way Valerie sees her. It's true, though. She's the one people always come to, whether it's for schoolwork, advice, or just a helping hand. But there's something different about this moment. She doesn't feel like she's in her usual zone of expectations. "I guess I get it done," she says, trying to keep things light.

Valerie nods and steps further into the living room, motioning for Natalia to follow her. "Come on. You want a drink or anything? I can offer you water or soda, nothing too fancy, though."

Natalia steps in, feeling a bit like an intruder in this personal space, but the vibe is calming, so she relaxes. "Water's fine, thanks."

The soft clink of a glass on the counter breaks her train of thought. Valerie returns, handing Natalia a cold water bottle.

For a brief moment, there's silence between them, a lull in the conversation as Natalia takes a sip of water and Valerie fiddles with the hem of her hoodie. Natalia notices a few moments where Valerie's eyes flicker down, almost like she's debating whether to say something more personal. But instead, Valerie just shakes her head, like she's pushing a thought away.

"Anyway," Valerie says, breaking the silence with a shift in her posture. "I appreciate you bringing this by. It's… really kind of you."

"No problem," Natalia replies with a soft smile. "It's really no trouble at all."

As Valerie steps back into the living room, she looks at Natalia, her voice quieter. "I always looked up to you back in middle school." She pauses, setting the envelope aside on the counter as she glances over at Natalia. "You were, like, the ideal student. Smart, athletic… You always knew what you were doing. I couldn't help but think, 'I wish I was like her.'"

Natalia is taken aback, her brows lifting slightly in surprise. "You looked up to me?"

She was used to inspiring people, but this felt different.

Valerie gives a small, almost embarrassed shrug. "I mean, everyone did. You were the one everyone respected. I was the quieter, more invisible one. I tried to get noticed, but it was always… you. You had it all together."

A soft, surprised smile appears on Natalia's face. "I had no idea you've known me for that long."

Valerie looks at her with a hint of humor. "Yeah, well, you wouldn't. You were too busy being the star athlete, the straight-A student. It wasn't until high school that I figured out we weren't all so different after all."

Natalia shifts her weight, clearly processing this new piece of information. "I always thought I was just doing my best to survive school," she admits, half laughing, half surprised. "I didn't think anyone would pay attention back then."

Valerie chuckles. "That's just how it works, I guess. People notice when you don't try to stand out, but you just... do."

There's a beat of silence as they both consider the change in perspective. Natalia speaks up again, but this time her voice carries a little more curiosity. "But I gotta ask, why are you home schooled? Why not just stick with school like everyone else?"

Valerie looks down, then back up at Natalia, a sigh escaping her lips. "I don't really like the school environment. I never have. It's too much, too much pressure, too many people pretending to be something they're not." She smiles softly, a little more to herself than to Natalia. "Homeschooling just made sense. I can work at my own pace, focus on what matters, without the extra distractions."

Natalia looks at her for a moment, considering the answer. "I get that. School is just... chaos, really. Everyone's just trying to outdo everyone else, acting like they have it all figured out."

Valerie nods slowly, her voice becoming more reflective. "I'm starting to think that's the way to go. I mean, I barely make it through school some days. The pressure, the noise... It's like everyone's always in competition."

"You probably are better off homeschooling, too," Natalia points out, her eyes twinkling with a hint of playfulness.

"Trust me, as someone who's really involved with school, it's tough." Valerie laughs softly. "Yeah, no kidding. I can't stand the school environment. The drama. It's too much. Maybe I just haven't figured out a better option yet." She looks away for a second, as if considering something, before returning her gaze to Natalia. "I guess it's kind of nice being here, though. Hanging out alone in my home, still getting the work done, no drama."

Natalia grins and looks around, "Yeah, it's pretty chill. I like the vibe you've made here."

Valerie's expression softens, she wonders what kind of vibe Natalia's talking about, but she thanks her for the supposed compliment.

There's a brief moment of connection, a sense that this simple exchange means more than just a school errand, before Valerie glances at the clock.

"Hey, I don't want to keep you. I'm sure you've got stuff to do today," Valerie says, pulling herself together.

"Yeah," Natalia agrees. "I should probably get going. But... if you ever need help with anything, let me know."

"I will, I'll probably find your Instagram and message you there, it shouldn't be that hard anyways." Natalia chuckled and thanked Valerie for the company and water, leaving her to herself again.

She walks out, reflecting upon her thoughts, whenever she glanced at Val at the restaurant, she'd expected Val to be some sort of secluded teenage girl, which she was, but the vibe she gave off was something unique. It was sort of mysterious, while also comfortable and sweet.

Meanwhile, Valerie locks the door and jumps onto her bed in her room, she taps her phone and follows Natalia on Instagram, hoping this could turn into something valuable.

Chapter 6

The next day, the last bell rung, sending students pouring into the halls like a flood breaking through a dam. Shawn swings his backpack over one shoulder, glancing at Alex as they step into the current.

"You heading straight home?" Alex asks, dodging a kid recklessly cutting across the hallway.

Shawn shrugs. "Yeah, for a bit. Might head out later."

Alex adjusts his books under one arm. "I was thinking of hitting the library. Got that project to work on."

Shawn raises a brow. "You actually care about that?"

Alex chuckles. "It's twenty percent of our grade, bro."

Shawn yawns lazily, shaking his head. "Yeah, alright. What time?"

"Six?"

Shawn nods. "Cool."

They step outside, the afternoon sun stretching their shadows across the pavement. Alex stretches his arms with a groan. "Bet you're gonna forget and show up late."

Shawn smirks. "Bet you're gonna be there early with, like, six pages of notes and a whole PowerPoint ready."

Alex grins. "I mean, do you want to fail?"

Shawn tilts his head. "Nah, but I also don't wanna be the guy who actually tries."

Alex snorts. "You try at the gym."

"Yeah, 'cause looking good is a grade that actually matters."

Alex rolls his eyes but laughs, shaking his head. "See you at six, idiot."

Shawn gives him a lazy salute before heading toward the bus stop. Alex watches him go, shaking his head with an amused smile before heading the other way.

Shawn steps onto the bus, slipping into his usual seat near the back. The ride is the same as always, too loud, too cramped, a mix of muffled conversations and music playing from someone's half-broken earbuds. He props an elbow against the window, watching the streets pass by in a blur of dull colors and neon lights. His mind drifts, half-listening to a group of freshmen laughing a few rows ahead, their energy too high for this late in the day.

At one stop, a kid nearly trips stepping off, earning a round of chuckles from the back. Shawn smirks, shaking his head. Same bus, same chaos.

As the ride stretches on, the crowd thins, leaving only a handful of students spread out in their usual spots. His stop finally comes up, and he pushes himself up, stepping off into the cool evening air. The wind cuts through his hoodie, but he barely notices. It's routine by now, home first, then out again.

His apartment isn't far, just a few minutes down the road. As soon as he steps inside, he kicks off his shoes, lets his bag drop carelessly by the door, and heads straight to his room.

He falls into his chair, powering on his console with a lazy flick of his finger. The screen glows to life, the familiar startup sound humming through his room.

By the time Shawn arrives at the library, Alex is already there, leaning back in his chair, earbuds dangling loosely around his neck, deep in conversation with Natalia. They're seated at the back table, a couple of textbooks and notebooks scattered between them. Natalia's eyes light up when Shawn walks in, and she gives him a small, welcoming smile.

"Yo, Shawn!" Alex calls out, looking up from the pile of papers. "You're late!"

Shawn grins, dropping his skateboard next to the chair across from them. "I'm never late. You're just too early."

Alex smirks, nudging Natalia with his elbow. "This is Natalia. You remember her from the other day at lunch?"

Shawn glances at Natalia, giving her a nod. "Yeah, we met briefly." His eyes narrow in a teasing way. "I didn't realize you two were already bonding over project stuff."

Natalia laughs softly, crossing her arms. "It's a project I have, not a therapy session." She looks over at Alex, raising an eyebrow. "Are you sure you don't want to add some 'dramatic flair' to this? Maybe a few memes for the target audience?"

Alex laughs and shakes his head. "Maybe if I want us to fail, but go ahead, pitch it." He gestures to her with a mock-serious expression.

Shawn interrupts, "Hang on, what about our project?"

Alex playfully assures him and smiles, "I've got over half of it done already, don't worry."

Shawn chuckles, "As expected, you big-brained moron. I'll count on you for the rest of the project then."

He slides into his seat, leaning back with a smirk.

"I'm intrigued. What's this project, then?

Natalia shrugs, glancing at the prompt sheet Alex had spread out. "I have an extracurricular project, I'm designing a marketing strategy for some ridiculous, over-the-top product. The school wants it realistic, though, so we're stuck with this... 'luxury pet bed' idea." She snickers. "You know, for the pampered pets with more style than us."

Shawn glances at Alex, then back at Natalia. "Luxury pet beds? Sounds like you're all about pampering the rich dogs." He taps his chin. "What's the budget for this thing? Like a few hundred for a mattress?"

Alex chuckles, shaking his head. "Yeah, that's the goal. We're supposed to make it seem like it's the next must-have thing. It's all about branding and who we're selling it to."

Shawn settles into the seat, crossing his arms with a relaxed smirk. "Alright, so we're designing a luxury dog bed for the rich, spoiled pups, huh?" He glances at both of them. "What's the plan then? Are we making this thing look like a throne, or are we going for some minimalist, eco-friendly thing with a price tag that could make anyone's head spin?"

Alex shrugs, scrolling through some notes on his phone. "Honestly, I'm leaning toward something more extravagant, something that screams 'money.' Like, imagine a pet bed lined with memory foam and wrapped in some kind of faux-fur material. We could brand it as the 'ultimate' luxury experience for dogs. But it's gotta look sleek, you know? Not too over-the-top."

Natalia raises an eyebrow. "Memory foam for dogs? That's... wow. How much do you think we can sell a dog bed like that for?"

Shawn chuckles. "Well, if we're aiming high, I'm thinking at least a few hundreds. Dogs deserve the best, right? Or are we trying to sell them the 'exclusive' lifestyle, like only the 'elite' can afford this level of comfort?"

Alex leans forward with a serious expression. "Exactly. It's all about creating that perception. We're not just selling a bed, we're selling a lifestyle. If it feels high-end, people will want it, even if their dogs can barely fit in it."

Shawn glares at him, "I was joking, genius."

Natalia nods, feeling the energy of the brainstorming session start to build. "I like it. Let's throw in a 'limited edition' angle. We can say it's only available to a certain group, maybe a special 'elite' membership for pet owners. People will eat that up."

Shawn laughs, shaking his head. "You guys are really taking this seriously." He grabs a notebook and starts jotting down ideas. "I'm liking the vibe though. Limited edition... Maybe we could tie it to an influencer campaign? Get a few high-profile pet influencers to back it."

She chuckles, "Now we're talking. A dog with more followers than me? That's the dream."

Alex snickers. "It's not about the dog, though. It's about the brand. We get the right influencer, the right image, and bam, you've got yourself a viral product. All we need is some high-quality visuals and catchy branding."

The three of them start bouncing ideas off each other, their energy rising as they get more into the concept. Shawn, usually laid back and distant, finds himself genuinely enjoying the brainstorming session. There's something about the way Natalia and Alex think, how they push and challenge each other, that brings out a sharper side in him.

It's not long before the whole table is covered in scattered papers, sketches, and notes, each person adding their ideas to the pile. The conversation flows easily, as if they've been doing this for years, not just an hour.

As they wrap up the session, Shawn leans back, looking over the ideas with a satisfied smirk. "I think we've got something here," he says. "A dog bed that's gonna make people question their life choices."

Natalia chuckles. "If anyone's questioning their life choices over a dog bed, we're doing something right."

Alex grins. "Exactly. Now, we just need to figure out how to sell this thing to a bunch of teenagers who probably don't even own pets."

Shawn shrugs. "That's what the influencer campaign is for. If a dog can have its own Instagram account, anything's possible."

The group laughs, the air light and easy as they wrap up. Despite the odd nature of their project, the bond that's starting to form feels real. It's not just about the assignment; it's about working together, exchanging ideas, and pushing each other to think bigger.

Shawn leans back in his chair, glancing around at the team. "Well, this was a lot less painful than I thought it would be."

Natalia smirks. "I can't get used to it. I still have to actually present this nonsense."

Alex laughs, shoving his papers into his bag. "We'll make it work. If we can make a dog bed sound like the next iPhone, we're golden."

The trio stands up, collecting their things, the conversation still light and easy as they walk out of the library, a little more connected than before.

Chapter 7

The next few days slip into an easy rhythm. Between school, gym sessions, and late-night gaming, Shawn finds himself settling into a new kind of normal, one where meeting up with Alex and Natalia at the library after class doesn't feel forced. The project gives them an excuse, but it's not the reason anymore. The conversations stretch beyond marketing strategies and branding; they joke, they argue over the best music to listen to while working, and Shawn finds himself, against all odds, not hating the company.

The group's brainstorming session stretches longer than expected, their conversation bouncing between actual work and playful banter. Alex sketches out rough designs for the luxury pet bed while Natalia critiques his artistic abilities, laughing at the exaggerated way he draws the product.

"Why does it look like a throne?" Natalia teases, nudging his arm.

"Because rich people love making their pets feel superior," Alex shoots back.

Shawn leans over, inspecting the drawing with an amused smirk. "I mean, I'd buy one for a dog if I had a million dollars to waste."

Natalia shakes her head. "See? This is why our marketing needs to be top-tier. We have to make people believe they *need* this, even if it's dumb."

They go back and forth, tossing around ridiculous slogans, "Because your dog deserves better than you," "A bed fit for a canine king," before finally jotting down a few serious ideas.

Eventually, as the conversation slows, Natalia taps her fingers against the table, suddenly thoughtful. "You guys ever think about how small our group is?"

Alex raises an eyebrow. "What, are you trying to start a club or something?"

Natalia smirks, propping her chin up with her hand. "Not a club, but... I do know someone who might fit in with us."

Alex raises an eyebrow. "Oh yeah? Who?"

Natalia glances at Shawn for a second, almost like she's expecting him to recognize the name before saying, "Valerie." She taps her pen against the table and leans back, "Apparently, she knew me since middle school."

Alex furrows his brows. "Valerie...? I think I've heard of her."

"She's homeschooled now," Natalia explains, glancing between them. "But she's cool. Smart. I think she'd vibe with us."

She hesitates for a second, "She could also use some company."

Shawn leans back in his chair, wondering if this girl Natalia is talking about is the same girl he used to sit with to eat.

Alex shrugs. "I mean, I don't mind. If she's chill and actually contributes, sure."

"Great," Natalia says, already pulling out her phone. "I'll tell her to come over."

Shawn watches as she types out a message, his curiosity slightly piqued. He wonders if the reason Natalia glanced at him while saying her name is because she knows that it is the girl he would eat with.

Just as Natalia finishes sending the message, her phone vibrates with a reply. She grins.

"She actually lives nearby. Said she'll stop by."

Shawn's fingers pause on his skateboard, his brow slightly furrowing. "Valerie?" he repeats, the name tugging at something familiar.

"Yeah," Natalia says, smiling, sliding her phone into her pocket. "I'm sure y'all have met."

Shawn shrugs, keeping his face neutral. "Maybe. Guess we'll see."

Alex leans forward, resting his arms on the table. "So, should I expect another Natalia type? All popular and overly confident?"

Natalia scoffs. "Please."

Before Alex can respond, the library doors slide open, and a girl steps inside. She scans the lobby before spotting them, hesitating for a brief moment before heading over to their secluded table a distance away from the entrance, Shawn's gaze sharpens slightly as she approaches, and for the first time in a while, surprise flickers through him.

It *is* her.

Valerie.

The quiet girl from the burger place.

Valerie reaches the table, her eyes briefly meeting Shawn's before she gives a shy smile to everyone else. "Hey." She stands awkwardly for a moment, as if unsure where to sit, but Natalia quickly gestures to the empty chair beside her.

Shawn leans back in his seat, arms folded casually across his chest, though his mind is elsewhere. The familiar feeling of her presence, the quiet energy she brings, it's all coming back to him now, the way she carried herself that night at the burger place, but he doesn't say anything yet.

Natalia tilts her head at him, noticing the slight recognition in Shawn's eyes, but she doesn't comment on it. Instead, she grins at

Valerie. "Welcome to the project. This is my project and these two fools here," she says, gesturing towards Alex, who nods at her with a genuine smile and Shawn, who stares into her eyes, as if communicating by just eye contact, "are helping me," she finishes.

Alex cracks in, "I'm just here to help, and by the looks of it, it seems like you already know Shawn?"

She nods her head and looks towards Shawn, who opens his mouth to say something but before he can, Alex speaks up.

"Well, I'm sure we'll make new memories today. We're about to make our mark with this project, right?"

Natalia laughs, "Save the corniness idiot"

Alex rolls his eyes and jokingly sticks out his tongue at her, signifying towards a playful yet close friendship between the two.

"Let's get to work. Alex and Shawn, y'all focus on the artistic details and drawing, I'll get Val caught up," Natalia announces.

They nod and get to work. Shawn watches Alex smoothly command the pencil's tip, sketching a design. Despite the small, unexpected reunion, he can't deny the feeling that something's starting to shift. This project, this group, there's potential here. And he's curious about what might come of it.

As the deep project work with friendly banter continues, the group slowly falls into a rhythm, the awkwardness dissolving as they start discussing their project again. Shawn leans in, listening to the dynamic between Alex and Natalia, both tossing out ideas with ease. Valerie, though still a bit quiet, seems to be warming up to them, offering thoughtful suggestions here and there.

Alex jots down notes, taking the lead on organizing their ideas while Natalia chimes in, her eyes bright with excitement.

Valerie occasionally glances at Shawn, and he can't help but notice the subtle shift in her demeanor. She seems like she's trying to figure him out, just as he is with her.

"Alright," Alex says, clapping his hands together. "We've got the bones of this thing down. Let's wrap it up for today and see what we can come up with next time. Sounds good?"

The others agree, and everyone starts packing up their things. Shawn stands up, grabbing his skateboard, and looks over at Valerie, who's collecting her things slowly.

"So," he starts casually, trying to keep the tone light. "How've you been?"

Natalia overhears him and looks at him, grinning, proud of herself for reuniting two potential friends, maybe more.

Valerie looks up, caught off guard for a moment. "Uh, good. Just… keeping to myself, mostly," she replies, her voice steady but soft.

Shawn nods, feeling the weight of the conversation hang between them. It's strange, this feeling of familiarity mixed with uncertainty.

"I guess we'll see how this group thing goes, huh?" Shawn says, grinning a little as he steps to the side, letting Val walk out first.

"Yeah, guess we will," she says, returning a small smile before stepping through the door.

As they walk out of the library, the cool air hits them, and Shawn breathes it in, glad to be out of the cramped room. He glances back at the other two, talking and laughing as they exit the building.

But there's something tugging at his mind, something he can't quite place..

Why does it feel like things are about to change?

He shakes off the feeling, determined to keep his focus on the project for now.

But deep down, he knows that there's more to this than just a school assignment. The group, these people, there's something more waiting for them. And Shawn isn't sure if he's ready for it. But he's about to find out.

Chapter 8

Monday feels like any other day. The group settles into their usual routines, school, studying, meeting up when they can. The library has become a common spot, but nothing feels out of the ordinary. If anything, things are more relaxed now that Valerie has joined them. She fits in naturally, blending with Natalia's energy while balancing out Alex and Shawn's dynamic. The conversations flow easier, the laughter a little more frequent.

The air in the school hallways feels heavier than usual, a mix of sweaty locker rooms, cheap cafeteria food, and the faint lingering scent of someone's too-strong cologne. The final bell has rung, and students spill into the halls, talking, shoving, laughing, just another chaotic end to the day.

Alex weaves through the crowd, sidestepping a half-open locker before someone slams it shut. His backpack tugs at his shoulder, weighed down with textbooks he knows he won't touch until last-minute panic sets in.

His mind is already elsewhere, thinking about meeting up with Shawn later, the project, and maybe squeezing in a few comments of banter before getting any real work done.

As he rounds the corner near the faculty office, making his way towards the school's dark hallways, something makes him slow down.

A man stands just outside the dark doorway, positioned like he's waiting for something. He's tall, dressed in unusual clothes, and completely out of place. No visitor's pass. No paperwork in his hands. He's not talking to anyone, just standing there, scanning the hallway like he's looking for someone.

Alex's stomach tightens. He doesn't know why, but something about the guy doesn't sit right. It's not just that he doesn't belong, he's too aware, like he's watching without wanting to be seen.

Alex keeps moving, but his steps slow. He debates getting a closer look, maybe even stopping at the water fountain nearby just to make it less obvious. But before he can decide, the man shifts. Without warning, he turns and starts walking toward the side exit.

Alex watches as he blends into the passing students, slipping away like he was never there.

For a second, Alex just stands there, fingers tapping against his backpack strap. Maybe he's overthinking it. Could've been a staff member, a janitor, some random parent. But then, why was he standing there like that?

Shaking off the feeling, Alex exhales and keeps walking. It's just been a long day. He's not about to let some weird moment throw off his whole week.

A few hours later, the four of them meet up at the library, nothing unusual about that. It's become a habit by now, studying together in the evening, half the time actually working on something, the other half joking around or getting distracted.

Natalia and Valerie are already there when Shawn and Alex arrive at the same time, Natalia leaned over a textbook, highlighter tapping against the page in thought. Valerie, meanwhile, is idly scrolling through something on her phone, looking vaguely bored.

"Look who finally decided to show up," Natalia teases as Shawn and Alex drop into their seats.

"Relax, we weren't even late," Shawn replies, setting his skateboard down beside his chair.

"Yeah, but we've been here long enough for Valerie to start reading *actual* study material out of boredom, so technically, you were late," Natalia counters.

Valerie raises an eyebrow. "I was *not* reading study material. I was looking up how long it takes to recover from caffeine addiction."

Alex smirks. "That's worse."

"Not if you think about it," Valerie argues, shutting off her phone and stretching her arms over her head. "I drink a *normal* amount of coffee. If anything, I'm enhancing my academic potential."

Shawn shakes his head, exhaling. "Y'all are a different breed."

For the next hour, the group actually gets some work done. The usual rhythm kicks in, Natalia keeping everyone on track, Alex doing most of the structuring, Valerie throwing in comments that somehow alternate between insightful and completely unhinged, and Shawn.. well, Shawn contributes when he feels like it.

It's easy. Comfortable.

Until Valerie nudges Natalia under the table.

"Don't look, but someone's staring," she mutters quietly.

Natalia, of course, immediately looks.

A man, middle aged, dark hoodie, sitting two tables away. He's not reading, not working on anything. Just sitting there, eyes locked in their direction.

The moment Natalia makes eye contact, the man casually gets up and leaves. Not rushed, not startled. Just… leaves.

Natalia exhales slowly. "Yeah, okay. That was weird."

Shawn, who was half-paying attention, glances between them. "What?"

"There was a guy staring at us," Valerie says, voice low. "Just got up and walked out."

Alex frowns. "How long was he watching?"

"I don't know," Valerie admits. "Long enough to creep me out."

Shawn rolls his shoulders, casting a glance toward the library exit. "Probably just some random dude."

"Yeah, maybe," Natalia says, but there's a tension in her voice that says she doesn't really believe that.

Alex leans across the table toward Shawn and Natalia, adding on to the suspicion of the guy earlier at school, "Earlier today, there was a guy near the faculty office. Just standing there. The second I looked at him, he dipped."

Natalia raises an eyebrow. "Like, he actually *ran?*"

"No, but he walked off quickly, like he wasn't supposed to be there."

Natalia stabs her fork into his food. "Think he's related to what happened right now?"

Alex shrugs. "I don't know. But I've been noticing things all week that don't feel right."

Shawn, who's been quiet up until now, speaks up. "Y'all are stressing it, just some old man, calm down."

Before Alex can answer, a couple of other students walk past, whispering to each other. The words are faint but catch Alex's attention.

"Did you hear? Emma Torres is missing. They found her stuff at the park, but no sign of her anywhere."

Shawn frowns, glancing at Alex. "Wait, Emma Torres? From our school? Nevermind keep stressing it."

Alex looks back to the students walking away. "Yeah man, they're saying she just vanished or went missing or something."

Shawn tilts his head. "Missing? What do you mean? How does someone just go missing?"

Alex shrugs. "They don't really know, I guess. But it sounds like something serious."

Natalia's gaze flickers between them. "Why do you think anyone didn't say anything sooner?"

"They probably don't want to cause a panic," Alex suggests.

Shawn looks a bit uneasy. "But it's not like they're keeping quiet about it. Rumors will be spreading fast."

The table falls quiet for a moment, each of them processing the idea of someone, someone they might've passed in the hall, suddenly being gone.

An hour or two later, they all left together. The air was colder now, the sky darkened, and the streets were quieter than usual.

Natalia and Valerie walk ahead, chatting about something random, some dumb joke Natalia made earlier. But even as they talk, Valerie keeps glancing over her shoulder, her face tense.

Shawn and Alex walk a little behind them, talking in low voices.

"So, did you hear anything more about Emma?" Alex asks, glancing at Shawn.

Shawn shrugs. "I barely even know her, but it's not something you just ignore."

Alex exhales sharply. "Maybe it's connected to that guy?"

Shawn nods. "It's getting a little too weird. Too many coincidences."

Then– footsteps.

At first, it's nothing. Just the usual background noise of a city at night.

But then, the pattern becomes obvious.

When they speed up, the footsteps speed up. When they slow down, the footsteps hesitate.

Valerie glances and pauses her gaze at Natalia, her expression tense. "It's the same feeling."

They stuck together walking as it got darker in the night, and that sense of someone following them got stronger, until one moment it got as loud as if it seemed like the footsteps were rapidly approaching them.

Valerie and Natalia increased their pace, walking in front of Shawn and Alex.

Alex looked down, hoping to see any shadows or signs of someone behind them.

Shawn didn't hesitate. He turned around fast and impulsively clenched his fists, ready for whatever is about to happen, but no one's there.

Alex stops, turns, scanning the street. The sidewalk is empty. The only movement comes from a few cars in the distance.

"Alright," Alex mutters. "The hell? That was weird."

Valerie hugs her arms. "Maybe it was just someone else walking home."

Shawn doesn't answer right away. He's still looking, scanning the street, the alleyways, the parked cars.

Something doesn't sit right with him.

Eventually, he exhales and turns back to the group. "C'mon. Let's just get home."

They keep walking, but the unease lingers.

None of them say it out loud. But tonight, they all feel it.

They're not just looking into something dangerous anymore.

Something dangerous is looking back.

Chapter 9

The next day, things get even stranger.

The school day passes in a haze. Nothing feels right, but no one can put their finger on exactly what it is. At lunch, Alex and Shawn sit together, exchanging quick glances every time a student walks by, half-expecting someone to approach them or maybe talk to them about the rumors.

"Dude," Shawn mutters, pushing his food around on his tray. "Did you hear anything else about Emma Torres? They still haven't found her?"

Alex shakes his head. "No. I checked some of the student boards, but there's not much new. It's like everyone's trying to act normal."

"Yeah, normal," Shawn replies, his voice laced with sarcasm. "Like when people go missing and everyone just keeps going to class like it's just another day."

"Maybe people are just in shock," Alex suggests, glancing around. "I mean, Emma wasn't exactly someone everyone knew."

"Doesn't matter," Shawn responds, his voice low. "It's still messed up."

Later that evening, the group meets up at the library again, more quietly than usual. Even with all the work they have, there's a quiet tension hanging in the air. No one speaks at first, each of them stealing quick glances at the others, trying to gauge if anyone else is feeling the same way.

Shawn, Natalia, Alex, and Valerie finally settle into their spots at the table.

Natalia sighs, breaking the silence. "So, I saw him. The guy. Again."

Valerie's eyes widened slightly. "Are you serious? What did he do?"

"Nothing," Natalia says quickly. "But he was just standing there. Watching. I couldn't get a good look at his face, but I'm sure it was him."

Shawn taps his fingers on the table. "We need to figure out who he is. This is too much to just ignore."

Alex leans forward, looking at the group. "We need to talk to people. Ask around. But we have to be careful."

"Yeah," Natalia agrees. "We don't know what we're dealing with yet."

Shawn nods, glancing at the window where the shadows stretch long across the pavement outside. "We've got to keep our eyes open. This guy… he's connected to something, I can feel it."

Friday.

The school trio is on edge the entire day, trying to avoid looking too suspicious while still piecing together the weird encounters and the rumors. As the day goes on, though, they start hearing bits and pieces from other students.

First, they hear someone talking about a girl named Emma Torres, the name is becoming more common, whispered among the halls. It's the same girl who went missing, but there's no confirmation of anything official.

The rumors just keep spreading.

Some say she was spotted leaving with a strange man. Others claim she just vanished without a trace.

None of it adds up.

By the end of the day, the tension between them is palpable. It's as if they're all afraid of what they might find if they dig too deep.

But they have no choice now. The pieces are falling into place, and the more they find out, the more they realize that the mystery is far bigger, and darker, than they originally thought.

Saturday

Shawn spent the day either gaming or working out. The group chat they had created was quiet, as if everyone had their own issues to worry about. At nightfall, he finally decided to get some rest, relieved from the constant activity, trying to focus on his usual gaming routine to take his mind off the whole situation. But every time he lowers the music, a chilling thought creeps in,

What if Valerie goes missing?
The idea lodges itself in his mind, unsettling and persistent. For someone who never feared anything, who lives recklessly, the realization shakes him.
Why does this scare me?
Why do I care?
Then his phone buzzes. It's a message from Alex.

Alex*:* "Dude, something's off. The guy was outside the school again. I'm not imagining this. He's been following us."

Shawn stares at the message for a long time. He doesn't respond immediately, not sure what to say.

He thought about going to the school to give Alex company along with the football team after their practice, but that idea waved off.

Instead, he gets up and walks to the window, tossing his phone on the bed, screen left open on Alex's chat. He looks outside, the shadows seem darker than usual.

And he knows. This time, it's not just a feeling.

They're not just dealing with someone following them. They're being targeted. But *why*? *Who*?

Shawn closed his eyes, struggling to suppress the storm of thoughts inside his mind. *You're too much, Shawn. Way too much.* The words dug into him like splinters, a reminder of what he'd been told, what he'd been, before he snapped. He winced, trying to push the memories back.

He imagines Valerie's eyes, zoned out, curious, always carrying some unspoken thought behind them. The way they flickered with amusement when she caught him off guard, or how they softened when she thought no one was looking. For a second, he can almost hear her voice, light, teasing, effortlessly slipping into their conversations like she'd always been there. He remembers the way she tilts her head when she listens, the way her laughter lingers for half a second longer than expected.

It's nothing special. It shouldn't be special.

But the thought of never hearing it again, of her becoming just another name whispered in the halls, another face on a missing poster, makes his grip tighten. His breath comes sharper.

His pulse spikes.

He opened his eyes, and they gleamed with a manic, almost predatory edge. A slow grin crept across his face, as if savoring the chaotic energy building inside him.

Let them try.

The thrill of the unknown surged through him, and for a split second, he felt the kind of excitement that had once driven him to the edge of madness.

His finger twitched involuntarily, an old, dangerous habit resurfacing, itching for a release. He couldn't help it.

Let them make their move, then it's our turn. My turn.

He grabbed his phone, fingers tapping quickly as he typed out a reply to Alex's message, eyes never leaving the screen. His thoughts darted from one violent idea to the next, a million possibilities flashing through his mind.

They don't know who they're messing with.

But just as quickly, his grin faded. He reread the message. His thumb hovered over the send button for a second before he erased everything, leaving only a simple thumbs-up emoji.

Better to let them think it's just another normal day. They had no idea what they were really up against.

Chapter 10

Monday

The soft light of early morning seeped through the white curtains of Natalia's bedroom, gently nudging her awake. Her phone buzzed on the nightstand, its glow just enough to disturb her peaceful slumber. With a groan, she stretched her arms above her head, the cool sheets brushing against her skin. The clock on her phone read 6:30 AM.

She opened her eyes, blinking a few times as her senses adjusted. The faint scent of lavender filled the room, thanks to the diffuser she had set up the night before. A small smile appeared on her lips as she let out a sigh of contentment.

But it didn't last long. The responsibility of the day ahead loomed in her mind. Today was no ordinary day, she had to finish an essay for school, run a few errands, and check in with the others about their investigation.

Natalia swung her legs out of bed, her bare feet hitting the cool wooden floor. She grabbed her phone and quickly scrolled through her messages.

One from Valerie. Another from Alex, giving her some info for the essay. The notifications about their investigation lingered in the back of her mind, but she quickly set it aside. She couldn't get lost in it right now.

With a deep breath, Natalia headed to the bathroom to start her morning routine. Her wavy blonde hair, slightly tousled from sleep, framed her face as she splashed cold water on her face to wake herself up. She stared at her reflection for a moment, her brown eyes looking back at her with a quiet determination. She wasn't the type to let the weight of the world show on her face, but beneath the surface, there was always something going on.

After brushing her teeth and freshening up, she changed into a casual outfit, black sweats and a slouchy cropped long sleeve top. She grabbed her favorite pair of sneakers from the closet and quickly slid them on.

In the kitchen, the smell of fresh coffee filled the air. Natalia poured herself a cup and sat at the small dining table, quickly eating breakfast, toast with avocado. She didn't need much, just enough to keep her going until lunch.

She checked her phone one last time. A message from Valerie: "Hey, do you want to meet up later?" Natalia smiled softly. She truly enjoyed her company.

There was something comforting about her presence, something easy. Maybe they could grab food after school.

With a quick sip of coffee, Natalia grabbed her bag, slung it over her shoulder, and walked out the door. As she headed to the bus stop, the chilly air of the morning hit her face. It was going to be another busy day, but Natalia was ready. One step at a time.

The bus ride to school was quiet for Natalia, as usual. She slipped her earbuds in, playing a mix of modern pop and some smooth indie tracks. Her mind was at ease this morning, no major stress weighing on her. Just the usual routine. As the bus pulled up to the school, Natalia put her phone away, preparing herself for the day ahead.

She met with her friends, Alex and some girls, just outside the school gates. Her old volleyball coach was always the one to unlock the gym, and she greeted her with a slight grin, looking a little too eager for a

Monday morning.

"Ready for another day?" she asked, her voice full of her usual energy.

"Yeah," Natalia replied, a small but genuine smile tugging at her lips. "Let's just get through it."

The bell rang, and they parted ways, heading to their first classes. Natalia's first stop was English, where she could always count on Mrs. Jacobs to make the lesson interesting. Today, they were discussing symbolism in classic literature, which suited Natalia just fine. She loved the way literature made her see the world in new ways.

Her next class was biology. They were studying cellular respiration, and Natalia found herself deeply engaged, answering questions with ease. Biology was one of her stronger subjects, and she appreciated the clarity it gave her in understanding the natural world around her.

When lunchtime came after other classes, Natalia headed to a quiet spot by the trees outside the cafeteria. Valerie had already sent her a text, asking about meeting up later. Natalia grinned and typed a quick reply, telling Valerie they should hang out after school. Valerie was home schooled, but they kept in touch regularly, and Natalia always enjoyed talking to her.

Natalia ate her lunch, more avocado toast and fruit, and glanced around the campus. It wasn't a huge school, but there was always a lot of activity during lunch hour. Some students gathered in groups, while others, like her, preferred to sit in solitude for a bit until her friends came. She didn't mind. She was always able to focus better when she had a quiet moment, but she enjoyed the company.

The afternoon passed in a blur of history, where they discussed ancient civilizations, and math, which Natalia wasn't as fond of but could still manage. The lessons were routine, but her mind kept wandering, trying to piece together the homework due at the end of the week. There was no rush to get through it, just the usual effort to balance everything.

At the end of the day, she walked to the bus, the quiet hum of the campus fading behind her. As she sat down, she glanced at her phone once more, Valerie had messaged again, confirming their plans to meet up soon. Natalia smiled, looking forward to a break from school.

Today had been another typical school day, and she was more than ready for the evening ahead, homework, a little relaxation, and then meeting up with Valerie to unwind.

The two met up later that day at the burger place, not knowing it could lead to a strange suspicion.

Valerie stared down at her burger, picking at it absentmindedly. She didn't look like herself. Her usual lively demeanor was gone, replaced by a subtle unease. Natalia noticed immediately.

"You okay?" Natalia asked, her voice quiet, sensing that something was off.

Valerie looked up, meeting her gaze, but there was a flicker of hesitation before she spoke. "I didn't tell you earlier... but I heard something last night."

Natalia's eyebrows furrowed in concern. "What kind of something?"

Valerie swallowed hard, her voice barely a whisper. "It was late, maybe two in the morning. I was lying in bed, trying to sleep, and I heard this sound. It wasn't like anything I'd ever heard before. Like a dragging, muffled yelling noise... and then footsteps. I thought maybe it was just an animal, but it didn't feel right. It was so close to my apartment building."

"Close to your building?" Natalia repeated, her stomach tightening. "What do you mean? Did you check?"

Valerie shook her head, her face pale. "I didn't want to. I just pulled the covers over my head and tried to ignore it. But later it felt like...

someone was trying to get in. I swear, I could hear the footsteps moving, and then that sound again. It felt like someone was right outside my window."

The words hit Natalia like a punch to the gut. "What? Who would be outside your window like that?" she murmured, her voice trembling slightly.

"I don't know," Valerie replied, her eyes wide with worry. "But it felt like they were watching me, waiting for me to do something. I've never been so freaked out in my life."

Before Natalia could respond, the TV hanging above the counter flickered on. The news anchor's voice echoed through the room, cutting through the quiet hum of conversations.

"...Authorities have confirmed that 16-year-old Emma Torres, a student from Riverside High, has gone missing. Last seen leaving school last Thursday afternoon, she never returned home. The police have issued a warning, as there are fears that the disappearance may be linked to a string of other recent cases..."

The news anchor continued, detailing Emma's last known whereabouts and urging anyone with information to come forward. But Natalia and Valerie couldn't hear the rest. They were too focused on the growing sense of dread swelling between them.

"Do you think..." Valerie started, but couldn't finish the sentence. She didn't need to. They both understood what was happening, and it wasn't just a simple missing person case. It was something much darker.

A flash of motion at the door broke their focus. Shawn stepped into the place, his usual confident stride making him stand out even in the busy restaurant. He spotted them immediately and made his way over to the table.

"What's up?" he asked, sliding into the booth beside Valerie with a casual grin. But as soon as he saw the serious expressions on their faces, his smile faded. "What's going on?"

Shawn's eyes narrowed, and he glanced at the TV, where the news report was still playing. He didn't need to hear more. His mind was already racing. "What could've happened?"

Valerie nodded slowly, her eyes filled with a mix of fear and frustration. "I think it's a bunch of kidnapping. That's what I've been thinking since last night. The noises I heard... It's too much of a coincidence. It didn't feel like just a random person outside."

Shawn's expression turned darker, his usually carefree attitude replaced with something more intense. "So trafficking huh? That's serious. And if it's happening here, it's not going to stay quiet for long." He leaned in closer, his voice low, almost like he was speaking to himself. "We need to figure this out. If Emma's just one of the girls... there's no telling how many others there are."

Natalia shivered at the thought. She could feel the weight of the situation pressing down on them. The noises, the missing girl, everything was starting to make sense in a way she didn't want it to. But she couldn't ignore the feeling that they were all connected, and they needed to act fast before it was too late.

"We're not just going to sit back and let this happen," Valerie said quietly, determination creeping into her voice.

Shawn nodded in agreement. "No way. We have to do something. This isn't over."

They all fell silent for a moment, each lost in their own thoughts. But one thing was certain: This was only the beginning.

Chapter 11

Tuesday

The morning started like any other for Alex. The soft buzz of his alarm echoed in the quiet room, pulling him from his dreams. He groggily reached for his phone, checking the time and scanning through his messages. There was one from Natalia asking if he'd heard about the missing girl from school, but he didn't respond yet. There was too much to focus on with the test he had later.

After a quick shower, Alex grabbed breakfast and made sure everything was set for school, notes, textbooks, and his laptop, ready for whatever the day threw at him. He was always prepared; it was part of the way he worked. Organizing his life kept things calm, and today, he needed all the calm he could get. He was popular for being a genius, so he had to maintain that reputation.

The bus ride to school was quiet. As usual, Alex sat near the back, headphones in, letting the music drown out the noise around him. The lyrics to his favorite tracks kept his mind busy as his thoughts drifted from coding projects to the upcoming exams. His life was all about finding balance, mixing the academic with the things that kept him sane.

When he arrived at school, he quickly made his way to his locker. The hallway was crowded, the usual noise filling the space, but Alex stayed focused. The day wasn't going to be long, and he had to keep his head in the game. First period was a breeze, just enough time to review some notes before the math test. The numbers and equations helped him zone out from everything else.

In between classes, Alex checked his phone. A message from Natalia appeared on his screen:

"Have you seen the news? They finally broadcasted the situation with Emma yesterday. "

Alex's heart skipped a beat as he read the message. He hadn't heard anything about it. He sent a quick reply:

"No, I haven't. Is it valid?"

Her response came almost immediately:

"Yeah, it's all over the news, and no one knows what happened. It's kind of weird."

Alex's mind instantly started working through the possibilities. A missing girl wasn't uncommon, but something about the way Natalia described it felt off. He couldn't shake the feeling that there was more to this.

At lunch, Alex sat with Natalia. The conversation started off normal, but it wasn't long before the topic shifted to Emma Torres.

"Hey Val, have you heard anything else about her?" Alex asked Valerie in the groupchat, looking at Natalia.

Valerie, who had the conversation via text, typed quickly,

"Yeah, they're saying she's been missing for days, and they're starting to get worried. No one knows where she went."

Natalia leaned in closer, lowering her voice. "I don't know... it just seems strange. You know what I'm saying? It feels like there's something we're not being told."

Alex frowned and typed up another message.

"It could just be a runaway thing, right? That's what they always say".

Valerie replied,

"I thought the same, but then I heard some weird noises a few nights ago. It sounded like scraping or someone dragging something... at first, I thought it was nothing, but then I started thinking about Emma, and the figures who were presumably watching us, and it didn't sit right."

Natalia chimed in, her voice serious. "I've heard things too. More than one girl's gone missing in the area recently. I think it's more than just a coincidence."

Alex felt the hairs on the back of his neck stand up. "Trafficking?" he asked, his voice tight with concern. He grabs his phone again and asks for Valerie's opinion,

"Do you think it could be trafficking?"

Valerie responded quickly,

"I don't know, but it's starting to feel like it. You know, a pattern."

The group chat fell silent, the gravity of their conversation settling in. Alex wasn't one to panic, but the possibility of something like trafficking happening so close to home was unsettling.

"We need to look into this," Alex said finally, his tone firm. "We can't just ignore it. If something's really happening, we need to be ready to figure out what's going on."

There was a pause as everyone processed what Alex said, and then Natalia responded, "We're not letting this go. I'll do some digging."

As the bell rang to end lunch, Alex stood up, his mind racing with possibilities.

The rest of the day was a blur. He tried to focus on his classes, but the thought of Emma Torres, the noises Valerie had heard, and the idea of trafficking kept coming back to him.

When the final bell rang, Alex was already on his way home, the weight of the conversation from lunch still hanging over him. He dropped his bag at the door and immediately sat down at his desk, opening his laptop. He needed to know more, anything that could help them figure out what was really going on.

Chapter 12

Valerie, while home schooled, has kept her ear to the ground. She hears bits and pieces from Shawn about what's going on in school, and she starts connecting the dots between this missing girl and the others Shawn has told her about. While she hasn't been directly involved in the discussions about these disappearances, she starts to feel a growing concern.

Wednesday, when Alex and Natalia return to the burger spot after making plans to meet up, they reveal that they've been investigating. They tell Shawn and Valerie about what they've uncovered from their own search, including disturbing patterns and the possibility of a trafficking ring operating in the area.

Natalia exhales sharply. "It looks like... like someone's picking targets. And it's not just kids disappearing. There are rumors of organized activity, maybe a trafficking ring." She swallows, her usual composure faltering for a split second. "We're not just talking about a missing student anymore. This could be much bigger."

Shawn leans back, running a hand through his hair. "That's serious. Really serious." He glances at Valerie, whose face has gone pale. "Val, you okay?"

"I... I think so," she murmurs, but she can't hide the unease in her eyes. "It's just... overwhelming. And the fact that the cops might not even be aware..." Her voice trails off, a shiver running down her spine.

Alex shakes his head. "Exactly. If the authorities aren't connecting the dots, then it's up to us to figure it out. Start small, but start somewhere."

Natalia nods. "We need to be smart about this. Talk to people, watch the area, document everything. It's dangerous, yes, but if we do nothing, someone else could end up missing. And that girl from last night... she's just the beginning."

Shawn's jaw tightens. "We've been talking about taking action for a while now, when do we actually take action, huh?"

Valerie feels a spark of resolve ignite inside her. She's still cautious, still hesitant, but hearing the fear and determination in the others' voices makes her realize she can't sit on the sidelines.

The group takes a moment, letting the weight of the situation settle. Their expressions mirror each other's concern: clenched jaws, furrowed brows, and the quiet, tense anticipation of what might come next.

They explain that, through their own research and conversations with others in the school, they've discovered multiple missing persons cases over the last few weeks. The girl from the night before is just one of many. The disappearances don't make sense, they all share similar circumstances, and the authorities seem to be dismissing them, or simply unaware of the bigger picture. It's starting to seem like these disappearances are part of something much larger than just a few isolated incidents.

Shawn, now feeling a stronger sense of urgency, shares what he and Valerie overheard earlier. The pieces start to fall into place. Natalia, who is always quick to act, starts making plans to look deeper into the disappearances. She suggests they start talking to people who might know more, like teachers, students, and even people in the local community.

Valerie, while feeling out of her element with this new danger, decides to use her skills to research what she can online. She's an antisocial diva, so her angle will be different from the others. She might find clues through social media or hidden connections that others might miss.

Alex leans back in his chair, eyes scanning the burger place like he's expecting trouble to walk through the door. "We can't just... sit around, can we?"

Natalia shakes her head, her fingers tapping against the table. "No. Too many things don't add up. If we don't do something, it's just going to keep happening."

Alex frowns, adjusting his glasses. "We're not trained for this. We could get ourselves hurt, maybe worse."

Valerie glances between them, biting her lip. "Yeah... but if we don't at least try, who will? We know too much already."

Shawn exhales, leaning forward. "So what, we make our own team? Like, unofficial, nobody else involved?"

Natalia nods firmly. "Exactly. We keep it small, stay under the radar. Work together. Pool what we know."

Alex hesitates, then shrugs. "Alright... I'm in. But we need rules. We can't just act recklessly."

Valerie straightens, a hint of determination in her voice. "Agreed. We watch, we document, we plan. But we do something."

They know they're not equipped to take down any criminal organization, but they can't ignore the nagging feeling that there's something sinister at play.

The group sets a date to meet up after school to brainstorm their next steps. As they work together to piece together their findings, they realize that the situation is much more dangerous than they could have imagined. Shawn and Alex, who have their own street-smart instincts, begin to notice suspicious people in the area, possibly connected to the disappearances. Natalia and Valerie's more methodical approach helps them trace connections they would have missed on their own.

The air between them felt heavier with each passing moment, the weight of what they'd uncovered pressing on their shoulders. Every glance outside, every stranger on the street, carried a hint of danger. They were starting to feel it, not just the fear of what might happen, but the realization that chasing the truth would pull them into a world far more complicated and risky than they'd imagined.

Chapter 13

Shawn knew something was off the second he stepped outside after the final school bell.

It was Thursday. The kind of day where everything looked normal, but today *felt* wrong. The sky was clear, the breeze was light, but the tension the past few days still clung to him like sweat. He could've taken the bus, like always. Instead, he slipped out the back gate and started walking.

He told himself it was for fresh air. Truth was, he needed space. Needed to move through the streets at his own pace, to think, to listen. The silence between footsteps helped him sort things out. His instincts had been buzzing ever since the meetup. Like something was pulling at the corners of his vision that he couldn't quite catch.

Across town, Valerie was buried in her laptop. Blue light flickered against her glasses as she scrolled through threads, posts, and obscure online forums. Her fingers paused on one disturbing comment:

"To the girl near Larkspur Ave– next time don't run. You got lucky."

It was by some bold teenager, could it be referencing some drama? A school fight?

A chill ran down her spine.

She screenshot it and immediately sent it to the group.

Valerie: "You guys… someone posted this before Emma disappeared. Same street."

Alex: "Timestamp checks out. Come to think about it, wasn't there a fight between Emma and some other girl before she went missing?"

Natalia: "Yeah but the school heads waved it off, it was just some beef. Where's Shawn? Val found something."

* * *

Shawn's walk eventually took as long as the length between midday and dusk, it was starting to get darker. He wandered to the edge of the warehouse district, near the abandoned units behind the gas station. He slowed his pace as he spotted it.

The **van**.

Same black van from the library night. Same dented bumper. Same feeling in his gut that screamed: *Wrong.*

He stepped off the sidewalk and ducked behind a dumpster, heart thudding in his ears. Then, there it was again.

A metallic clink. Something dragging.

A voice, loud and annoyed:

"…should've wrapped it tighter."

Shawn's mind didn't panic. It calculated. Cold. Sharp.

He quietly slid into a dark corner behind a dumpster.

His fingers twitched. Not with fear, but with instinct.

He hadn't told the others much about what he used to be. The anger. The way he *used* to solve problems. The things that came naturally when cornered.

His teeth clenched. If he stepped out now, he could-

"Don't."

The voice came from behind him: soft but sharp, steady enough to cut through the chaos in his mind.

Shawn froze, his shoulders tensing. He turned slowly to see a girl standing just a few feet away, her eyes calm but fierce.

Her presence was quiet power itself.

"I'm serious," she said, voice low, almost a warning. "If you move toward that fence, you're walking into something you won't walk out of."

Before Shawn could respond, a tall figure stepped forward from the shadows beside her, a boy with a composed expression, hands tucked casually into his jacket pockets.

"I'm Zayn," he said, voice even, confident. "We're not here to cause trouble, but you need to listen. That place, what you're chasing, it's dangerous. More than you know. You know that."

Shawn narrowed his eyes, instinctively sizing them up. "Who are you?"

Zayn shook his head slowly. "We'll tell you, not here. We've been tracking the same thing you have, the events, the disappearances. It's bigger than your town, and it's getting worse."

The girl stepped slightly forward. "We don't want to fight. But if you get in too deep, you won't like what you find."

There was something about the way she spoke, it was convincing.

Shawn glanced between them, then back toward the dark alley.

His pulse was loud in his ears. Finally, he nodded.

His phone in his pocket buzzed, he pulled it out, keeping an eye on the strangers in front of him.

It was Natalia,

"Meet at Val's tonight, here's the location."

She sent the address pin.

"Alright," he said, voice rough.

He wasn't sure if he should bring them with him, but he thought it would be better to introduce the others to these new mysterious, potentially helpful, strangers.

"Come with me."

And just like that, everything changed.

Chapter 14

The air inside Valerie's room was thick with tension, lit only by a desk lamp and the cool glow of her laptop screen. Lines of text scrolled up as she tracked forum chatter and archived posts. Natalia sat cross-legged on the bed, chewing the end of a pen, her expression tight with concern. Alex stood by the window, tapping his fingers against the sill in a rhythm that betrayed his nerves.

Valerie's apartment sat on a quiet corner lot at the edge of a tired neighborhood, too far from the main streets for traffic noise, but close enough to feel exposed. The apartment itself was small, single-story, with peeling white paint and a porch light that flickered like it was blinking out some forgotten code. The kind of house that blended into the background, harmless, forgettable.

But behind it, things changed.

The backyard ended abruptly at a chain-link fence tangled with dry weeds and creeping vines. Beyond that fence was a sloped patch of untamed trees and brush, leftover land the city forgot to level.

Everyone called it the "back pocket," a dip of old woodland barely wide enough to be called a forest, but dense enough to drown out sound if you stepped just a little too far in.

In the last two years, it had been whispered about. Kids from the neighborhood said someone tried to lure a girl back there with a fake lost dog. Another went missing after cutting through late at night. Valerie didn't let the rumors bother her, until she started hearing things. Small things. Shifts in the leaves. The soft metallic sound of something moving where nothing should be. She told herself it was raccoons. Sometimes she believed it.

Inside, the house was still. The scent of lavender oil drifted faintly from the diffuser on her desk. The hallway lights were off, just the lamp in the living room giving the house its soft glow. No TV. No music. The quiet was almost too complete.

Valerie's room, though, was bright and precise.

Soft LEDs traced the edge of the ceiling. Her desk was organized in a beautiful kind of chaos, printed screenshots, maps, highlighters, sticky notes, and a corkboard filled with ideas still in pieces. Her hanging chair swayed slightly from earlier, when she'd been pacing. In the corner, a small tank of fish shimmered in the dim blue light, the hum of the filter soft and rhythmic.

The blinds were drawn tight over the window, but she could still feel the weight of the dark outside pressing gently against the glass.

"Shawn's late," Natalia muttered.

"He said he's coming," Valerie replied, not looking up.

"Hopefully alone," Natalia added.

That made both Valerie and Alex pause.

Before either could ask what she meant, the front door creaked open downstairs. The murmur of voices. Then the slow tread of feet up the stairs.

The bedroom door opened.

Shawn stepped in first, tense, alert, his eyes flicked across the room, then the hallway, then the corners of the ceiling, like he was scanning for something out of place.

He had never been inside Valerie's house before.

It felt… soft. Lived-in. Almost too peaceful for someone like her. But what struck him wasn't how cozy it was– it was how vulnerable. Thin curtains. A back door with a lock that looked like it could be picked with a bent coin. Windows too close to the tree line. No fence worth mentioning.

The place looked like it *should* have been broken into by now.

And yet it hadn't.

That made his skin crawl more.

Shawn looked tense, more than usual, but composed.

Behind him, two unfamiliar faces stepped into the room: the girl from the alley, calm and alert, and the boy with dark eyes and a measured presence.

Valerie's hand froze on her track pad.

Natalia stood.

Valerie blinked. "…Who are they? Why are they in my house..?"

"I know, don't worry, they're not the problem," Shawn reassured her simply, stepping aside. "They're here because they're tracking the same thing. The disappearances. The posts. Everything."

The girl offered a small nod. "I'm Nora. This is Zayn."

Zayn gave a single wave, casual. "I'm from Holloway. Other side of the state. We've seen this pattern before."

Holloway was a great distance away from Meadowcrest, it was surprising.

Alex raised an eyebrow. "You tracked this all the way from Holloway?"

"I didn't track it," Zayn said. I followed it, just like it's following you now."

There was a silence, heavy and electric.

Valerie finally spoke. "What do you mean by 'it'?"

Nora's gaze settled on her. "Not a person. Not exactly. A system. A network. Disguised in plain sight."

Shawn leaned against the wall. "Start from the beginning."

Zayn exhaled, slow and controlled. "Last year, students disappeared from our town. Most unrelated on paper. But a few times, it started with the same thing, strange posts.

One was a direct message. One a forum thread.

It could have been anything, to disguise a hint.

Alex pulled out his phone. "Wait... the comment Val screenshotted, about the girl near Larkspur– "

"Same phrasing," Zayn nodded. "It's not a threat. It's a signal."

Natalia sat down slowly. "A signal to who?"

"To whoever's behind this," Nora said. "Recruitment. Targeting. Both. We don't know exactly, but we know it escalates.

One post turns into tracking. Then fear. Then... vanishing."

"Just like Emma," Valerie whispered.

"And maybe not just her," Shawn added grimly. "There was a van. Assuming it was the same one Alex saw one night at school, and I saw it again tonight."

Valerie looked sharply at him. "You didn't follow it, right?"

Shawn hesitated and looked away.

"He was going to," Nora said. "Until we stopped him."

Zayn crossed his arms. "If you get too close too early, you scare them off. Or worse, you get killed."

The room went quiet again.

"What do you want from us?" Natalia asked finally, voice quieter than usual.

Zayn glanced at Nora, then back at the group. "We want to work together. You've seen things too. You've got connections here. But we've got patterns, intel, names they tried to wipe. You don't need to trust us completely. But if we don't combine what we know, we're not just risking more disappearances."

Nora finished the sentence for him:

"We're risking one of you being next."

CHAPTER 14

Holloway
3 Months Back

Zayn.

Chapter 15

The gym was electric, bright lights casting long shadows, sneakers pounding against the hardwood like thunder.

The crowd's roar was a low rumble in Zayn's ears, distant and muffled, as if the world had narrowed down to the court beneath his feet.

The Holloway Hawks were down by one. The clock ticked relentlessly toward zero.

Zayn caught the ball with practiced ease, fingers spreading wide as the leather bounced into his hands. His eyes scanned, the defenders pressing close, the clock's unyielding countdown. No hesitation.

He planted his left foot, then exploded forward with a fluid burst, weaving through a wall of moving bodies. Sweat slicked his brow, but his focus was locked. His breath was steady and controlled.

A defender lunged to block his path. Zayn shifted, spinning on his heel, the ball floating just above his outstretched fingertips. He arced backward, creating space as time slowed.

With a breath, he leapt backwards. The spin move back, the leap, the form, it was perfect. He flicked his wrist, curving the ball on its way to the rim. The ball sailed in a perfect curve, spinning softly toward the rim. The gym seemed to hold its breath.

The ball slipped through the net with a whisper as the buzzer screamed its final note.

Silence shattered into a thunderous uproar.

Zayn didn't smile or shout. Instead, he turned calmly and jogged back, sweat mingling with the heat of adrenaline. He'd expected a victory. Around him, teammates surged forward, clapping and shouting.

But Zayn's eyes were already scanning the court, alert for what came next, or rather, for someone special, even as victory washed over him.

Zayn slowed as he reached the corner of the court, the roaring crowd blurring into a wall of sound pressing against his skin. Schoolmates, spectators, and even parents were celebrating with joy of home victory. His chest heaved, sweat dripping down the sides of his face, but his eyes stayed sharp, scanning teammates as they rushed toward him with triumphant shouts.

"ZAYN! THAT WAS SICK!" someone yelled, slapping him on the back with a force that nearly knocked the breath from him.

He nodded, voice caught somewhere between exhaustion and satisfaction. The weight of the win was heavy, but not the kind that made him want to celebrate. It was a different kind of weight. One that settled deep in his gut, reminding him this was only one battle in a longer war.

The coach's whistle cut through the noise, sharp and commanding. Zayn's teammates started to shuffle toward the benches, their adrenaline slowly ebbing away.

Zayn stood a moment longer, catching his breath, letting the last bits of tension loosen from his muscles. The gym lights glared off the glossy floor, reflections shimmering like a fading dream. His hands brushed the ball absently, tracing the leather's worn grooves as if trying to remember every second of the play.

Then came the familiar buzz in his pocket.

He pulled out his phone, thumbs already swiping past notifications.

A message from someone flashed on the screen:

"Meet me outside."

A grin broke through his tired expression.

Pocketing his phone, Zayn grabbed his bag and headed for the exit, the cheers still echoing behind him but already fading into the night.

He got compliments and praise every few seconds as he cut through the people in his way on his way outside.

The parking lot lights flickered overhead as Zayn stretched out a hand to a fist bump, steady and sure. He had that calm confidence that came from countless hours on the court, but beneath it, something quieter, a patient determination that didn't need to shout to be noticed.

He stood tall, with a lean, athletic build honed by years of pushing his limits. His skin was a warm bronze, smooth but marked here and there by faint scars, small reminders of hard practices and close calls. His dark wavy hair fell just over his forehead, loose enough to catch the breeze but never out of place. His eyes, sharp and steady, were a deep brown, almost black, framed by thick lashes that gave him a thoughtful, serious look.

His jaw was strong, clean-shaven, and the faintest dimple appeared when he smiled, rare but genuine.

He moved with the fluid grace of someone used to controlled bursts of speed and precision, each step measured but ready to explode into action.

There was a quiet intensity about him, the kind that made you pay attention without him ever having to say a word.

Mira waited just a few steps away, her silhouette framed by the amber glow of the streetlight. She was the opposite of calm, fiery, quick, and impossible to ignore. Her hair, pulled back into a high ponytail, bounced with every step she took, strands of dark chestnut catching the light like flickering flames. Her eyes, bright and sharp, sparkled with determination and a hint of mischief.

She was shorter than Zayn, but there was a fierce energy about her that filled the space between them. Athletic too, her lean frame shaped by years on the soccer field, every movement confident and purposeful.

When she smiled at him, it was a full, easy smile that reached her eyes, warm and unguarded. It was clear they were close, connected by years of shared victories, defeats, and silent understandings.

Zayn and Mira had a bond forged through years of sweat, early mornings, and late-night talks under fading streetlights. They knew each other's strengths and weaknesses like the back of their hands, unspoken cues passing between them on and off the court.

They weren't just friends; they were each other's anchor in a world that often felt unpredictable. When Zayn played, Mira was the first to cheer, loud and relentless. And when Mira pushed herself on the field, Zayn was the steady presence waiting at the sidelines, ready to catch her if she stumbled.

There was no need for grand declarations or clichés between them. Their friendship was quiet but unbreakable, a constant that made the chaos of life easier to bear.

They were *best friends.*

Chapter 16

The crowd's noise still hummed faintly behind them as Zayn and Mira made their way through the parking lot. They walked side by side, shoulders nearly touching, moving with a rhythm that felt familiar, like they'd done this a thousand times before.

"You crushed it out there," Mira said, her voice easy, a teasing lilt to it. "That last shot? Pure magic. You had me holding my breath."

Zayn smiled, brushing a lock of hair back from his forehead. "Just did what I had to. Can't win games solo, though. Everyone did their part."

She bumped his shoulder playfully. "Don't sell yourself short. You've been on fire lately. Ever since the season started, you've been locking in. What's up with that?"

Zayn's grin faded just a little, his gaze drifting ahead. "I don't know. Just… focused. Got something to prove, I guess."

Mira glanced at him, her eyes softening with knowing. "You don't have to prove anything to anyone. Especially not to me."

There was a pause, a quiet space between them where years of friendship spoke louder than words. Zayn looked over, catching the earnestness in her eyes.

"You're the only one I told about the tournament invite," he admitted, voice low.

Mira's lips curled into a smile that was more warmth than mischief.

"Guess that means I have to make sure you don't back out."

He laughed, a short, genuine sound that eased the tightness in his chest. "Good luck with that."

They rounded a corner and Mira nudged him again. "Seriously though, what's going on? You've been different. Distant."

Zayn hesitated. "It's nothing bad. Just... stuff I'm trying to sort out."

"Stuff that you can't talk about?"

This question hit him, it was as if she was referring to all those times he'd vent to her, with nothing but trust.

He glanced at her with a flicker of vulnerability. "I want to, but it's complicated."

Mira reached out and gave his arm a quick squeeze. "Hey. When you're ready, I'm here. Always. You know that, ya big doofus."

Zayn's smile deepened, the weight lifting just a little. "Thanks, Mira. That means everything."

She bumped him again, this time with a grin. "Don't get all sappy on me now. We still have a game to celebrate."

They stopped near the end of the parking lot, the night air cool against their skin. Mira pulled her phone from her pocket and glanced at the screen. "Hey, when are you heading to that tournament?"

Zayn shrugged. "In a couple days. Not sure if I'm ready yet."

Mira's eyes narrowed playfully. "Not ready? Since when did you get cold feet?"

He smirked. "Maybe I'm just scared."

"Scared? Of what?"

"Failing. Letting myself down."

Mira gave him a look that said she'd heard it all before. "You won't. And if you do, I'll be right there to pick you up."

He shook his head with a soft laugh. "I'm lucky to have you."

"You're stuck with me," she said with a wink.

They stood in comfortable silence for a moment,

two best friends bound by more than just sports,

a quiet understanding that no matter what, they had each other's backs.

They walked together all the time, it was normal for them, he often walked her home after her soccer drills.

Mira opened the car door, sliding in with a practiced ease that made Zayn smile. He leaned against the hood for a moment, watching her settle into her seat. The glow from the streetlamp caught the strands of her hair, casting them gold.

"Remember that time in eighth grade when I convinced you to try out for the school team?" Mira asked, her voice teasing but warm.

Zayn laughed, the memory sharp and clear. "How could I forget? I was terrible. You were the one running drills with me every afternoon until I didn't want to quit."

She shrugged, eyes gleaming. "I knew you had it in you. Just needed someone stubborn enough to push you."

"That's you, all right," he said, shaking his head with affection. "The relentless motivator."

They fell into easy silence for a beat, the weight of years stretching between them like a thread.

"You've been my teammate in more ways than one," Zayn said quietly, "on the court and off."

Mira's expression softened. "We've always had each other's backs. Even when things got messy."

Zayn's fingers drummed lightly against the car hood. "Like the time after the state finals last year, when my knee gave out?"

She grinned. "You limped all the way to practice the next day. Didn't want to let the team down."

He shook his head, smiling ruefully. "That's what you get for being stubborn."

"And you learned from the best," Mira said, winking.

The breeze stirred the leaves, carrying the faint scent of freshly cut grass and distant barbecue smoke. It was the kind of night that made you want to believe things would always be this steady.

Mira turned to him. "Promise me something?"

Zayn raised an eyebrow. "What's that?"

"That no matter where this tournament takes you, you don't lose sight of why you started playing in the first place."

He looked at her, eyes serious. "I promise. It's never just about the game. It's about the people I play for, and those who stand beside me."

She smiled softly. "Good. Because you've got a whole team behind you. Me included."

Zayn felt the weight of those words settle warmly inside him. In a world that was fast and uncertain, Mira was the constant. The friend who knew every up and down without needing explanation.

"Best friends," he said quietly, "through every shot and every stumble."

Mira reached over and bumped his shoulder. "Always."

He got into the driver's seat, he was the man, the big guy, but ironically, he felt safe.

There's a different type of peace you get when you know you have someone to count on, he had someone he could trust.

Mira's eyes softened, her voice steady. "Same here. You don't have to carry everything alone. We're a team, on and off the court."

They sat in comfortable silence for a beat, the kind that only years of friendship can create.

Then Mira nudged him again, grinning. "So, what's the plan for after tonight's win? Celebration or ice cream to cool off that buzzer-beater heat?"

Zayn laughed, the tension easing from his shoulders. "Ice cream sounds good. But only if you're buying."

Mira smirked, "Deal."

The quiet warmth between them was a steady pulse, a reminder that no matter how fast life moved or how hard it got, they weren't facing it alone.

Chapter 17

The days since the game blurred into a steady rhythm of practice, school, and long walks home that Zayn barely remembered. Everything was on repeat, like muscle memory. Only one thing stood out: Mira.

It was late afternoon, and the sun painted long shadows over the field. The soccer goalposts gleamed silver in the fading light, nets swaying lightly in the breeze. Zayn leaned against the chain-link fence, a sports drink in hand, watching as Mira sprinted down the field, weaving past cones, cutting angles with ease.

"Alright, let's go again!" she called, breathless but energized.

Zayn jogged toward the sideline, picked up the ball, and threw it toward her. "You sure you're not part machine?"

She smirked and caught it with her foot mid-air, bouncing it before placing it down. "Only the cool part. Now stop slacking and gimme something with pace."

He laughed and fed her a fast ground pass. Mira stepped into it, delivering a perfect strike that smacked the back of the net. She pumped her fist, then turned to him, grinning. "Told you. Golden foot."

Zayn raised an eyebrow. "You keep saying that like I didn't help you train."

"Please," she said, jogging over. "You just stood around and looked pretty."

"Guilty," he said, bowing with mock pride.

They continued for a while, the ball flying between them with ease, no pressure, just the kind of rhythm only best friends could find. The world felt quiet out here. Safe.

Eventually, Mira flopped down on the grass, panting. Zayn joined her, sitting cross-legged as he passed her the drink.

"Thanks," she said, taking a long sip. "You've been quiet lately."

"Just tired," he said, but she gave him a look that said she didn't believe it.

His phone buzzed. A new message. Zayn checked it and made a face.

"What is it?" Mira asked.

"Tournament's tomorrow," he said. "Coach just confirmed."

She sat up straighter. "That's the big one, right? Across town?"

"Yeah."

Mira tilted her head, noticing his hesitation. "You're not going?"

Zayn rubbed the back of his neck. "I don't know. Something about it… just doesn't feel right."

She nudged him. "You're just overthinking. It's a chance to be seen, Z. To show what you've got. And I'll be fine."

He didn't answer right away. Mira shifted closer, voice softer.

"Hey. You've been working toward this. You miss this, you'll regret it. I know you."

He met her eyes. "You'll be okay while I'm gone?"

She scoffed. "I'm not the one who's nervous. I'll run drills, binge a show, maybe annoy my neighbors with my playlist. Go. Win. Then bring me something from the vending machine."

Zayn chuckled. "You always bribe me with snacks."

"And it always works."

He stood, offering her a hand. She took it, and he pulled her up with ease.

They walked over to the bleachers, where Mira kept her essentials. Her duffel bag with a pair of shoes to wear after practice, a bag for her dirty cleats, a large sized metal water bottle, and her phone, along with its charger.

They took off, but didn't part ways immediately.

Zayn walked her home, like he always did after her late practices. The streets around the college campus were calm this time of evening, painted in gold by the dipping sun.

Students passed by in pairs or small groups, some laughing, some with earbuds in, the usual college chaos mellowed by the hour.

Mira lived in a small off-campus apartment complex just a block away from their college's south entrance. It wasn't fancy, cracked sidewalks, flickering porch lights, a bit worn, but it had a kind of quiet charm, and she made it hers. Posters in the windows. A half-dead plant she refused to give up on.

They stopped at the steps.

Zayn hesitated like he always did, lingering, not from awkwardness, but the kind of comfort that makes you want to stretch every moment. Mira leaned on the railing, keys jingling in her hand.

Mira smiled, leaning her shoulder against the door frame. "Text me before the game. And after. Don't make me hack your phone just to get an update."

Zayn chuckled, the sound low and warm. "I'll let you know when I leave tomorrow. Promise."

She squinted at him playfully. "You'd better. Or I'm showing up at that gym in full mascot gear just to embarrass you."

"That actually sounds terrifying," he said, grinning.

Mira pointed a finger at him, her tone mock-bossy. "Now go home, Captain Holloway. Hydrate. Stretch. Sleep. You've got a game to destroy."

He gave a small, joking salute. "Yes, coach."

She started to turn the knob, but paused, glancing back one last time. "Hey, Z?"

He turned, "Yeah?"

Her voice softened. "You've got this. And whatever weird feeling's messing with your head? It's just nerves. You're going to kill it out there."

Zayn looked at her, the dim porch light catching her eyes just enough to make him want to memorize them. "Thanks, Mira. For everything."

She gave a quiet smile, the kind that meant more than words. "Always."

The door clicked shut behind her.

Zayn lingered for a second longer, standing alone in the quiet hallway outside her apartment. The campus around him was peaceful, still breathing with the last warmth of the day.

Then, finally, he turned and began walking. Step by step, into a night that already felt a little colder.

Chapter 18

The morning sun had just started to stretch across the sky when Zayn's alarm buzzed. 6:45 a.m. Sharp. The golden hue seeped through his blinds, catching on the dust motes dancing in the air.

He lay there for a moment, still under his sheets, before sitting up with a deep breath. Today wasn't just another game. It was the one Mira had told him not to miss.

He moved through his morning routine in quiet focus, cold shower, protein shake, gear check. Every motion was mechanical, but it carried a weight of purpose. His duffel bag sat neatly by the door, already packed. He grabbed it, slung it over his shoulder, and headed out into the crisp morning.

The walk to the campus gym was quiet, just the sounds of birds, rustling trees, and the soft hum of waking traffic. At the gym, a few teammates were already there, joking, stretching, tossing a ball around. Zayn gave them nods and brief smiles, exchanging handshakes and a few shoulder bumps.

"Yo, Holloway's golden boy," one of them teased. "Ready to carry us again?"

Zayn smirked. "Only if you catch my passes this time."

Their coach walked in, clapping his hands. "Let's go, boys. Bus leaves in ten."

By noon, they were loaded and on the road. The drive to the

tournament took just about an hour, winding past stretches of pine trees, old towns, and quiet highways. Zayn sat near the front, headphones in, nodding slightly to music, but his eyes stayed fixed on the passing landscape.

When they arrived, the parking lot was already buzzing with energy. Families, students, rival teams. The building was a regional complex, taller than Holloway's gym, with shining banners and glass panels reflecting the afternoon sun.

As Zayn stepped off the bus, a familiar voice called out.

"Yo, Z!"

He turned to see his older cousin, Damian, walking over with a grin. Mid-twenties, short beard, fitted jacket, sunglasses perched in his hair.

"Didn't think I'd miss your big day, did you?"

Zayn smiled wide. "You drove all the way out here?"

Damian clapped his shoulder. "Of course. You've been grinding for this since middle school. I wanted to see it."

Zayn nodded, the nerves settling a little more. "Glad you came."

Damian jerked a thumb toward the lot. "I parked near the back. You need anything, call me. I'll be around."

The team moved inside. The locker room was cool and clean, the walls lined with wooden benches and rows of neatly numbered hooks. Zayn laced his shoes slowly, thoughtfully. The air buzzed with the typical pre-game tension, but he was calm. Focused.

When it was time, they emerged into the court's bright lights, the bleachers filled with fans and camera phones. The stadium wasn't massive, but it felt *alive*, bigger, louder than Holloway's.

The game began under a late afternoon sky, sunlight spilling in through tall gym windows and casting golden slashes across the hardwood. The stands buzzed with quiet anticipation. You could hear every footstep, every breath, every heartbeat between whistles.

Zayn was focused, steady. He moved with quiet precision, like he was always one second ahead. When others hesitated, he was already in motion. The ball came to him often, not by chance, but because people trusted him with it. He didn't waste a single movement. When he passed, it felt deliberate. When he ran, it looked effortless.

In the second half, things started to slip. The other team pushed harder, faster, louder. Holloway's grip on the game faltered. Mistakes crept in. Energy dipped.

But Zayn didn't rattle.

He found his rhythm again, darting into open space, drawing eyes, opening chances for others. He picked his moments carefully. He read the floor like a map only he understood.

Then came the final minute.

Tied game.

The ball ended up in his hands one last time.

He took a breath.

There were voices in the crowd, stomping feet, a rising hum of tension, but it all faded into a low, distant echo.

This was his chance to prove himself to the scouts watching him, to make his team proud, to win, for himself, his journey, and for Mira.

He slipped past a defender and dashed towards the hoop.

Two defenders held their ground in front of him, under the hoop, holding their hands up. Zayn suddenly stopped, all the momentum from his sprint came rushing into him, and he jumped up.

The momentum helped him jump higher, he raised the ball, held it for a split second, and shot it.

It hung in the air for a heartbeat.

Swish.

The buzzer sounded.

And the gym erupted.

The crowd roared to life. His teammates surged toward him, shouting and grabbing his shoulders. Somewhere in the noise, the coach's voice cracked from shouting. All around him, celebration. Relief. Joy.

Zayn didn't scream or raise his fists.

He just stood there for a moment, quiet in the center of it all. A half-smile pulling at his lips.

Victory.

Zayn smiled, finally letting the moment reach him. He skipped the celebration, and ran to the locker room to tell Mira about the victory, his last shot, his hard work.

He was stopped by people and teammates, but he threw fist bumps back, showed his gratitude to their praise, and slipped past into the locker room.

He opened his locker and pulled out his phone to text Mira.

Then he saw it.

A message, sent about thirty minutes earlier.

zayn, im being followed, pleas-

And then nothing. No follow-up. Just the typing bubble, frozen in time.

Zayn's stomach dropped.

He stared at the screen. Tried calling. No answer.

Again.

Straight to voicemail.

He turned quickly, hearing his team roar through the hallway entering the locker rooms. He ignored his teammates jumping up and down with glee, over their victory. He saw his coach.

For someone who just made a game-winning shot, Zayn's eyes

screamed fear, anxiety.

The only thing in his head was the message, heart beating fast, his mind drifting through countless possibilities, and the crowds coming in to celebrate with the players.

This meant a lot for him, but back home was someone else that meant a lot more.

Chapter 19

"Coach, I need to go. It's urgent."

The coach's celebratory expression changed.

"Dinner's in thirty-"

"I can't. Something's wrong."

The urgency in his voice shut down any argument.

He left his things in the locker and ran out, sprinting.

Dashing through crowds, praises, avoiding any conversations, he needed to be somewhere.

Outside, he sprinted across the parking lot, scanning.

Damian was leaning against his car, with a proud smile and a look of approval.

"Damian!" He jumped over the stairs and ran towards him.

His cousin shouted. "Zayn! You did insan-"

Zayn cut him off, "I need your car. Something's wrong back in town, I need to be there urgently, please."

Damian sensed the urgency in his voice and tossed him the keys without hesitation. He slipped into the passenger seat as Zayn jumped into the driver's seat and slammed the door shut.

Damian was confused, but was here to back his cousin up. "You've got enough gas, but be careful, let's move."

Zayn didn't wait. He peeled out of the lot. The engine roared, tires screeching as he merged onto the open road. His hands were steady, but inside, panic clawed up his spine.

The sun dipped low behind him.

And ahead, back in Holloway, something was about to change him.

Damian glanced over and noticed the rush in Zayn, "Tell me everything."

Zayn recounted the chilling message, the incomplete plea that had haunted him since he saw it. "She sent it about thirty minutes ago. Then nothing. No calls, no follow-up. I tried calling her. No answer."

Damian's jaw clenched. "That's bad, man. She'll be okay.

Don't worry about pushing the car, let's just get there asap.

My car's built for this."

The speedometer climbed steadily.

Sixty miles per hour. Seventy. Eighty. Ninety.

The evening blurred past in streaks of shadow and light. Trees whipped by like ghosts, their limbs reaching out in silent warnings.

Zayn's heart pounded in his chest, syncing with the rhythmic thrum of the engine. His mind raced, replaying the message over and over.

Zayn, I'm being followed, pleas–

The incomplete sentence echoed in his ears, a scream frozen in time. Why hadn't she finished? Was she still in danger? Was she hurt? Was she even alive?

The weight of those questions crushed him.

His eyes flicked repeatedly to the rearview mirror, half expecting to see headlights trailing behind him. The empty road stretched endlessly, offering no answers, no comfort.

Every red light he ran felt like a risky hammer blow, every turn a desperate gamble to shave seconds off the clock.

He tried to silence the chaos inside his head, focusing on the road, on the small details, the way the dashboard glowed faintly, the loud roar of the engine.

But his thoughts kept breaking through.

What if this was a trap? What if Mira was hiding, terrified?

What if he was too late?

The familiar streets of Holloway began to slip into view, the clusters of streetlights guiding him home. The town felt too quiet, as if holding its breath for what was to come.

He whipped onto the narrow road leading to the sports complex where Mira practiced. The field was surrounded by tall chain-link fences topped with barbed wire, a faint glow from the floodlights washing over the empty turf.

The night air was still, filled only with the whisper of leaves and distant sounds from a late-night diner. The parking lot was empty except for a lone car, lights dimmed, the engine off.

Zayn killed the engine and sat for a second, the silence pressing in.

His hands trembled slightly as he stepped out, the cold biting through his thin jacket.

The scent of fresh-cut grass and damp earth filled the air. The floodlights illuminated the field in stark, almost unnatural brightness, casting long shadows.

He walked toward the edge of the turf, eyes scanning for any sign of her. The soccer balls lay scattered, some near the goalpost, others by the sidelines, untouched.

Then all of a sudden, a sheriff cruiser pulled up into the parking lot, with flashing lights. Zayn saw the glow of the red and blue and looked at Damian, who also noticed, and nodded at Zayn, reassuring him not to worry.

"I'll deal with them, you go find her!" He shouted.

Zayn nodded, turned, and ran to the field. His breath hitched.

The place where Mira had trained just hours ago was frozen in time, still, silent, empty.

Zayn's chest tightened. The adrenaline had pushed him this far, but now a cold knot settled deep in his gut.

He pulled out his phone again, checking for missed calls or messages.

Nothing new besides a few text messages and calls from his teammates, asking where he went.

Zayn's fingers trembled slightly as he locked his phone and pocketed it, forcing himself to breathe steady and slow. His eyes scanned the open space, searching for any sign, any clue that Mira might still be here, waiting, lost, or trying to reach him.

But all that greeted him was silence.

He clenched his fists, swallowing the rising panic. This was just the beginning. He wouldn't let the silence win.

With resolve hardening inside, he stepped forward into the growing dark, ready to fight through whatever lay ahead.

Chapter 20

Zayn's footsteps felt impossibly loud as he paced with purpose, each step fueled by a desperate hope.

His heart hammered painfully in his chest, an unrelenting drumbeat that echoed in his ears louder than the quiet night around him. The adrenaline that had driven him through the frantic ride here now settled into a cold, heavy knot deep in his stomach. His breath came in sharp, uneven bursts as his eyes swept over every inch of the field.

Then, near the far goalpost, his gaze caught something out of place, a water bottle, half-crushed and lying on its side. Nearby, a pair of cleats, tossed carelessly as if dropped in a hurry. And just beyond, a crumpled sweatshirt, its fabric stained with grass and dirt.

Mira's things.

His breath caught in his throat. The quiet around him suddenly felt suffocating, every sound distant except for the thundering in his ears.

Zayn crouched slowly, trembling hands reaching out to brush the sleeve of the sweatshirt. The fabric was rough under his fingers, but the reality it carried was sharper than any blade. This wasn't a joke. It wasn't a cruel prank. This was real.

"Mira!" His voice cracked, raw and desperate, slicing through the night. "Where are you? Talk to me!"

Only silence answered back. The kind of silence that pressed down on his chest, making it harder to breathe.

His fingers fumbled for his phone, hands slick with sweat. He dialed her number again, the ringtone ringing out, sharp and hopeful. And then, a faint tune from a shadowed corner beyond the goalposts, near the edge of the field. A quiet rustle, barely audible over the beating of his heart.

Zayn's pulse spiked. Without hesitation, he followed the sound, eyes darting between the darkness and the path ahead. The night seemed to hold its breath with him.

Between the overgrown bushes and a rusted chain-link fence, half-hidden beneath dead leaves and tangled vines, lay Mira's phone, ringing from Zayn's call. His stomach dropped as he scooped it up.

He hung up. The screen was dark, locked. But Zayn knew the password by heart. Years of trust, endless secrets shared in whispered conversations and quiet moments.

His fingers shook as he entered the numbers, the screen flickering to life.

Multiple missed calls from him, countless texts, all unanswered. The last message she'd sent, cut off mid-sentence. The typing bubble froze in time, like a silent scream trapped inside the phone.

He swiped through her photos, searching for anything, anything that could explain.

He knew his best friend, he knew she would leave something behind, he knew she wouldn't just let herself be taken away.

Then he found it: a single image, blurry and grainy. A figure lurking just beyond the frame, a shadow in the corner. He made the image out to be a masked figure, it seemed like the figure was chasing her down.

She wasn't just gone. She had been taken.

A cold wave of panic crashed over him, but Zayn clenched his fists hard, forcing the chaos back down. He was no good to her if he lost control now.

But why? who? how? She didn't do anything bad to anybody?

His thoughts destroyed him.

He looked back to the field. Everything was left behind exactly as if she had stepped away for a moment, her cleats resting on the grass, water bottle tipped over, sweatshirt abandoned mid-drill.

His whole body trembled, not with tears, but with an angry storm swirling inside. A storm of fear, helplessness, and rage.

"Zayn." The voice was calm, steady, breaking through the night like an anchor.

He turned to see Damian, his cousin, approaching through the shadows. The light from the stadium caught on his face, serious, eyes sharp but filled with quiet reassurance.

"I've told the cops everything," Damian said. "They're already on it. They're searching the area."

Zayn nodded, swallowing hard. The weight of the situation pressed down on him, but his cousin's presence grounded him.

Damian clapped a hand on his shoulder. "You're not alone in this."

Zayn's mind spun with a thousand questions, fears, and what-ifs. But beneath it all, a fierce determination blazed brighter than any doubt.

This wasn't the end. It was only the beginning of a fight he was ready to face, no matter what it took.

The night stretched on, cold and endless around them. But in Zayn's chest, a fire burned steady and unyielding. He would find Mira. He had to.

And nothing, no darkness, no silence, no shadow would stop him from bringing his favorite person home.

Chapter 21

Zayn woke up with a sharp breath, the dim light outside his window telling him it was late.

His room was quiet. Too quiet. A silence that didn't feel peaceful, it felt heavy.

He shook his head, jumped a few times, and wrapped his head around to the moment.

It was the evening of the next day, he'd slept through a lot.

The memories rushed back all at once. The late-night drive. The field. The abandoned cleats and phone.

The cops pulling up behind him as he sprinted through the grass.

He had passed out sometime after Damian came up to him. His body giving up under the weight of everything, panic, dread, exhaustion. His head had fallen against Damian's shoulder as they sat near the edge of the field.

A while after he passed out, the team came back to town.

Damian had called the coach from Zayn's phone, and informed him of the events.

When they returned later that night, his coach, a few teammates, and Damian helped him get back to his dorm. Zayn hadn't said a word the whole way. He was out of it.

When they reached his building, he nodded, forced a small thank you, and collapsed into his bed the moment the door shut.

His cousin had taken care of everything. He drove back and picked up Zayn's things from the locker. Said he'd hold onto them until they meet again. He kept quiet, didn't tell anyone.

Just like Zayn had asked.

After recollecting the previous night's events, Zayn looked around. He hadn't even noticed Mira's things, her cleats, her bag, her phone charger, set neatly by his desk. They'd brought them back. He didn't remember asking them to.

Now, they sat there. Like a ghost of her.

His stomach growled, but he ignored it. Food didn't matter. Nothing did.

He threw on a hoodie, pulled the strings tight around his face, and stepped out.

The distant campus was muted in the early evening haze, light winds, and the golden sunlight slanted through the trees, casting soft shadows on the sidewalk. Students laughed somewhere in the distance, but it all sounded far away. Like it belonged to another world.

Zayn walked. Nowhere in particular. Just forward.

Every few steps, flashes of the night before crept in. The way Damian's voice had stayed calm when the cops questioned them. The way the lights from the cruisers lit up the field. The way Mira's phone buzzed in his hand, the photo of the masked figure.

He called the police station when he reached the edge of campus, asking for any updates. The response was short.

No leads. Missing person report filed. They'd follow up.

He hung up and called Damian next.

His cousin picked up on the second ring.

"Someone's finally up huh? All good?" Damian asked with a laugh.

Zayn stared at the sky with a blank expression. "Define good."

Damian sighed. "I figured. I've informed your coach, and a few of your teammates may know about the situation, but the cops have posted missing person alerts, if you need me, call me, I'll be there."

"Thanks," Zayn said. It came out quieter than he meant it to.

They waited in silence for a while.

"We'll find her," Damian said finally. "I know it."

Zayn didn't respond. He just ended the call and kept walking.

An hour later, he was back in his room.

He sat at his desk, Mira's phone in front of him, screen dark.

And something snapped.

He didn't know where to start. But he knew this wasn't over.

Not even close.

Holloway
1 Month After the disappearance of Mira.

Nora.

Chapter 22

The campus air still held the warmth of the afternoon sun, soft and golden as it filtered through the rows of maple trees lining the walkway. Nora walked alone, backpack slung over one shoulder, her headphones silent for once. The buzz of the week was behind her, lectures, labs, the weight of expectations, and ahead was the only place that felt remotely like home.

She reached the second floor, turned the key, and opened the door to a familiar sight.

Layla was curled up on the couch in a hoodie three sizes too big, a bowl of popcorn balanced on her lap, eyes locked onto the TV screen. Something bright and ridiculous was playing. Cartoons, maybe, some colorful show with chaotic dialogue.

Aliya sat nearby, half-focused on her laptop, legs tucked under her, one headphone dangling out.

"You two look suspiciously relaxed," Nora said, setting her bag down by the door.

Layla turned, flashing a grin. "We're in recovery mode."

Aliya gave a small wave, not looking up. "Survived the school week. Deserve the peace."

Nora raised an eyebrow. "Pretty sure that popcorn was mine."

Layla held it tighter. "Possession is nine-tenths of the law, big sis."

Nora laughed under her breath and walked over, ruffling Layla's hair on her way to the mini-fridge. "How'd school go?"

"Boring. But I got a ninety on my chem quiz."

Aliya glanced up at that. "She did. We celebrated with iced coffee and zero remorse."

Nora pulled out a bottle of water, unscrewing the cap. "Proud of you, Lay."

Layla beamed. "Thanks."

It had taken time for this routine to settle in.

Layla staying weekends.

Aliya making space without hesitation.

The three of them creating something small but real between beige dorm walls and tangled charger cords.

No one questioned it anymore. Not professors, not housing. Layla loved it here, no one made her feel like she was in the way.

Nora sat on the edge of the desk chair, sipping her water, watching them. Aliya looked peaceful, her long hair tied up, wearing an oversized band tee and fuzzy socks. Layla, a whirlwind of sarcasm and spark, tucked into the cushions like she belonged there.

Because she did.

"Any plans tonight?" Aliya asked after a moment.

"None," Nora said. "And I'd like to keep it that way."

Layla perked up. "What if we changed that?"

"Great," Nora said, already wary.

Aliya closed her laptop slowly, mock-serious. "We were thinking… hot chocolate run. Maybe that corner café with the fairy lights. Then movie night. Pajamas required."

Nora squinted. "Movie night I'll consider. Fairy light café? Too much serotonin."

Layla gasped. "Wow. You hate joy?"

Nora stood and stretched. "I tolerate joy in moderation."

Aliya tossed her a pillow. "You'll come around."

Nora caught it with one hand and smiled. "You two are relentless."

"And you love us," Layla said, reaching for more popcorn.

Nora didn't answer. She just sat back down and pulled out her laptop, a smile ghosting on her lips.

Layla flipped through shows with one hand, clearly not watching any of them.

"You know," she said, eyes still on the screen, "if we leave now, we can catch that café before the line gets insane. They do that marshmallow drizzle thing you like."

Nora raised an eyebrow. "You remembered that?"

Layla scoffed. "Please. You talk about it like it's a spiritual experience."

Aliya smiled. "She really does. You should hear her mid-finals week. 'I just need marshmallows and silence.' Like a monk in combat boots."

"I do not sound like that," Nora muttered.

"You do," they said at the same time.

Nora sighed. "Fine. I'll come."

Layla sat up, victorious. "We leave in ten."

"Twenty," Aliya corrected. "I'm not wearing shoes right now, and I need to look like I've slept this week."

"You have slept," Nora said.

"Not mentally."

Nora laughed.

She glanced at Layla. "You good with your school stuff?"

Layla nodded. "All done. I told you, I'm getting good at this balance thing."

Nora's expression softened, "Yeah, You are."

They got ready together, Layla raiding Nora's hoodie stash, Aliya changing her bun three times, Nora pretending not to care but adjusting her jacket in the mirror more than once.

It was simple, quiet fun. The kind that you don't realize matters until it's gone.

On their way out, Layla stopped by the mirror in the hall.

"You two are my favorite people," she said casually.

Nora chuckled. "You say that now. Wait till we run out of whipped cream and have to share a table with college couples doing eye poetry."

Aliya made a face. "Oh no. The unspoken date night."

Layla laughed and pulled the door shut behind them.

The café was exactly how Nora remembered it, warm lights draped across the ceiling, the windows fogged just enough to make the world outside feel distant. Inside, soft jazz hummed under the quiet clinking of mugs. The place was small, tucked between a laundromat and a plant shop, but it had heart.

They found a table near the corner, cramped, a little wobbly, but perfect.

Aliya slid into one side of the booth, Layla beside her. Nora took the other seat, tugging off her gloves and tucking them into her pocket.

Layla leaned forward, eyeing the menu with way more excitement than necessary. "Okay, so. I'm getting the deluxe cocoa. Extra whip. And the cinnamon swirl muffin."

Aliya squinted. "Isn't that like… dessert on dessert?"

"Exactly," Layla said proudly.

Nora rolled her eyes. "Sugar coma incoming."

"And you'll love me through it," Layla grinned.

They placed their orders and sank into the evening.

It was peaceful.

Aliya scrolled through her phone, showing Layla a meme that had them both in stitches. Nora mostly watched, her sister laughing without restraint, her friend half-choking on a sip of hot tea.

She didn't say much. She didn't need to.

This was enough.

Even when Nora let her gaze drift out the window, toward the quiet sidewalk, toward the dim orange glow of the streetlights, there was no tension. Just the hum of distant traffic. The occasional passerby. The city breathing around them.

For the first time in a while, Nora felt something like stillness.

It was late when they finally stepped back onto the street. The wind had picked up, but the cold didn't bite. Layla's laugh echoed down the block as they walked, linked arm-in-arm. Aliya tossed a crumpled napkin at her and missed.

They reached the dorm an hour before midnight.

Inside, the heater kicked on with a soft groan. Nora hung her jacket, Layla collapsed onto the bed with a dramatic sigh, and Aliya stretched like a cat, already yawning.

"Tomorrow," Layla said, muffled into a pillow, "we make pancakes."

Nora smiled, pulling her blanket over Layla. "Sure," she whispered. "Tomorrow."

She turned off the lamp.

The room went quiet.

Chapter 23

Saturday morning came slow and golden.

The soft hum of the dorm's old heater filled the room as sunlight spilled through the slats of the blinds, casting quiet lines across the carpet. Aliya had claimed the corner of the couch, half-wrapped in a blanket, lazily flipping through a magazine. Layla was still asleep, curled up on Nora's bed with one leg hanging off the edge like she'd just melted into it.

Nora moved quietly, brushing her teeth at the sink by the bathroom mirror, hair tied up in a messy bun, hoodie halfway zipped. Her eyes were tired, but there was peace in her posture, like she hadn't felt this kind of quiet in a long time.

College had its chaos, but weekends like this made it worth it.

She walked back into the main room with a small box of cereal in her hand and tossed a few pieces at Aliya. Aliya dodged dramatically, scowling with her eyes still on the page.

"Hostile behavior before ten AM? That's a new low."

Aliya grinned. "You've survived worse."

From behind them, a groggy voice mumbled, "Can someone tell the sun to shut up…"

Layla blinked awake, pulling the pillow over her head with a groan.

Aliya laughed. "She lives."

"Barely," Layla muttered. "Someone turn down the brightness on the day."

Nora tossed a rolled-up sock at her. "Get up. I'm making pancakes."

That got Layla moving. A little.

The morning stretched lazily. Layla made milkshakes and spilled them twice. Aliya put on a playlist that shuffled from pop to sad indie without warning. Nora cleaned her desk, then messed it up again looking for a charger she never found.

Around noon, they ventured out. Nothing big, just a walk downtown. Some thrift browsing. A slice of pizza. Layla talked the whole time, telling them about a weird substitute teacher who pronounced mitochondria like "mickey-dondria," and how she got a detention for correcting him too loudly.

Aliya nearly choked on her drink laughing.

It was easy. Warm. A simple Saturday no one thought to treasure.

Not yet.

That night, they watched a movie none of them actually finished. Nora fell asleep first on the armchair, then Aliya, and finally Layla, curled under a blanket with her phone still lit up beside her.

The dorm was quiet again, and outside, the city kept breathing.

Sunday evening came too quickly.

The sky was turning that burnt orange shade it always did around this time, when the weekend felt like it was already slipping away. Shadows stretched long across the sidewalks, and the streets looked half-asleep, like the world was tired too.

Nora drove in silence, both hands steady on the wheel. Layla sat beside her, legs folded up onto the seat, hoodie sleeves pulled over her hands. The windows were cracked just enough to let in the breeze, that in-between temperature that wasn't quite warm anymore. Their playlist had ended a while ago, but neither of them had bothered to start a new one.

Layla let her head lean against the glass. "It's quiet."

Nora glanced at her. "You want me to put something on?"

Layla shook her head. "No. I like it. Just feels weird going back."

Nora didn't answer right away. The road curved ahead, a few kids riding bikes in the opposite lane, the soft hum of their tires on pavement blending with the buzz of late-summer bugs.

"It's only for a few days," she said finally. "Then you're back with us again."

Layla smiled faintly, but didn't look away from the window. "I know."

A moment passed.

"Do you think Mom's gonna say anything about my math grade?"

"She might," Nora admitted. "But that's not your whole report card. It's one class."

"She's gonna make it sound like the end of the world."

"She makes everything sound like the end of the world," Nora muttered, then added more gently, "It's not about you. She's just… tired. Bitter. Something. I don't know. But it's not you."

Layla was quiet for a while after that. The kind of quiet that didn't need to be filled. She watched the neighborhoods shift through the window, the houses getting older, yards messier, porches more crowded with rusted bikes and forgotten toys.

This wasn't the nice part of town.

"I wish I could stay all week," Layla said suddenly.

Nora's heart clenched.

"I know."

The car rolled to a stop at a red light. Nora looked at her little sister, really looked. Fourteen years old, hoodie zipped to the top, hair in a loose braid, face still round with youth but eyes a little too aware. Too sharp for her age. She was growing up faster than she should have.

"I mean," Layla continued, "I know I can't. But I wish.

It just feels… easier. When I'm with you and Aliya."

Nora exhaled slowly, her fingers tightening on the wheel. "You don't have to explain that. I get it."

They passed a gas station, a laundromat, then the little corner market Nora used to walk to as a kid. Layla sat up a bit straighter as they turned down their old block, the house coming into view at the far end. Nothing had changed. Same chipped paint. Same overgrown lawn. Same porch light that never worked.

Layla let out a breath that sounded too heavy for someone her age. "I feel bad sometimes. Like I'm ditching her."

"You're not," Nora said immediately. "You're surviving. That's not the same thing."

Layla didn't answer. She reached down to retie one of her sneakers, her fingers slow and distracted.

The car rolled to a stop in front of the house.

Neither of them moved.

Finally, Layla unbuckled her seat belt but didn't reach for the door. "If she says anything about my hair or my clothes, I'm gonna scream."

Nora smiled a little. "Tell her it's my fault."

Layla smirked. "I always do."

They sat there in that pause, the kind that stretches and stretches but doesn't quite snap.

Then Nora turned toward her fully. "Hey."

Layla looked over.

"You are good," she said, her voice low but firm. "And strong. And smart. And you don't owe her some perfect version of yourself just because she can't handle her own life."

Layla blinked, eyes shining just barely.

"I mean it," Nora added. "You're not the issue here. You're the light in this mess."

Layla swallowed hard, then reached over and hugged her tightly. It wasn't just a goodbye hug. It was the kind that clung, quiet, desperate, full of things neither of them had words for.

When they pulled back, Layla wiped her eyes with her sleeve and nodded.

"I'll text you."

"Anytime," Nora said. "Even if its three in the morning, I'm here."

Layla opened the door, stepped out, and adjusted her backpack on her shoulder. She gave a little wave, then jogged up the steps.

Nora didn't drive away right away. She waited until the front door opened, Layla stepping inside.

The porch light never flickered on.

Nora stared at the house for a long moment, jaw set.

Then she shifted into drive and pulled away.

She didn't turn the music on.

She didn't call anyone.

She just drove.

She felt at peace, the kind of peace that hits hard with gratitude and excitement for what's next.

What could possibly go wrong?

Chapter 24

The days slipped by in a steady rhythm, textbooks stacked beside half-empty coffee mugs, late-night study sessions stretching deep into the quiet hours. Nora and Aliya settled into their groove, part scholars, part sisters by choice.

Their dorm room became a sanctuary, filled with whispered jokes, shared playlists, and the steady thrum of mutual support. Between pages and flashcards, they found space to breathe, to be themselves, to carry each other through the stress of midterms.

When Friday finally arrived, Nora found herself driving toward Layla's school with a mix of relief and anticipation. The afternoon sunlight spilled golden through the trees as she pulled up to the curb.

Layla was already waiting, her backpack slung casually over one shoulder, eyes bright and laughing as she waved.

The car ride back was easy, filled with the comfortable banter that only siblings and those who have built their own kind of family can share. Layla teased Aliya, who was already on speakerphone, plotting their weekend adventures. Nora laughed more than she had in days, the sound light and free, a small reprieve from the weight she usually carried.

Back at the dorm, the three sank into familiar routines. Layla kicked off her shoes by the door, her energy contagious as she moved through the room. Aliya pulled out snacks while Nora spread her notes across the table, but their conversation wasn't about studying. It was about everything else.

Plans for Saturday night floated between them: a quiet movie marathon, homemade popcorn, no big crowds, just a chance to relax before the storm of exams picked up again.

That night, as Nora watched Layla drift off on the couch with Aliya reading softly nearby, she felt the deep comfort of belonging. It was the kind of peace that felt fragile and precious. They were safe here. For now.

But beneath that warmth, a quiet knot of worry twisted in Nora's chest. Layla's smile was a little too bright, her laughter a little too quick. Nora caught herself wondering how long this calm could last. The world outside their door was a place of shadows they couldn't yet see, but Nora knew it was closing in.

Still, tonight wasn't the night for fear. Tonight was for holding close what they had, this fragile bond, this moment of light before the darkness crept closer.

The next day, the morning light crept softly through the blinds, casting thin stripes across the dorm room walls.

Nora sat on the edge of her bed, surrounded by scattered notes and textbooks, the quiet hum of campus life filtering faintly through the window. Aliya was sprawled on the desk chair, earbuds tucked in, half-listening to a playlist while reviewing flashcards. Layla lounged on the small couch, flicking through her phone with a distracted smile.

The day stretched ahead, filled with the familiar comfort of routine and the anticipation of evening plans. Outside, the air held the crisp edge of early fall, leaves already turning golden and fluttering lazily from the trees.

Nora finally looked up from her notes, eyes meeting Layla's across the room. "So, you're really set on going to the park this afternoon?"

Layla stretched, propping her head on one hand. "Yeah, it's just a few of us from school. A little fresh air, some soccer, maybe a picnic if we get hungry. Nothing wild."

Aliya exchanged a glance with Nora, the worry unspoken but thick in the room. "That park's a bit far from campus, right?"

Layla laughed softly, brushing a loose strand of hair behind her ear. "I know what you're thinking. But trust me, we'll be together the whole time. Plus, I have my phone on me. Fully charged."

Nora bit her lip, her fingers drumming lightly on her notebook. "We just want you to be safe. It's not that we don't trust you, but just be careful."

Layla's smile softened, and she swung her legs off the couch, standing up. "I get it. And I appreciate it. I promise I'll be careful. I'll check in when I get there and before I head back."

Nora stood too, moving to stand beside her sister. "Okay. Just remember, if anything feels off, you call us."

"Deal," Layla said with a reassuring grin. She grabbed her jacket from the hook by the door, slinging it over her shoulder. "Now, don't spend all day buried in those books. You both need breaks too."

Aliya pushed herself upright and gave Layla a quick hug. "Have fun. And don't let the boys steal you away."

Layla rolled her eyes playfully. "I'll try not to."

With a final wave, she stepped out into the hallway. The door closed softly behind her.

For a moment, Nora and Aliya stood quietly in the room, the absence of Layla creating a subtle void.

Nora sighed, sinking back onto her bed. "I hate feeling like this. Like I'm not doing enough to keep her safe."

Aliya pulled her chair closer, resting her chin on her hand. "We're doing what we can. And Layla's smart, she knows the risks."

Nora nodded, but the knot in her stomach didn't ease.

"Come on," Aliya said, nudging Nora gently. "Let's get back to these midterms before we drive ourselves crazy."

The hours slipped away in a mixture of focus and whispered distractions.

Flashcards were flipped, formulas scribbled, and study guides highlighted with methodical care.

Occasionally, Nora would glance at the door, as if expecting Layla to walk back in early.

By late afternoon, the sun dipped lower, painting the sky in soft shades of orange and lavender. Nora closed her laptop with a tired smile. "I think we've earned a break."

Aliya stretched, cracking her knuckles. "Absolutely. But don't forget, we have plans tonight."

"It's been a week since we *actually* went out."

Nora smiled at the thought, the promise of a night out lightening the weight of the day. "Yeah. We deserve it. Just a few hours to unwind."

They moved around the room, setting aside notes and tidying scattered papers.

Aliya rummaged through a drawer, pulling out scarves and hair ties, while Nora flipped through her wardrobe, debating what to wear.

"So, what's the outfit vibe tonight?" Aliya asked, holding up a navy sweater. "I'm thinking comfort."

"Comfort sounds perfect," Nora said, holding a black jacket against herself. "Plans made. Outfit decided. Now we wait for Layla."

The sound of the hallway door caught their attention. Nora glanced at the clock, it was nearly mid-evening, Layla should have been back by now.

They exchanged a quiet look, a mix of anticipation and the lingering worry neither wanted to voice aloud.

Nora's phone buzzed suddenly on the desk, the sharp ring breaking the calm.

Nora reached for it and picked it up.

It was one of Layla's school friends.

She picked it up and put it on speaker.

"Yes?"

There was noise on the other side of the call, probably just the group running around.

"Hi Nora, has Layla gone back to your place?"

Nora raised an eyebrow and looked at Aliya, who met her gaze, "No, not yet. Why?"

"Oh, we were playing a game of hide and seek, and we ended the game a while ago, but nobody has found Layla, and we've called her multiple times, but she hasn't picked up, nor is her location updating."

Nora glared at Aliya, signaling her to grab the car keys, and replied with a sense of rush in her tone, "I'm coming, stay there."

Chapter 25

The parking lot by the park was nearly empty when Nora's car skidded into a space, headlights slicing across the cracked pavement. The moment she killed the engine, she and Aliya jumped out. The air was sharp and cold, heavy with the smell of pine and the faint smoke of distant barbecue pits. But something was off. Too still. Too quiet for a weekend evening.

A small cluster of teens stood near a wooden bench at the park's entrance, their faces pale in the low light of a flickering streetlamp. One of them– Emma, if Nora remembered correctly from pictures, stepped forward the moment they approached.

"She still hasn't answered," Emma said. Her voice trembled. "We thought she was messing around at first, just hiding too well, but it's been almost forty minutes. We've searched the entire park."

"Did anyone see her leave?" Aliya asked, glancing around.

"No," said one of the boys, arms folded tight against his chest.

"She was it during hide-and-seek. She said she was going to count behind that oak tree over there– " he pointed toward a large tree near the edge of the field, "but no one ever saw her after that."

Nora's eyes darted across the field, to the walking paths, to the dark line of trees beyond the picnic tables. "And her phone?"

"Calls go straight to voicemail," Emma said. "Last time we checked her location, it pinged once… then stopped."

Nora looked back at Aliya. No words were needed, only a nod.

"Alright," she said quietly. "We fan out. Check the entire park again. The bathrooms, the playground, the field. Everywhere."

The group scattered. Nora and Aliya moved quickly, flashlights sweeping through the shadows. The bathroom stalls were empty. No shoes behind benches. No familiar voice laughing from behind a tree. Aliya called Layla's phone again. Still nothing.

Fifteen minutes passed.

Nothing.

Aliya turned to Nora, breath coming quicker now. "This isn't right."

"I know," Nora whispered. Her stomach twisted. She turned toward the tree line at the far end of the park, the edge of the woods. Thick and overgrown, it bordered the park like a curtain, a sliver of wilderness that most kids avoided after dark.

"She wouldn't go in there," Aliya murmured.

"Unless someone made her," Nora said, already moving forward.

Aliya hesitated. Then followed.

The trees swallowed them fast. Branches hung low, roots curled like fingers across the dirt. Their flashlight beams bounced off twisted trunks and fallen leaves. The deeper they went, the more the sounds of the park faded. Until only their footsteps and the soft crunch of twigs remained.

Nora stopped. "Call her again."

Aliya hit redial.

Ring.

Ring.

And then,

A faint sound.

To the left.

A soft buzz. A ringtone. Muffled. Close.

Nora froze. "Did you hear that?"

Aliya nodded, stepping carefully toward the sound.

They pushed past a low tangle of brush.

Then Nora saw it.

A phone.

Faced down in the dirt. Layla's.

And beside it, a pale purple hair tie, the one she'd been wearing around her wrist all day.

Nora's chest tightened. She knelt slowly, fingers trembling as she reached for the phone. It was cold. The screen was cracked, smeared with dirt.

Aliya's voice cracked. "Nora..."

Nora stood, silent, gripping the phone.

Behind them, they heard the others shouting their names, Emma, the others– they were catching up.

When they arrived and saw the phone, the group fell silent. The reality began to settle like dust on their shoulders.

One of them pulled out their phone and dialed 911.

Aliya stood behind Nora, her hand on her shoulder. Nora didn't move. Her eyes were locked on that patch of earth. That little piece of her sister left behind.

Not a trace of Layla.

Only silence.

And the dark.

The police arrived twenty minutes later. Flashlights, questions, tape.

Aliya gave her jacket to Nora. Someone tried to ask if she was okay.

She didn't answer.

They took the phone. Said they'd run diagnostics, see if they could trace it.

Nora didn't argue. Didn't blink.

When she got home that night, she sat on the edge of her bed, legs numb, face blank.

The room was silent except for the hum of her mini-fridge and the dull drip of the leaky sink.

She stared at the purple hair tie in her palm.

Layla never took it off. Not once.

Nora clenched her hand around it until her nails dug into her skin.

Then stood, walked to her desk, and pulled open the drawer.

She reached under a stack of books and took out her old journal, one she hadn't touched since Layla moved in.

She flipped to the first blank page.

And with a pen that shook at first, she wrote:

"They took her from me. Whoever they are. I don't care anymore. I will find her.

Even if I have to disappear too."

She closed the journal. Sat in the dark.

And something inside her shifted.

The girl who once blamed herself was gone.

Now, there was only purpose.

Chapter 26

The dorm room felt emptier than it ever had.

His textbooks lay untouched on the desk, dust settling over half-open notebooks.

The basketball posters on the wall looked faded, almost forgotten.

Zayn sat on the edge of his bed, hands folded, eyes hollow.

Zayn stopped going to practice.

Stopped seeing his teammates.

Stopped talking to Mira's parents.

Everywhere he looked, he saw shadows, reminders of the empty seat where she should be.

He lay awake in his dorm, replaying the previous few nights, her smile, the look in her eyes, the way she told him, "I'll be fine, just go."

He hated the silence that followed.

One evening, while scrolling aimlessly, a message popped up on his burner-phone: a flyer shared by Damian.

A new missing person, a kid, much younger, same eeriness, same silence.

The flyer read:

"Gabriella Mendez, Age 15, Missing from Ledgeville."

His chest tightened.

He stared at the flyer, memorizing every detail.

This wasn't just another case.

This was a sign.

He texted Damian:

"I'm leaving. Need to see this for myself."

Damian replied immediately:

"Be safe."

Zayn left him on read.

He packed a small bag. Took his keys. Left the dorm behind.

His heart still ached, but something inside shifted.

Not hope. Not closure.

Just a raw determination to stop the silence from swallowing another life.

***

The fluorescent lights buzzed overhead, flickering just enough to remind Nora they were still in the dorm room, still in the city, still trapped by silence she couldn't break.

Aliya sat on the floor against the far wall, legs crossed, eyes on a book she wasn't really reading. Every few minutes, her gaze flicked toward Nora, who sat curled on the bed with a thin blanket wrapped around her knees.

Nora didn't speak. She barely moved.

She stared out the window at the flickering street lamps, their orange halos blurred by rain on the glass.

The small room smelled faintly of dry shampoo and cold coffee.

Aliya shifted, then spoke quietly, like she was afraid to shatter the stillness.

"Nora, you didn't eat breakfast. You didn't eat lunch either."

Nora blinked, then looked away.

"I'm not hungry." Her voice was thin.

Aliya didn't argue. Instead, she pulled a small plate from her bag: some sandwiches she'd made earlier. She placed it gently on the desk beside Nora, who barely glanced at it.

Night crept in slow and heavy.

Aliya lit a single candle. Its flame flickered shadows across the peeling wallpaper.

She reached out, tentatively, and touched Nora's hand.

Nora flinched but didn't pull away.

"I'm here," Aliya whispered.

Nora closed her eyes and exhaled, small and ragged.

After what felt like a lifetime, she pulled her phone close. Her fingers trembled as she typed Aliya a message, knowing she was right in front of her:

"I'm okay."

Aliya smiled softly, but didn't say a word. Instead, she pulled out a folded piece of paper from her pocket, wrote something on it, and laid it beside Nora's phone.

It was a note:

"I'll carry your grief if it means you don't drown in it."

Nora's breath caught. She let the tears come, slow and quiet.

For the first time in weeks, she *cried*.

Aliya sat near her and gave Nora a tight hug as she wept in Aliya's arms like a child. There was something so comforting about this.

Days slipped by. Nora skipped classes, meals, even her midterms.

Nora barely spoke but never left Aliya's side, occasionally helping Aliya study.

Aliya carried the weight of the world for the both of them, making calls, bringing food, setting gentle reminders to drink water or stretch. One rainy afternoon, Aliya's phone buzzed. She showed Nora a screenshot: a missing child alert for a girl in a nearby town.

Nora's eyes lingered on the photo.

Something deep inside stirred, like a faint spark beneath ashes.

"I have to go," Nora said quietly, voice raw with hesitation.

Aliya nodded.

"I'll come with you."

Nora shook her head.

"No. This one... I need to do this."

Aliya squeezed her hand.

"If you find anything, call me. Promise?"

Nora's eyes met hers.

"Promise."

The hour before leaving, Nora sat by the window again, the note from Aliya still folded in her palm.

She took a pen and carefully wrote Layla's name on her wrist, deliberate, like a vow.

Then packed a small bag, the emotional weight of it heavier than any physical suitcase.

Aliya watched silently, ready to support but letting Nora take this step alone.

Chapter 27

The road out of Holloway faded behind Zayn as the sun slipped low, bleeding orange and purple across the sky. The town ahead looked small and quiet, swallowed by shadows creeping fast.

He drove past a "Welcome!" sign, now noting he'd entered the town. He stepped out into the cooling air, pulling his jacket tighter, the missing girl's flyer folded deep in his pocket.

The streets were silent. Faint crackles of distant traffic reached his ears, but the immediate world around him felt still, as if holding its breath.

He walked slowly toward the park where the girl was last seen.

He noticed the faded paint of a small basketball court glowed dim under flickering streetlamps. Something in him stung. He hadn't touched a basketball in a while. The goal that once meant everything to him now meant nothing.

His fingers brushed over the flyer again. The girl's face stared back at him, eyes wide with something lost.

Zayn took out his phone and opened the maps app, scanning the geography around him, the shadows pooling beneath the streetlights.

As the evening deepened into the night, he found a low rooftop overlooking the block, settled down with his back against the rough brick. A cigarette flicked to life, smoke curling upward in the chill air.

His mind drifted. Mira's smile, the way she was, he wanted his other half back.

Meanwhile on the other side of the town, Nora's car rolled quietly just as the last light drained from the sky, the horizon bruised with deep purples and fading gold. The air outside was cool and damp, the kind that settles softly on skin and carries the faint scent of earth and distant rain. Streetlights blinked awake one by one, their weak halos casting long pools of light on cracked sidewalks and worn asphalt.

She eased the car into a parking spot near a small motel nestled at the edge of town, the casual ragged broken place that had seen better days. The building's paint was peeling, windows fogged and cracked in places, and the flickering porch lights cast uneven shadows that danced faintly in the gentle breeze. The quiet hum of cicadas filled the silence, a slow, rhythmic song that seemed to mark the passing of another day.

Nora sat for a moment, hands gripping the steering wheel a little too tightly, her breath shallow and uneven. The weight of the bag resting on the passenger seat felt heavier than it should, she reached over and lifted the bag gently, then opened the door and stepped out into the cool evening air. The ground beneath her feet was rough, scattered with dry leaves and small stones that crunched softly with each step.

Her eyes traced the jagged outline of rooftops and telephone wires, lingering on a few flickering porch lights still stubbornly glowing despite the coming night. The silence was thick, almost tangible, broken only by the faint rustle of wind through leaves and the distant bark of a dog.

From her bag, Nora pulled out a small pen and, with deliberate care, traced over the fading name *Layla* on the inside of her wrist. The ink smudged slightly as her hand trembled. It was more than a name; it was a vow written in silence, a promise to remember and to fight.

Night crept in slowly. Nora's thoughts drifted unbidden to the past, the sound of Layla's hearty laughter echoing faintly like a ghost, the warmth of her smile, the way her hand fit perfectly in hers. Memories both painful and precious tangled in her mind.

Each step Nora took was careful, her eyes scanning the streets, watching the ordinary scenes of daily life with a mixture of longing and detachment. She walked slowly, absorbing the quiet, aware of how distant she had become from this world that went on without her sister.

Her path led her finally to the narrow alley beside a small convenience store, the place where the shadows gathered and silence screamed louder than words. There, Nora paused, breathing deeply, steeling herself against the heavy weight of the unknown.

As the night fell deeper, the last tendrils of twilight slipped away, and streetlights flickered hesitantly to life, their pale glow barely penetrating the gathering shadows.

Nora moved carefully along the edge of the alley, her footsteps muffled against the cracked pavement and scattered leaves. The air was thick with the scent of damp earth and distant smoke, heavy and still, as if the night itself held its breath.

Ahead, perched on a low rooftop that overlooked the narrow street, sat a solitary figure. Cloaked in a dark hoodie pulled tight against the chill, his silhouette was hunched and still, almost blending into the worn bricks behind him. His gaze was fixed downward, unblinking, scanning the quiet street like a sentinel waiting for a sign.

Nora's breath caught in her throat. She froze, the sudden pulse of adrenaline sharpening her senses. The stillness of the man unsettled her far more than any movement would have.

Her mind raced. *Who is he? Why is he here?*

A thought flickered unbidden, *Is he involved?*

The suspicion was like a sharp edge cutting through the fog of her weariness, unwelcome but insistent.

Without making a sound, Nora melted back into the shadows, her footsteps light and careful as she retreated to a narrow corner just out of sight. The rough brick wall pressed against her back, cool and grounding beneath her fingertips. Her breathing slowed, matching the quiet rhythm of the night, but her heart hammered fiercely in her chest.

From her hidden vantage point, she kept the figure in sight. The man remained seated on the rooftop, his posture tense but still, shoulders hunched beneath the dark hoodie. His gaze never wavered from the street below, sharp and searching.

Nora's eyes narrowed. She tried to steady the swirl of suspicion and fear twisting inside her. *What is he doing here?* The question hung heavy in the air, unanswered.

The alley was cloaked in silence, broken only by the occasional distant sound, a creak of a loose shutter, the faint rustle of leaves stirred by a soft breeze. Shadows pooled thickly, offering cover and concealment alike.

Meanwhile, Zayn's senses flickered like a sixth sense. A prickle at the back of his neck, the subtle shift of the air. He tensed, slowly turning his head, scanning the darkness just beyond the edges of the streetlight's reach.

There, movement. A shadow slipping silently behind a wall, blending into the night.

His breath caught, muscles coiled tight. The weight of unseen eyes settled like a stone in his chest.

He didn't speak. Didn't call out. Instead, he shifted slightly, watching, waiting.

Nora held her breath, frozen against the wall, the cold seeping into her skin. Her pulse slowed but the tension remained, electric and raw.

Neither of them moved for several long moments: two figures locked in a silent, cautious standoff, each waiting for the other to make the first move.

The night deepened, wrapping them in its quiet embrace, as suspicion and unspoken grief wove a fragile thread between them.

Nora waited until the figure on the rooftop finally rose, moving with a deliberate, measured pace. She stayed pressed against the wall, shadowed and silent.

Her steps were careful and light, matching his direction but keeping a safe distance. The town's dim streetlights cast long, trembling shadows, stretching and shrinking as she moved through the silence.

Every sound, the soft scrape of her shoes against gravel, the distant murmur of traffic felt magnified in the stillness. She forced herself to stay calm, steady, eyes sharp.

Zayn's senses, now tuned to danger and the unknown, prickled with awareness. A fleeting feeling, like a breath on the back of his neck. He glanced over his shoulder, catching a flicker of movement, a shadow slipping behind a fence, a silhouette momentarily framed against a cracked wall.

He jumped off, and walked toward a sign. His pace slowed, cautious but unyielding. He didn't turn fully but kept his gaze flickering to where the shadow had been.

Nora's heart hammered, but she held her ground, blending with the night like smoke. Or so she thought. She needed answers, and though she didn't trust this stranger, she couldn't ignore the pull, the unknown, shared grief and the silent questions.

They moved like ghosts through the empty streets, two haunted souls bound by loss, suspicion, and the fragile hope that maybe, just maybe, they weren't alone.

Chapter 28

The streetlight flickered overhead, casting a pale circle of light onto the cracked pavement where Nora stepped from the shadow.

Zayn turned, his breath catching as their eyes met, two haunted souls laid bare in the quiet night.

For a long moment, neither moved nor spoke. The world seemed to hold its breath.

Nora's hands clenched at her sides, trembling slightly, not from fear, but from the weight of everything unspoken.

Zayn's gaze searched hers, searching for a trace of truth, of understanding.

Then, slowly, he took a tentative step forward.

"Who are you and why are you following me?" he yelled.

Nora's jaw tightened, eyes narrowing but her voice was calm, steady.

She hesitated, then met his gaze fully.

"Because I don't know if you're part of…"

She didn't know if she wanted to bring up the reason she was here.

The silence returned, heavier now, filled with shared pain and fragile trust.

Finally, Zayn exhaled slowly, nodding once.

"Same reason I'm here."

Nora didn't answer at first. Her eyes flicked past him, scanning the dark street as if something might leap out and prove them both wrong.

But nothing moved.

Only the soft hum of a faraway honk and the sigh of wind between old buildings.

She looked back at him, noticing the same pain in his eyes.

"You lost someone too," she said. Not a question.

Zayn's expression didn't change, but something inside did, like a door creaking open, just an inch.

He gave the smallest nod. "Yeah."

Nora took another step closer, still cautious. The distance between them narrowed, but the weight between them stayed.

They stood there, two strangers bound by grief and suspicion, the first fragile bridge between their worlds.

The town had gone still.

* * *

They sat across from each other on the edge of a rusted bench beneath a busted streetlamp that flickered now and then, casting light and shadow in uneven pulses.

Neither of them spoke right away.

Not because they didn't have questions, but because silence was safer than saying the wrong thing.

Zayn leaned back, hood down now, fingers laced in front of him, elbows on his knees.

Nora sat upright, guarded. Arms crossed. Eyes sharper than before. "You first," she said quietly. "Who was it?"

Zayn stared ahead for a second, then said, "Her name was Mira. My best friend. It's been over three months."

Nora's eyes softened just slightly, not expecting him to open up.

"My sister. Layla. I was supposed to be watching her. I wasn't. Few weeks back."

A long pause. They sat a few feet apart, but felt each other's emotional weight just from the few spoken words.

"That alley, or rather, the roof" she said. "Why were you there?"

"I've been following flyers," Zayn said, still holding his cigarette.

"There's a pattern, one that Holloway PD didn't care about."

Nora glanced at him, "You're from Holloway."

Zayn glanced back, "Yeah, rural side."

Nora nodded slowly. "Ledgeville, for college. Came here for clues, I want to find my sister."

Zayn looked at her now, not just glanced. *Looked*.

"Most people stop looking after a month."

Nora's voice was barely above a whisper. "Most people have something left to go back to."

The light flickered. Neither of them moved.

And for the first time, they didn't feel entirely alone.

Chapter 29

They didn't decide to stay in a motel together because it was safe.

They chose it because it was *nothing*. No memories. No friends. No ghosts. Just four walls, two beds, and a door that locked.

Zayn and Nora had just met. Not as friends, not even as allies, but as two people too stubborn to stop looking.

They came from different ends of pain, but in that quiet, broken town, both of them stood on the same cracked pavement, looking into the same unknown.

That was enough.

There was no dramatic moment where one said, "Let's get a place."

It was simpler than that. Zayn had cash. Nora had a list of safe spots. Neither of them wanted to go back to their cars.

So they found the motel.

Two floors. Rotten siding. Vacancy sign flickering like a dying star. But it was close to the last known location. It was cheap, and it had two beds.

That was the rule.

Always two beds.

No matter how tired. No matter how desperate. They weren't here to heal. They were here to search. Trust wasn't assumed. It had to earn its place like everything else.

The room was small. Beige walls. A heater that clicked every few seconds.

Zayn threw his duffel on the far bed and opened the curtain halfway. Nora dropped her bag near the desk and didn't say a word.

They didn't talk that first night. Not really.

He scrolled. She stared at the walls.

The silence wasn't awkward. It was heavy.

Weighted.

* * *

Zayn started waking up early. Walking the streets. Staring at flyers, talking to locals, following threads that didn't go anywhere.

Nora stayed in. She mapped out patterns. Traced timelines. Collected interviews like puzzle pieces no one wanted to fit together.

They weren't partners.

But they didn't leave.

Day after day. Same room. Same quiet rhythm.

They took turns buying food. Shared coffee in the mornings, even if it went cold.

Sometimes he'd come back late, wet from rain, and find a sandwich waiting.

Sometimes she'd fall asleep at the desk and wake up with his hoodie on her.

Nothing was said.

But something was happening.

Not friendship.

Not yet.

Just this small, strange rhythm:

One searching through streets, the other through shadows.

Both pretending they weren't afraid.

Both chasing someone they couldn't bring back.

And maybe, just maybe, starting to believe that if they kept going… they might not have to do it alone.

There wasn't a single reason they stayed.

Not comfort. Not trust. Not even progress.

Just this:

They didn't leave.

And that mattered more than either of them said.

Zayn came back one night later than usual, his jacket soaked, his knuckles scraped. He didn't explain why. Nora didn't ask. She just left the motel door unlocked.

Inside, the room felt dimmer than usual, the air heavy with the kind of quiet that settles after another dead end.

He sat at the edge of the bed, leaned forward, elbows on knees, water dripping onto the stained carpet.

"I hate this town," he said finally, not looking at her.

Nora, across the room, looked up at him, taking his jacket off.

"I hated it first," she replied.

That was the closest they came to a confession.

Week Two passed like that.

Small shifts. Half-conversations. Tiny gestures that didn't ask for anything in return.

They ate together. Not at the same time. But leftovers and portions were always in the mini fridge. Notes scribbled on napkins.

"Don't eat this. Tastes like dirt."

- Z.

"Too late. You owe me water."

- N.

* * *

One night, the power went out for three hours. The heater died. The only light came from a candle Nora had packed without reason. They sat there, backs against opposite walls, the silence loud enough to hear each other breathe.

"Were you always like this?" Zayn asked suddenly.

"Like what?" she replied.

He paused. "Empty."

Nora didn't answer right away. She looked down at the name written on her wrist. Still there. Faded, but there.

"No, but I'm good at becoming what I need to be," she said quietly.

He nodded, like he understood too well.

Chapter 30

The next day, they got their first real lead.

Nora was cross-referencing dates in the motel's yellow notepad while Zayn paced, staring at the map he'd taped to the wall.

She stopped suddenly. Her finger traced over two circles: Ledgeville and Meadowcrest.

"This one," she said, pointing at Ledgeville, the town they were in. "Gabriella. The missing girl. She was seen at a bus stop the night before she vanished. But it's not the closest stop to her school."

Zayn walked over. "So she was already running."

"Or being led," Nora said, looking up.

A beat passed between them, the first spark of sync.

Like maybe, just maybe, their puzzle pieces were part of the same picture.

They didn't hug. Didn't high-five. That wasn't who they were.

Zayn suggested, "Let's check the stop."

She shook her head. "It's not about finding something. It's about where they don't want us to look."

Zayn leaned against the wall, squinting at her with surprise. He looked at her, *really looked*, and said, "You always think like that?"

She shrugged. "It's how I cope with losing her."

Then, quieter:

"It's how I still survive."

The silence returned. But it didn't feel as heavy.

They went back to the motel.

Same two beds. Same two shadows on the wall.

But something had shifted.

For the first time, the room didn't feel temporary.

It felt like something was beginning.

Not healing.

Not yet.

But something real.

The days had started to blur.

Same streets. Same flyers. Same looks from people who had already stopped caring. It didn't matter how many times Zayn retraced the girl's last known steps, or how often Nora scoured the town's message boards: nothing changed.

That morning, he'd gone out again. Another lead. Another maybe.

A man at the gas station claimed he saw someone matching the girl's description. "Three days ago, I think. Or last week?" he'd said, scratching his head. "Could've been someone else."

Zayn thanked him anyway and walked out into the cold.

He didn't even tell Nora.

Back at the motel, her voice met him as soon as he stepped in. "Anything?"

He shook his head.

"No," she muttered, flipping through a folder filled with scribbled notes and maps. "But there's this trail near the edge of town. Gabriella used to hike with her older brother. Locals say she was seen there once."

Zayn sat down on the bed, staring at the ceiling. His body ached. His head pulsed.

"We'll check it tomorrow," she added, quietly, already planning the route.

And that was it. No time to rest. No time to break.

But Zayn *was* breaking– slowly, silently, without permission. He hadn't slept more than four hours in days. He couldn't remember the last time he'd eaten a full meal. Every time he looked in the mirror, he saw less of the person Mira used to know and more of someone haunted.

That's when it slipped.

He didn't plan to say it. Didn't even realize it was coming out until it already had.

"I'm done," he said suddenly, voice sharp. "I can't keep chasing shadows. This town, the flyers, the dead ends... It's killing me."

Nora looked up, startled by the sudden eruption. For a moment, the walls echoed his frustration.

"It's killing me too," she said quietly, voice steady but tired.

He stopped pacing and faced her. "Then why do you keep doing it?"

"Because if I don't, then what? I let her go like everyone else?"

Zayn's jaw tightened. "We're not going to find them. Not this way."

"We're not going to find them if we don't try," she snapped back.

For a heartbeat, their eyes locked, two storms colliding.

Then Nora looked away, biting her lip, the tension breaking into something fragile.

"I'm sorry," she whispered. "I didn't mean- "

"Neither did I," Zayn said, rubbing his head. "I just... I hate feeling this powerless."

Nora nodded. "Me too."

The room fell silent again, but this time it was different. It wasn't empty, it was raw.

They were broken.

They were afraid.

And for the first time, they weren't pretending.

* * *

Later that night, the motel room was dark except for the glow of Zayn's laptop and the night lamp near Nora's bed. Their cork board was cluttered now, a mess of scribbled timelines, blurred maps, pinned photos. Faces that never came home.

Nora sat cross-legged on the bed, scrolling through online missing persons logs like a habit. Same patterns. Same dead ends.

Until she stopped.

Her finger hovered over a name.

Emma Torres

Age 16

Disappeared: *Meadowcrest, 2 weeks ago*

Nora frowned. "Hey. I've seen this before."

Zayn looked up. "Who?"

She turned the screen. "Emma Torres. She was on one of the older posters in Ledgeville. I remember her face. But I thought she was from here."

Zayn came over, took the laptop, started digging.

Click.

Another tab.

Click.

Zayn sat back slowly.

"Meadowcrest," he muttered.

Nora leaned forward. "That's two towns. Two girls. Same timeline?"

Zayn added, "How do we know this is a valid lead? It's been two weeks since the incident.

Nora didn't blink. "Because someone out there still believes she didn't run."

Zayn didn't argue.

She stood and started pulling papers off the wall. "We leave at dawn."

Zayn zipped his bag. "We don't even know who's still looking."

Nora looked him dead in the eye.

"Then it's time they know that we are."

Chapter 31

The morning air was crisp, the kind that sharpens senses and clears heavy thoughts.

Zayn leaned against his car, glancing over at Nora, who was gathering the last of her things.

"So," he said, breaking the silence, voice low but steady, "you think Meadowcrest's ready for us?"

Nora looked up, a faint half-smile tugging at her lips. "Ready or not, it's where we have to go. No use waiting around here."

Zayn nodded. "Yeah. Feels like we're finally stepping into the real game."

She zipped her jacket up and slung her bag over one shoulder. "Don't get cocky. We still have a lot to figure out."

He grinned. "You're always the cautious one."

She shook her head, eyes softening. "Someone has to be."

There was a pause, comfortable, honest.

"I guess we should roll," Nora said, turning toward her car.

Zayn straightened, keys jingling. "I'll see you there. Same place, same fight."

Nora climbed in her car and started the engine.

Zayn jumped in, and honked to get Nora's attention.

She looked at him, hearing the honk, and saw him gesturing towards his steering wheel. He turned the ignition and started his car, the engine *roaring* from a cold start.

He looked over and let out a small chuckle as he saw her roll her eyes with a faint smile and pull out of the parking lot, following her.

As Zayn sped up a bit, catching up to Nora, he looked over until she looked at him a few seconds later. Their eyes met one last time.

He put weight on the gas pedal and put a distance between them.

Nora shook her head, smiled, and followed.

They were ready to fight together.

No grand promises. No heavy goodbyes.

Just the quiet understanding of two people carrying the same burden, heading toward the same unknown.

Zayn was already ahead by a few miles, driving with steady focus. They'd left at the same time, but his pace was faster, a mixture of humor between the two and determination pressing him forward.

The road stretched out before them, winding through sleepy towns and empty fields bathed in the soft golden light of early morning.

Nora's thoughts floated between past and present: memories of Layla's laughter, the ache of absence, the reason she couldn't turn back now.

Zayn's mind raced with thoughts of Mira, the pattern they'd been chasing, and the unknown that awaited them.

Hours slipped by.

The quiet companionship of the road bridging the distance between two broken souls searching for answers.

By late morning, Meadowcrest appeared on the horizon, a small city resting beneath a sky brushed with soft white clouds.

Zayn pulled into a parking spot near a cafe just as Nora rounded the corner, pulling up beside him.

"Took you long enough," he said, jokingly.

She smiled, "Shut up, we got here at practically the same time." Together, they stepped inside the cafe. The warm scent of coffee and baked bread greeting them like a small comfort.

"Hungry?" Nora asked, breaking the silence.

Zayn cracked a small smile. "After so long, starving."

They settled into a booth by the window, eyes tracing the gentle bustle of Meadowcrest waking up around them.

The weight of the road eased a little, replaced by the quiet beginning of something new.

The afternoon sun faded as Zayn and Nora left the cafe, stepping out into the cool air of Meadowcrest. The streets here felt less familiar, the city's edge creeping in with faded sidewalks and occasionally flickering streetlights.

They found a modest motel nestled between shuttered shops and quiet houses, a place that seemed just right for laying low, regrouping, and planning.

Inside their shared room, the silence settled comfortably between them. The weight of the day's drive still hung heavy, but the space offered a moment of calm.

Zayn pulled out a worn map, spreading it across the small table, while Nora organized her scattered notes and photos.

Neither spoke excessively. There was a time for jokes, and a time for work.

They had plans to walk around, hoping to notice something, a clue, a lead, any suspicious people, or activity.

Together, they stepped into the chill of dawn, ready to face the shadows that had haunted them for too long.

The chilly air bit softly at their skin as Zayn and Nora moved through the waking streets. The world was quiet, still catching its breath before the bustle of day.

They walked side by side, eyes sharp, scanning the cracked sidewalks, shuttered storefronts, and empty alleys for anything that didn't belong. Every stray paper fluttering in the breeze, every flicker of movement in a window drew their attention.

The town felt heavy with silence, a quiet that seemed to stretch too long, hiding secrets in its folds.

Then, from a block ahead, a lone figure appeared, slipping out from the shadow of a narrow side street. His gait was purposeful but guarded, hands buried deep in his jacket pockets, head low.

Nora's eyes narrowed. "Who's that?"

Zayn's jaw tightened. "Someone who's been around."

They exchanged a look, neither fully trusting, but both certain they needed to know more.

Without a word, they fell into step behind the figure, keeping a safe distance but closing slowly.

The man didn't glance back, but his pace didn't quicken. He moved with a familiarity that told them this was no random passerby.

As they followed, the darkness of the early night and late evening emerged. Streets grew quieter still. The city's edge gave way to empty lots and forgotten warehouses, the kind of places where shadows lingered and whispers could hide.

The figure stopped near an alley, casting a quick glance around before continuing on.

Nora's breath hitched. "We should keep up."

Zayn nodded, muscles coiled like a spring.

They moved cautiously, slipping through the dim light, two shadows tailing a third.

Chapter 32

Zayn and Nora moved quietly through the thinning streets of the warehouse district, the shadows stretching longer beneath the dying light. They kept a careful distance behind the figure ahead, his pace steady but cautious, slipping in and out of pockets of shadow like someone used to being unseen.

Neither spoke much, both their eyes sharp, ears tuned to every faint sound: the scrape of shoes on gravel, the distant hum of traffic, the clink of metal echoing faintly from up ahead.

This time, a metallic clang rang out, loud. Something dragging against concrete. The faint murmur of voices: low, tense.

The figure slid into a hidden corner, behind a dumpster ahead of him.

Something about the way he moved told them he wasn't just another curious bystander. He was hunting too, or maybe running from something.

From their hidden vantage point, Zayn whispered, *"He's like us."*

Nora nodded, barely daring to breathe. "Why else would he hide from that noise? He's watching, investigating."

They watched him, and the scene in front of him, noticing a black van on the other side of a chain-link fence.

They quietly moved closer, hoping the figure wouldn't notice them, and he didn't.

Then they heard a voice, loud, and irritated:

"Should've wrapped it tighter."

Zayn and Nora glanced at each other, eyes squinted, sharing similar thoughts.

The two realized they were *not too far away from a scene they had been hoping for so long now.*

Then suddenly the figure moved, rising slightly from his squat, controlled and stealthy, as if he was going to jump into something dangerous.

Nora stood up and approached the figure.

Before Zayn could stop her, Nora had come to a conclusion and boldly yelled,

"Don't."

Meadowcrest
Present Time

Chapter 33

The room smelled faintly of old carpet and sunlight filtering through blinds. Dust hung in the beams, caught in the air like tiny sparks. Zayn and Nora had just finished speaking about their pasts, and the words still lingered, heavy and raw.

Shawn leaned back in his chair, fingers drumming lightly on the armrest. His gaze didn't leave the floor. "I can't say I understand... not fully. But I feel it. The way it clings to you, even when you're moving forward."

Nora shifted, letting the silence stretch. She noticed the subtle tension in Shawn's posture, the way he folded his hands tight, as if holding in more than he said. She wondered how long he'd been carrying his own weight.

Alex spoke next, voice careful and quiet. "It's... a lot to hear. And to watch you two go through it all alone. Makes the rest of us feel..." His words trailed. He shrugged, a little helpless. "Small. Powerless. Like we should've done more, earlier."

Valerie's gaze flicked between Nora and Zayn, thoughtful. "We're all small sometimes," she said softly. "But maybe what matters is what we do now. How we move forward, together. Not alone."

Zayn rubbed the back of his neck, still tense from retelling. "We didn't come here to show off or get pity. Just... wanted you to know the stakes." His eyes scanned the room, landing on Shawn briefly. "You get it, right?"

Shawn looked up slowly, deliberately. "I get it. Maybe more than you think." His voice was low, dark, but steady. "You've been dragging yourself through hell alone. We've all been scraping the walls of it in our own ways. But hearing it out loud… it changes things. Makes it real."

Nora's fingers fidgeted with the hem of her jacket. She felt the tension in the room, but also something fragile beginning to grow. Maybe it was relief. Maybe it was trust. She wasn't sure yet.

Natalia finally spoke, her voice soft but firm. "So we're here. You two, and us. Not friends yet. Not even allies fully. But at least we know where we each stand." She paused, scanning their faces. "That counts for something."

Alex tilted his head, exhaling slowly. "It does. Maybe enough to start figuring out what comes next."

Valerie leaned forward slightly, hands resting on her knees. "We don't need answers right away. Just… presence. Seeing each other, hearing each other. That's the first step. Everything else comes later."

Shawn's lips twitched into a faint smile. "Presence," he repeated. "A funny word. Simple, but it carries weight. Most of the time, that's all you get before the rest of the world pulls you under again."

Zayn watched, noticing the way Shawn's dark eyes carried history and loss he rarely shared. He felt a strange relief, knowing they weren't the only ones who'd carried ghosts quietly, each of them tucked under their ribs like a second heartbeat.

Nora's voice came out softer this time, almost to herself. "I don't think I've ever just… stopped, and let myself sit with it. Not like this." She glanced at Zayn. "Not like this with anyone else."

Zayn's jaw softened and he nodded. "Me neither. But maybe that's why we're here now. To stop running for a minute. To see who we are when the chasing isn't all there is."

Natalia exhaled, shoulders relaxing slightly. "Then let's make that count. Even if it's just this hour, this room. We can figure out the rest later."

Shawn leaned forward, elbows on his knees. "I don't expect it to be easy. Nothing worth it ever is. But... hearing it all out loud, seeing you two... it makes me think maybe it's not pointless. Not yet."

Valerie nodded, quietly. "Not pointless. That's something."

The room fell into a calm rhythm, subtle but profound. No one spoke excessively for a few minutes, letting their own thoughts breathe. The weight of flashbacks, of danger, of loss, hung in the corners of the room, but it wasn't suffocating. Not yet.

Nora finally looked at each of them. "So... we start from here. From this moment. Not the past. Not the fear. Just... here."

Zayn's lips curved slightly. "Here."

Shawn's dark gaze swept the room, resting briefly on Nora and Zayn. "Here, for now. That's all we can promise. But it's enough."

Alex drummed his fingers lightly on the table in a tentative rhythm. "Enough to keep going, I guess."

Natalia let out a small, relieved laugh. "We'll see how long it lasts before one of you starts panicking again."

Valerie shook her head but smiled faintly. "That's probably inevitable."

Nora leaned back in her chair, eyes closing for a brief moment. The room felt warmer, somehow, like the first breath after a long run. Shadows still lingered, ghosts waiting outside, but for now... they were together.

And that, she realized, was enough.

Chapter 34

The apartment was quiet again, even the hum of the fridge sounded loud.

For the first time in hours, it felt like the group could breathe. The air had softened, almost peaceful, almost normal.

Then came the first crack.

It was faint, like glass shifting somewhere in the next building. The kind of sound that made you stop mid-breath, unsure if you really heard it.

Shawn's head turned first, eyes narrowing. "That wasn't just me, right?"

Nobody answered.

Then came the second one. Sharper. Closer.

This time, everyone froze.

Zayn's mind kicked into overdrive, mapping the space, counting exits. Nora's hand twitched toward her phone. Natalia sat perfectly still, listening. Valerie blinked, already half-standing, the familiar unease settling in her chest.

It wasn't the first time strange noises echoed through her building, but this one felt different. Heavier. Intentional.

Shawn moved toward the door, quiet but alert. "That came from next door. Maybe from a building nearby."

Alex, meanwhile, wandered toward Valerie's shelf, mumbling,

"Alright, so, if someone's breaking in, I need a weapon. Something blunt. Something effective."

Valerie frowned. "Alex–"

But he was already holding up a pink plush cat, squinting at it like it might transform into a sword. "This'll do. Emotional damage weapon."

Zayn looked at him, eyebrows raised. "You serious?"

Alex shrugged, "You ever been hit with a plush cat? Hurts emotionally."

Natalia sighed, fighting a small smile. "You're unbelievable."

Shawn turned his head just enough to see Alex standing there, stuffed cat in hand, expression flat. "We might be in danger," he said. "And you brought backup from Build-a-Bear."

Alex grinned. "She's called emotional support, bro. Learn to accept help."

Zayn snorted, shaking his head. "You're a menace."

Valerie didn't even speak. Just stared at Alex, who grinned back at her.

Then another sound cut through the room, this time, a deeper crack, followed by a faint, metallic clatter.

The smiles vanished.

Shawn straightened instantly.

"Alright now that's too suspicious."

Zayn grabbed a flashlight off the counter. Nora picked up a heavy book. Natalia wrapped her hand around a candle holder, holding it like it weighed more than it did. Valerie just stood there, half grounded, half listening, to the night, to the walls, to whatever waited outside.

Alex, of course, gripped the plush cat.

They crept out of the door, the cozy air of Valerie's apartment fading into something sharper. The faint vanilla scent from a candle mixed with dust and old carpet. The apartment had felt cozy until now.

Shawn glanced around the corner. He couldn't see movement, but the faintest reflection caught his eye, as if someone was pulling away.

Nora's pulse quickened. "You see anyone?"

"Maybe," Shawn murmured. "Maybe not. But someone was there."

The air grew still again.

Alex, whispering: "Maybe it's the wind."

Shawn didn't look at him. "If the wind starts throwing rocks, sure."

Zayn exhaled slowly. "So... we checking it out?"

Shawn's eyes stayed fixed on the alley. "Yeah. Together. Stay close."

They didn't know what was waiting out there. But as the night pressed closer to the window and the last fragments of glass caught the light, the six of them stood in the quiet, ready to move.

And for the first time in hours, the silence didn't feel safe anymore.

The night air hit them as soon as they stepped off the threshold of Valerie's apartment. Cold, damp, smelling faintly of rain that had fallen hours ago. The narrow street was almost deserted, lit by a few weak streetlights that cast pools of yellow over cracked concrete.

Zayn immediately moved toward the middle of the group, flashlight sweeping slowly across the street. The broken glass glittered faintly on the ground, tiny pieces that caught the light like fragments of stars. He knelt, crouching low to examine them. They were jagged and fresh, clean edges. Someone had used force, that much was obvious.

Nora bent slightly, hands brushing against her knees. Her pulse was steady but alert. She glanced at the others, seeing the tension in Shawn's shoulders, the way Valerie's eyes flicked constantly from shadow to shadow, and the slight stiffening of Natalia's posture. Everyone had gone quiet, but their attention was absolute.

Alex trailed behind, holding the plush cat in one hand. He was trying not to look ridiculous, but he could not stop himself from whispering under his breath. "You are going to protect us, right?" He shifted the cat's head as if it could see better in the dark.

Zayn glanced at him and shook his head with a faint smile. "That thing is not helping anyone."

Shawn gave a dry hum, shoulders tightening. "You brought a stuffed animal into a tense situation. This is what passes for your contribution?"

Alex shrugged without looking up. "Vibes matter."

Valerie gave a small exhale, one eyebrow raised, her eyes settling on Alex just long enough for him to notice the silent 'bruh' of disbelief. He met it with a sheepish grin, but even she allowed a faint smile before returning her attention to the street.

The quiet outside was not comforting. Somewhere far above, a window rattled faintly, sending a shiver down everyone's spine. Another crack of glass sounded, this time further down the block.

Nora stiffened. "That was the same building as before," she said. "Someone is moving around there."

Shawn squinted toward the noise. "Maybe. Maybe not. Either way, we stay aware."

Zayn's beam swept along the adjacent building, following the patterns of the broken windows. He felt the faint prickling of being watched, that instinct that had been there ever since the first crack of glass. Whoever it was, they knew someone had noticed.

Natalia shifted her weight from one foot to the other, glancing down the street. "Feels like we're walking into a spotlight," she muttered, half to herself. "Like every shadow is looking at us."

Valerie stayed quiet, letting them talk while keeping her eyes scanning the tops of windows, the edges of roofs, the spaces where someone could hide.

The apartment complex had always felt a little off to her, but this was different. Real movement, real attention.

Shawn finally spoke, voice low. "We check the immediate area, no farther. Just enough to see if someone is there. We won't run after shadows."

Alex moved the plush cat slightly in front of him, muttering, "Safety in numbers, right?"

They began moving down the street slowly. Each step was careful, each sound amplified in the otherwise quiet night. Broken glass crunched lightly underfoot, making everyone pause for a second longer than necessary.

A trash can lid shifted somewhere ahead, maybe wind, maybe not. Every small noise set them on edge.

Nora kept glancing above, thinking about the broken windows, trying to determine if anyone was watching from above. Her mind ran through every possible explanation, but she refused to voice them aloud. It would only make everyone else more tense.

Shawn stayed near the front, eyes trained on shadows, posture rigid but controlled. He moved with deliberate caution, aware of every reflective surface, every shape that could mask a person. He felt the tension in the group, and kept it contained, knowing a single word could escalate nerves unnecessarily.

Zayn crouched slightly over a patch of shards. "Footprints," he said quietly. "Fresh. Someone was moving fast. This way."

Nora followed, peering at the shards and faint impressions in the concrete. "So it was definitely someone," she said.

Valerie's gaze swept the tops of windows again. "If they're still there, they are probably watching from above, waiting for us to make a move."

Alex muttered, "Okay, maybe Mr. Whiskers is just symbolic after all."

Zayn glanced at him with a grin. "Symbolic is exactly what it is."

Shawn allowed the faintest twitch of his lips, part disapproval, part amusement. "Next time, leave the cat behind," he said flatly.

Valerie shook her head, eyes narrowing at the faint shadows on the building across the street.

The group paused at the edge of the next block. Another faint metallic clang echoed from the other building. Their eyes followed the noise, tense but calm.

No figure emerged, but the evidence was clear: someone had been here, someone had broken the glass, and someone had probably noticed them watching.

The night air pressed heavier now, closer. They could hear the distant hum of the city, the faint scuff of shoes on concrete, the subtle whisper of wind against windows. Every detail mattered.

Shawn finally nodded. "We won't go farther tonight, but we know someone is here. That's enough for now."

Alex held the plush cat a little higher. "I knew you'd appreciate this, bro."

Zayn shook his head, smirking. "You really do not get it, do you?"

Shawn glanced back at them, lips twitching again. "We are lucky this is a quiet night."

Valerie's eyes lingered on the broken windows, her hands tight at her sides. The city felt alive in a way it had not before, watching them, testing them.

They turned slowly back toward the apartment. Every step was measured, every glance deliberate. The broken glass still shone, a reminder that the calm they thought they had was gone.

And outside, somewhere above, someone was still watching.

Chapter 35

They gathered back inside Valerie's apartment, the door closing softly behind them. The small space felt almost cozy again, but the shadows in the corners were heavier than before. Every chair, every lamp, every stack of books seemed more solid, more present, as if they were trying to anchor themselves against the tension outside.

Zayn set the flashlight down on the table and rubbed the back of his neck. "Fresh footprints, broken glass, someone watching from up there. That is exactly what we thought it might be."

Nora sank onto the edge of the couch, hands pressed to her knees. "Yeah, but the thing is… I didn't see anyone, at least not clearly. Just shadows and reflections."

Alex perched on the arm of another chair, still holding Valerie's plush cat. "Shadows can be suspicious. They can also be absolutely nothing. But the footprints make it harder to ignore."

Valerie leaned against the counter, arms crossed. "The building across the street had every window intact except those two. Someone moved quick. That's too specific to be random. And if they were testing us…" She paused, frowning. "Then they know we're aware now."

Shawn ran his hand across his jaw, thinking. "Or they got careless. Could be a neighbor, could be someone trying to scare people away. Either way, it's enough to keep us alert."

Natalia sat on the floor, knees drawn up, eyes tracing the ceiling. "I hate this feeling. Like someone's watching but won't let you see them back. Makes everything else feel fake. Like the walls are moving."

Alex tapped the cat's nose and nudged it toward her knee. "He sees everything. Trust him."

Valerie gave him a slow look, caught between disbelief and amusement. "Why my cat, bro," she muttered under her breath, quiet but loud enough to make Nora hide a smile.

The tension cracked for half a second, a flicker of warmth through the unease.

Zayn exhaled. "We need to figure out what to do next. We can't just sit here waiting for the next sound. They could be back any minute."

Shawn's gaze moved toward the window. "We watch quietly. We don't go out there unprepared. If someone's testing us, we don't panic."

Nora tilted her head. "And what if they come closer? What if they're still watching right now?"

Shawn shrugged, his tone level. "Then we're ready. And we're not going to act like we're alone."

Alex adjusted the cat in his arms.

"And if all else fails," he raised the cat plush into the air, "emotional damage."

Zayn let out a quiet laugh. Even Shawn's mouth twitched before he sighed through his nose.

Valerie shook her head, moving to the window. The blinds swayed slightly as she peeked through. "I don't see anyone now. But that doesn't mean they're gone. And if they're patient, they won't show themselves. Not yet."

Natalia spoke softly from the floor. "We need a plan. Something small. If they're watching, we should at least know what we're willing to risk."

Shawn nodded. "We observe. We document. No rash moves. And

we make sure everyone here knows what the others saw. Communication is our edge."

Zayn leaned against the wall, flashlight tucked under his arm. "Still feels like we're sitting ducks."

Nora glanced up. "Feels like we're being tested. Like they're waiting to see how far we'll go before we panic." She looked around the room. "And I really don't like being part of that test."

The apartment went quiet. The only sound was the low hum of the city outside and the occasional creak of the old floorboards.

Then–
A sharp crash. Glass shattered violently from Valerie's bedroom.
The sound ripped through the apartment. Everyone jumped.
Valerie screamed, hand slamming to her mouth.
Shawn shot up and snatched the flashlight off the table, already moving toward the door. Zayn followed, pushing past the others with a quick glance.

"Cover yourselves!" Shawn barked, adrenaline tight in his voice.

The others froze, panic rising instantly. Nora's knees shook. Natalia hugged herself, pressing against the wall. Alex crouched down, clutching the plush cat like it might do something useful. Valerie stood rooted, wide-eyed, staring at the smashed window.

Shawn and Zayn sprinted out the door and onto the street.

They moved fast, scanning the alleys, rooftops, and the faint glow of the city beyond.

Empty.
Nothing stirred. No shadow, no figure. Just the cold, quiet street.

A tense minute passed before they returned. Their eyes swept the room as they stepped back inside.

"Nothing," Shawn said, voice firm and disappointed.

Zayn nodded, flashlight beam cutting across the apartment.

"Didn't see a single thing."

The group had huddled near Valerie's desk. On top of the scattered shards lay a small, roughly wrapped object tied with string. The edge of a note peeked from beneath it.

Valerie stepped closer, frozen. Nora reached for the corner. Slowly, the words became clear.

Stay out of it.

The room went silent.

Every heartbeat seemed louder than the crash that had brought the note here.

Valerie stared at the paper, her face pale, lips pressed tight, as if the words had physically pushed the air out of the room.

Shawn and Zayn instinctively shifted toward the door, bodies tense, muscles ready, eyes sweeping every corner.

Alex muttered, "Well… that escalated fast," gripping the plush cat tighter, almost like holding on to something solid might steady him against the panic crawling up his spine.

Nora and Natalia hovered near the desk, glancing between the note and the others, uncertainty in their movements, hesitation in their breathing. Valerie stepped forward, placing herself protectively in front of it, her hands curled slightly as though she could physically shield the message from anyone else.

Outside, the city seemed quieter than it had moments ago. The street looked empty, the faint hum of traffic distant, as if the world itself had been muted, waiting. But everyone inside knew better. The silence was temporary. The threat had only just begun.

Someone had crossed the line.

And now, the warning was real.

Stay out of it.

Chapter 36

The note sat on the desk.

Stay out of it.

Nobody touched it. The words pressed down on the apartment, heavier than the shards of glass glittering on the floor. The soft hum of the city outside seemed sharp and intrusive now, each distant car, each flicker of streetlights magnified.

Valerie's eyes kept returning to the broken window. Her voice trembled slightly. "I... I can't stay here tonight. Not like this. Anyone could–"

"Nobody's going to hurt you," Natalia said, stepping closer. Her hand rested lightly on Valerie's shoulder. "We'll make sure of it. You're not staying alone."

Valerie shook her head. "It's not just the window. The street... the corner apartment... they know exactly where I am. Anyone could see everything inside."

Alex shifted the plush cat nervously. "Well... they already did. And that was terrifying."

Shawn's hand rested on the windowsill, scanning the street outside without a word. Zayn stayed near the door, alert but quiet, letting his presence speak for him.

Valerie pressed her hands against her cheeks, exhaling shakily. "I can't... I can't be here. Not tonight. Maybe... maybe not even for a while."

Natalia nodded. "Then we move you somewhere safer. My place. It's a little walking distance, far enough to be out of sight, close enough we can get to you if we need to. You'll be safe there."

Valerie's shoulders slumped. Relief and fear tangled together in her chest. "Okay. I trust you."

Zayn spoke up. "I'll drive both of you there. Walking isn't safe. Just to make sure you get inside safely. Nora and I can stay in touch."

Shawn gave a flat look. "The rest of us should stay here. Just in case. Keep eyes on this apartment, on the street. If they're still out there…" His jaw tightened, voice low. "We need to know."

Alex groaned, clutching the plush cat. "Perfect. Emotional support on patrol duty, still working overtime."

They spent the next few minutes quietly gathering what Valerie could carry. Every movement was deliberate, careful not to disturb the fragile calm that had barely settled over the apartment.

Natalia slipped her arm around Valerie's shoulders. "We'll set up a group chat. All of us. If anything happens, we're connected. Even if we're not all together."

Valerie nodded, trying to steady herself. "I just… I don't want to feel like this again. Not in my own home."

Shawn glanced at the note on the desk one last time. "Leave it there," he said softly. "It's evidence. And a warning."

Valerie swallowed. "I used to feel safe here," she whispered.

Nora knelt beside her. "Nothing is safe anymore," she said, voice low.

The apartment settled into a tense quiet. Not calm, but careful. Every creak of the floorboards, every faint hum from the city outside, every flicker of streetlights made their hearts tighten.

When Zayn and Natalia were ready, Valerie took a deep breath. "I'm ready," she said, clutching her bag.

The three of them left quietly. Zayn had the car parked a not too far away, out of sight. The streets were empty, but each passing shadow, each distant sound, made Valerie's pulse quicken. Natalia stayed close, a steady presence guiding her.

Back at Valerie's apartment, Shawn, Alex, and Nora watched from the windows, alert, silent. The broken glass and the lingering shadow of the note pressed on their minds, but for now, they were staying put, ready for whatever came next.

Inside the car, Valerie exhaled slowly. The familiar fear was still there, but Natalia's apartment was just far enough away to feel safer. Zayn parked and Natalia led them towards her place.

"You're here," Natalia said softly, letting Valerie step inside. "Safe. For now."

Valerie let herself be guided in, "Thank you," she admitted, voice quiet but steadying.

Zayn pulled out his phone. "Group chat. All six of us. If anything happens, we're connected instantly."

Valerie nodded. "Thank you. Really."

Outside, the street looked ordinary, empty, quiet. But inside, Valerie, Natalia, Zayn, and the distant presence of Shawn, Alex, and Nora all understood: the night had shifted everything. The note, the broken window, the invisible threat; it had drawn them into a bigger problem.

And there was no going back.

Stay out of it.

Even now, Valerie realized she couldn't ignore it.

Chapter 37

Valerie sank onto the couch, clutching the plush cat tightly. Her hands were trembling slightly. "I don't think I could've stayed at my apartment tonight. Not after everything that happened."

Zayn gave a reassuring nod. "You're safe here. I'm going to pick up the others and bring them here. Stay put. Don't open the door for anyone else. Keep things quiet. I'll be back soon."

Natalia nodded and moved closer to Valerie, placing a gentle hand on her shoulder. "You're going to be okay. And..." She hesitated, then continued, "I think it would be a good idea if the others stayed here tonight as well. Just for safety. That way, you're not alone, and we can all watch each other's backs."

Valerie's eyes widened slightly. Relief, mingled with worry, crossed her face. "You really think that's necessary?"

Natalia smiled faintly, the kind of smile that gave quiet authority. "I do. It's a short distance from your apartment, enough that you're out of immediate reach, but close enough we can check in if needed. We'll make room. You won't be alone tonight."

Valerie nodded, feeling the first genuine relief of the night. The tension had not left entirely, but a tiny anchor had been set.

Zayn left swiftly, slipping into the streets, his eyes scanning constantly, every flicker of movement making him pause. The drive to pick up the other three was tense, measured, and silent, with only the faint hum of the engine and the city at night keeping him company.

When he arrived at Valerie's apartment, the others were waiting, already alert. Zayn motioned for them to be quiet.

"Doors locked? Windows closed? No distractions. Quick in and out. We're going to Natalia's."

Shawn gave a short nod. "Alright."

Alex smirked, holding the plush cat slightly too tightly. "We're basically moving a queen. Don't worry, your majesty, I've got you covered."

Shawn shot him a flat, unimpressed look. "Focus, Alex."

Nora rolled her eyes but moved quickly to help gather essentials: clothes, toiletries, snacks, and a few personal items Valerie had. Alex added the plush cat dramatically, muttering, "Cannot survive without him."

The drive back was deliberate and quiet, tension in every glance at passing shadows. Small talk broke the monotony, but carefully, as if even a laugh could attract attention.

"So, Alex," Zayn asked quietly, "the cat is really that important?"

Alex smirked at the plush, patting it with exaggerated seriousness. "Absolutely. Emotional support, tactical genius, backup plan. You don't know what you're missing."

Nora laughed softly. "Backup plan? Really?"

Alex's grin widened. "Every mission requires redundancy."

Shawn shook his head subtly, eyes flicking toward a flicker of movement in a distant alley. "Redundancy, sure. Just don't drop it."

When they reached Natalia's apartment building, she was already at the door, gesturing them inside. "Come in, we think y'all should stay here tonight. It's safer, and…" She glanced at Valerie, "I think it's better if you all stay as well. Just for the night. No one should be alone."

Shawn exhaled, almost quietly. "Alright. Better safe than sorry."

Alex dropped the bags and laid down by the couch dramatically. "So on the floor, huh? Honestly... I kind of like it anyway."

Nora rolled her eyes, a faint smile tugging at her lips. "Better than being out there getting yourself killed."

Valerie exhaled slowly, leaning back. "I feel safer already."

Natalia nodded, her eyes sweeping the room. "Good. That's the most important part. You're not alone, and we have eyes on everything. We'll adjust the furniture, make space for sleeping, make it comfortable, but most importantly, safe."

The group began unpacking, distributing bags, adjusting couches and chairs to create small zones for each person. Despite the lingering tension, small moments of humor and quiet chatter filtered through.

Zayn finally spoke, drawing their attention. "Now, for future plans. Natalia, if you're fine with it, Nora stays with you and Valerie for safety. And Shawn, I move in with you for the time being?"

They nodded. Shawn hesitated a bit over the fact that there would be another person in his fort of independence, but agreed.

Alex smirked, patting the plush cat again. "Best plan I've heard all night. Emotional support mandatory, check. Solo living, check."

Natalia added, "Each of you has a place to stay now, so we stay connected."

Shawn nodded slowly, gaze steady. "We stay alert, communicate clearly. We have a group chat.

If anything happens, we respond as a team."

Alex leaned back, a grin spreading. "Freedom, emotional support, tactical coverage. Honestly, I can work with this."

Nora laughed softly, shaking her head. "Mandatory emotional support, Alex. Don't forget that."

The group settled into the arranged spaces, bags tucked neatly, small sleeping zones created. The city outside continued its quiet rhythm, unaware of the tension, the warnings, and the plans being made within Natalia's apartment.

Valerie exhaled slowly, hugging the plush cat and leaning against Natalia. "I feel safe. At least for now."

Zayn scanned the windows one last time. "Keep alert. Nothing is guaranteed. But tonight, we are together, and we are prepared."

Even with the laughter, the small jokes, the reassurances, the note, the broken glass, and the taps outside lingered in their minds. The night was far from over.

And for the first time since the evening began, Valerie felt that maybe, just maybe, they could face whatever was coming, together.

Chapter 38

The night in Natalia's apartment was quiet in a way that felt strange. Too still, like the city outside had paused just long enough to listen.

Valerie slept near the couch, wrapped in a blanket that still smelled faintly of her old apartment. Nora and Natalia shared the bed, heads turned in opposite directions, the flicker of the streetlight outside tracing lines across the wall.

Zayn lay near the window, half awake.

Sleep didn't come easily. His mind wandered, not to the warning, not to the note, but to something older. Someone.

Mira.

He could still see her in fragments, the way she laughed too quickly, the way she'd rest her chin on her hand when she was pretending to listen. The last time they spoke had been before his tournament.

He'd told her he'd call. She said she'd wait. Neither of them had kept that promise.

Now the thought of her came like fog, slow, unwanted, but impossible to shake off. He wondered where she was. If she was safe. If she'd ever think of him when nights got too quiet like this. If she was even alive.

He turned over, pulling the thin blanket higher over his shoulder. The hum of the city outside was dull, distant, like an engine behind a wall.

That was when he noticed movement, soft, deliberate.

Zayn opened his eyes a little. In the dim light, he saw Shawn slipping his jacket on, careful not to make a sound.

For a moment, Zayn thought of saying something. But Shawn's expression, calm, focused, almost cold, stopped him.

Shawn glanced once toward the sleeping group, then toward the door.

Zayn's thoughts stirred.

Where's he going at this hour?

The door clicked softly behind him.

Zayn stayed awake for a few minutes more, eyes open to the ceiling, debating whether to follow or ignore it.

He let out a slow breath and turned back over. The city outside stretched, restless, but his eyes finally gave in.

Sleep caught him halfway between thought and worry.

* * *

It was barely sunrise outside when the first sound came, the gentle clatter of dishes from the kitchen.

The smell of eggs, toast, and something faintly sweet drifted into the living room.

Natalia and Nora were already up, both quietly moving around the counter. Natalia flipped something in a pan while Nora set out plates. Valerie sat near the table, hair messy, eyes still tired but more at peace than the night before.

Zayn blinked awake, rubbing at his eyes. "What time is it?"

"Barely sunrise," Natalia said softly. "We didn't want to wake anyone, but we figured food might help after last night."

Zayn sat up slowly, nodding. "Smells like heaven."

Alex was still asleep, tangled up in his blanket and the plush cat, snoring softly.

Nora smiled faintly. "He was talking to that thing in his sleep. Tactical genius or something."

Zayn chuckled under his breath, but it faded quickly when he looked around the room again.

"Where's Shawn?"

The question landed heavier than he meant it to.

Valerie frowned, glancing toward the door. "He was here last night, right?"

Zayn nodded slowly. "Yeah. I saw him before I fell asleep."

He hesitated, then added quietly, "Actually... I saw him leave. Didn't think much of it. Thought he might've gone to get air or something."

Natalia turned off the stove, her tone suddenly alert. "When?"

"Late. Past two, maybe."

For a second, no one spoke. The quiet stretched again, not tense, but curious in a way that felt uneasy.

Then came the sound of a knock on the door.

Shawn stepped in, jacket dusted faintly with dirt, face unreadable. His eyes flicked over the group like nothing was wrong.

He dropped a folded piece of paper onto the counter beside Natalia.

"Morning," he said simply.

Nora crossed her arms. "You disappeared."

Shawn shrugged, grabbing himself a water bottle. "Went to check something out."

Zayn raised an eyebrow. "So late at night?"

Shawn didn't look at him. "Just making sure we weren't followed.

We weren't."

Natalia stared at him, searching his face for more, but his tone gave nothing away.

She sighed, setting down the spatula. "Next time, tell someone before you go off on your own. We've had enough surprises."

Shawn gave a small nod, not defensive, just distant. "Noted."

Zayn leaned back, watching him.

There was something different about Shawn's eyes, not fear, not exhaustion, but something sharper. A kind of focus that didn't match the calm around them.

Alex finally stirred, voice muffled from the floor. "If anyone left the house without emotional support cat authorization, I'm gonna be disappointed."

That broke the tension, slightly. Nora rolled her eyes, Valerie exhaled, and Natalia's frown softened.

Shawn finally sat down, quiet. "Let's eat. We've got a long day."

The morning light crept across the room, soft but unsteady, like it was waiting for something to happen.

None of them said it out loud, but they all felt it.

Whatever Shawn had gone out for, it wasn't just a walk.

Chapter 39

"So what now?"

Alex leaned back in his chair, tapping the side of his mug. "Well, technically, it's Friday. So school is happening. Somewhere. Not here. Not for us. Lucky us."

Nora rolled her eyes. "You're leaning into this skipping-school thing, huh?"

"Of course," Alex said solemnly, pointing a finger at her like a lecturer.

"This is an educational experience. Life skills, survival strategy, conflict avoidance, tactical coffee consumption. Curriculum approved."

Valerie chuckled softly, tugging the blanket tighter around her shoulders. "Tactical coffee consumption?"

"High-level," Alex replied, nodding seriously. "Hard to quantify. Definitely not in any textbook."

Shawn, who had been quietly eating his toast, raised a brow. "You've got a weird way of motivating people."

"I'm a modern educator," Alex said, shrugging. "Also terrifying in multiple ways. Don't forget that part."

Natalia let out a small laugh, shaking her head. "If your teachers knew their favorite student was applying his 'methodology' here, they'd lose their minds."

Zayn smiled, setting down a plate of fruit. "Honestly, I think you're just avoiding homework."

Alex gave a dramatic gasp.

"Homework? What is this... medieval torture? You expect me to sit in a classroom, answer questions about someone else's world, and write essays? Madness!"

Valerie laughed softly, and even Shawn smirked just a little. "You're unbelievable," he muttered.

"Unbelievably excellent," Alex said, puffing his chest. "I consider it my duty to raise the bar for academic performance, by not showing up. Revolutionary."

Nora shook her head, smiling. "You're lucky you're funny when you do this."

"Lucky or cursed?" Alex countered, leaning back in mock philosophical contemplation. "The world may never know."

Valerie glanced at the window, sunlight spilling over the small kitchen table. "I don't miss school at all. Not even a little."

Zayn nodded, picking at a piece of toast. "Me neither. I'm not from here, anyway, but it feels like everything else was more... urgent. More real than sitting through lectures about things that don't matter right now."

Shawn finally spoke, quietly, as he pushed his plate away. "Life lessons are happening whether we sit in class or not." His gaze flicked across the group, lingering on each face briefly. "Some of us are just paying attention differently."

Alex leaned forward, grinning, "See? Even Shawn approves of my method. Skipping school for life lessons, tactical coffee, and emotional support. Truly, I'm ahead of my time."

Nora snorted, reaching for a piece of fruit. "Ahead of your time or just procrastinating?"

"Both," Alex said with a flourish, holding up the plush cat in mock salute. "Always both."

Valerie shook her head but smiled faintly. "I guess… for now, this is enough. We don't need school. Not today."

Natalia nodded, her eyes sweeping the room. "We have breakfast, a place to stay, and a real-life conflict. That's more than enough for today. Lessons can wait."

Valerie exhaled slowly, leaning back. "Yeah. We'll deal with normal life when normal life is ready for us."

Alex seized the opportunity.

"Normalcy? Perfect! Then I declare this an official mental health day. School is canceled. Curriculum: survival skills, tactical snack acquisition, and emotional support studies."

Nora rolled her eyes. "And who gave you authority over that?"

Alex pointed at himself solemnly. "I did. As appointed chaos philosopher and life skills consultant."

Valerie groaned, hiding her smile behind the plush cat. "You're ridiculous."

"Unquestionably," Alex said with mock pride. "But think of the benefits. We're learning time management, coffee before chaos, bread before danger, and teamwork. We even have a practical module on hiding from glass missiles."

Natalia chuckled, shaking her head. "I suppose this counts as an advanced elective in real life."

Zayn exhaled, leaning back in his chair. "I haven't even thought about school in… forever. Feels weird. Like the world moved on, and we're… paused."

Valerie's eyes softened. "Maybe it's good we're paused. Gives us space to breathe, to think… to plan."

Shawn, quietly nibbling on the last piece of toast, finally spoke. "Plans are important. We're not just drifting. We observe, we adjust, and we stay aware. Even if school isn't happening, that's a lesson in itself."

Alex smirked, holding the plush cat close. "And when we return, I expect a full report on who actually passed trigonometry without crying."

Shawn allowed a faint chuckle to escape, though his voice was soft. "I'd rather not."

The group fell into a comfortable rhythm after that, light conversation, small jokes, quiet laughter. Plates were passed again, toast buttered, fruit eaten, coffee sipped. The sunlight climbed higher, spilling over them, warming the room and their tired bones.

Even with the memory of broken glass, the strange note, and the long night, for this moment, everything felt safe. Normal enough.

And Alex, naturally, found the perfect moment to lean back, grin at everyone, and declare, "I think we just redefined what a school day looks like. History books will be jealous."

Nora rolled her eyes, but the corners of her mouth twitched in a smile. Shawn's gaze softened as he watched the group, letting himself relax just slightly.

For now, the world could wait.

Chapter 40

Natalia's apartment had that soft, lived-in perfection that somehow managed to feel both meticulous and welcoming. Every surface gleamed just enough to suggest care without being sterile. Cushions were plumped on the couch, pastel curtains fluttered faintly in the breeze, and small potted plants lined the windowsills, catching the sunlight that spilled through the living room. Posters of concerts, abstract art, and a few quirky motivational quotes decorated the walls, but nothing felt forced.

The group moved slowly through it, like they'd entered a quiet bubble outside the world.

Valerie perched on the arm of the couch, curled in a blanket, sketchbook in her lap, tracing idle patterns that didn't need to mean anything.

Alex sprawled on the floor near the coffee table, meticulously arranging snacks and pretending to grade them on a scale of importance.

Shawn and Zayn leaned against a windowsill, focused on a multiplayer mobile game on their phones, one occasionally whining about losing against the other.

Nora lounged in a chair, half reading, half observing, smiling faintly at everyone else's antics.

Despite the careful order and aesthetic charm of Natalia's apartment, the day felt slow, almost sleepy, the kind of sluggish comfort that made hours stretch without urgency.

Natalia herself moved lightly between the kitchen and living area, tidying, adjusting cushions, humming softly to herself, her presence a quiet anchor.

"Feels... weirdly normal here," Valerie murmured, almost to herself, as she traced the edge of her sketchbook.

Alex glanced up, raising a brow. "Normal? Pfft. Normal is overrated. We're in a safe bubble of curated perfection. Curriculum: tactical snack management, emotional support, and window-staring proficiency."

Shawn smirked faintly, and looked up. "You find a way to make even normal seem absurd."

Alex puffed his chest proudly. "It's a gift. And a duty. Someone has to keep chaos academically interesting."

As the morning slowly bled into afternoon, the group found ways to pass the time.

Zayn and Shawn got into a quiet debate about the best methods to win in their game, occasionally interrupted by Nora's commentary or Valerie's dry observations.

Alex tried to rope everyone into a makeshift card game on the coffee table, claiming it was "critical tactical training" disguised as leisure.

Natalia hovered nearby, offering rules clarifications, snacks, and the occasional sigh at Alex's insistence that the plush cat had to be dealt into every hand.

Valerie found herself wandering through the apartment at one point, pointing out small quirks she'd never noticed before, a plant with leaves slightly too long, a crack in the windowsill, the way the light hit Natalia's organized bookshelves.

"You've got a good eye for detail," Natalia remarked, smiling softly.

Valerie shrugged. "I notice things. Makes me feel grounded, I guess."

By mid-afternoon, the group had settled into a lazy rhythm. Coffee refills, whispered jokes, soft laughter spilling into the bright apartment.

Shawn lounged in a corner, back pressed against the wall, eyes locked on his screen, while Zayn sat cross-legged on the floor nearby, equally absorbed.

They celebrated small victories with quiet nods and groaned at each defeat, the game keeping them half-immersed in competition and half in distraction.

Every few minutes, Alex drifted over, offering unsolicited commentary on their moves, only to be met with sharp scoldings for "leaking strategies" or "ruining the suspense."

The room hummed with a lazy, comfortable rhythm, their focus punctuated by laughter, groans, and the soft tapping of buttons.

Alex, never one to truly rest, wandered between the kitchen and living area, checking on snack supplies and offering commentary on the "critical balance of caffeine to sugar ratio" necessary for mental performance. "I declare this a highly scientific study," he said solemnly.

"Also, anyone touching the chips without my approval will be considered an act of war."

Nora laughed softly, shaking her head. "You really treat everything like a battle strategy."

"I am a scholar of chaos," Alex replied without missing a beat, plopping down on the floor again.

"Every day is an exercise in emotional resilience and tactical negotiation.
Today's lesson: keeping your hands off my Pringles."

Valerie smiled faintly, curling back into her blanket. The slow, comforting rhythm of the apartment, the quiet camaraderie, the tiny annoyances and soft jokes, felt almost like a balm.

Even with the tension from the previous night lingering, the sunlight spilling in and the careful order of Natalia's space made it feel normal enough, at least for now.

As the day waned, shadows lengthened across the pastel walls. Natalia paused by the window, drawing the curtains slightly.

"We should probably start thinking about dinner soon," she said softly.

"And, well, just keep an eye out. It's easy to forget we're not completely safe yet."

The group nodded, but no one felt the urgency, not yet.

The city outside carried on, unaware of their quiet haven.

Valerie hugged her sketchbook to her chest, Alex reorganized his snacks for the fifth time, and the two boys in the corner of the room occasionally yelled, mourning their virtual defeats.

By the time the sky had deepened into evening, the apartment felt like a cocoon.

The sun dipped low, spilling golden light across the walls, and the group gathered together, blankets and mugs in hand. Outside, the faint hum of the city continued, ordinary and unsuspecting.

Chapter 41

As the sunlight waned, spilling a golden glow across Natalia's apartment, she stretched and glanced at the group.

"Alright, we should start thinking about dinner now. Some of us can head out to the store, the rest can prep here."

Alex jumped immediately to his feet.

"Mission: grocery acquisition. Stealth, speed, and tactical snack optimization. I volunteer as tribute!"

Nora groaned but smirked. "Someone has to make sure you don't get distracted by literally everything on the shelves."

She stood and stretched, her hair catching the last streaks of sunlight through the window.

Zayn shrugged, tossing his phone onto the counter. "I'll come. Fresh air might be good."

Shawn stood silently, sliding his phone into his pocket.

Valerie stayed behind, pulling her blanket a little tighter around her shoulders. "We'll stay here and start on dinner. Chop, stir, clean… you know, cooking stuff."

Natalia smiled faintly. "Sounds like a plan. We'll have the home front covered, and the others can handle the fieldwork."

The group split naturally: Alex, Nora, Zayn, and Shawn stepped out, the evening air cool but gentle.

The sky had shifted to a warm amber, and the streetlights began flickering on, casting long, soft shadows across the pavement.

The air smelled faintly of flowers from nearby gardens and the distant hum of the city carried softly on the breeze.

Alex, of course, treated the walk like a covert mission. "Eyes open, people. Strategic scanning is essential. Sidewalks are potential ambush zones. Watch the snack displays for enemy placement."

Nora shook her head, laughing. "You literally can't walk two feet without a mission briefing, can you?"

Shawn remained quiet, shoulders relaxed, letting the breeze glide through his hair.

Zayn, leaning back slightly with his hands in his pockets, seemed almost meditative, letting the warm glow of the sunset wash over him as he followed the group.

They arrived at the store, Alex immediately darting between aisles with exaggerated military precision. "Okay, team. Objective: secure carbohydrates, proteins, and caffeine. Prioritize chocolate for morale."

Nora grabbed a basket, laughing as she tried to corral Alex's energy. "Focus on what we actually need before you fill the cart with half the candy aisle."

Shawn silently examined the shelves, methodically selecting items, occasionally glancing at Alex to make sure the chaos didn't escalate beyond control. Zayn wandered more freely, letting his mind drift, occasionally checking the shelves, occasionally just enjoying the warm glow of late afternoon sun through the store's large front windows.

Meanwhile, back at Natalia's apartment, Valerie and Natalia set to work. The kitchen smelled faintly of garlic and herbs as they chopped vegetables, stirred sauces, and arranged ingredients.

The sound of knives against the cutting board, the occasional sizzle from the pan, and the warm aroma created a cocoon of domestic comfort.

Valerie, tracing the edge of a chopping board with her fingers, noticed the little details she hadn't before, the pattern of the tiles, the way sunlight streaked across the countertops, the organized but personal touch Natalia had applied to every corner.

"It really does feel perfect here," Valerie murmured, as she chopped a pepper. "Not fake, not forced. Just... calm."

Natalia smiled softly, glancing at her. "That's what I wanted. Somewhere you can feel at peace."

Alex, Nora, Shawn, and Zayn returned not long after, bags in hand, sunlight fading behind them in streaks of pink and gold.

They dropped their groceries on the counter, laughter spilling as Alex demonstrated an over-the-top inspection of the items, nodding solemnly at each. "All items accounted for. Morale boosts secured. Victory is ours."

Dinner preparation became a shared, almost playful task.

Chopping, stirring, stirring sauces, seasoning, all accompanied by soft jokes and small teasing remarks.

Alex insisted the plush cat needed its own tiny plate, much to Valerie's quiet amusement. Shawn offered rare commentary on the seasoning, while Zayn and Nora quietly coordinated timing so nothing would burn.

As the food simmered, Natalia suggested, "After dinner, maybe a walk? The evening light is beautiful. It would be nice to step outside for a bit."

They agreed, and once plates were filled and dishes passed around the table, they ate together.

The meal was simple but hearty, a small island of normalcy after the tension of the past few nights.

Conversation drifted from shared memories, silly hypotheticals, and small observations about the city glowing under the last light of day.

After clearing the dishes, they bundled up lightly and stepped outside.

The air was warm with a soft breeze carrying the scents of nearby gardens and the distant city. Streetlights glimmered faintly in the distance, their glow blending with the deepening twilight.

They walked in pairs or small clusters, occasionally brushing shoulders, sharing small jokes.

Alex continued his "strategic commentary" in a hushed, playful tone, earning quiet groans and laughter from the others.

Valerie and Natalia strolled together, quietly observing the city, while Nora and Zayn trailed slightly behind, talking softly about nothing and everything.

Shawn trailed a bit behind them, observing others, families, couples, and groups of kids cycling around, yelling and laughing.

For a while, the city felt distant, the tension of the previous night softened into the warmth of companionship. Golden light spilled over the streets and buildings, casting a spell of calm that made even the most alert in the group relax, if only for a little while.

As they rounded a quiet corner, the group stumbled upon a small neighborhood park, tucked between low apartment buildings and flowering hedges. The late evening sun painted the swings in amber, outlined the edges of the basketball court with warm gold, and lent a soft glow to the empty benches scattered across the grass. A gentle breeze ruffled the leaves of the trees, carrying the faint scent of grass and distant flowers.

"Wow… this is nice," Valerie murmured, her eyes sweeping the park. She paused on the swings, brushing her fingers over the worn chains as if tracing memories of happier times.

Nora glanced at the basketball hoop, then at Zayn. "Bet you lost all your skills," she teased lightly.

Zayn's lips curved into a small, confident smile. "Depends. Back in college, I was the ace on our intramural team. Not exactly the same as playing a casual game here, but I haven't lost my touch."

Shawn's brow arched, and a smirk tugged at his lips. "Ace, huh? Think you can handle two of us?"

Alex immediately leapt in, bouncing on the balls of his feet. "Oh, two-on-one? I call dibs on being the distraction specialist. Zayn doesn't stand a chance."

Valerie laughed softly, shaking her head. "You two are going to somehow turn it into a tactical exercise."

The group quickly split up naturally. The girls drifted toward a picnic table and the swings nearby, settling in comfortably.

Valerie eased herself onto a swing, letting it sway gently as she traced patterns in the air with her fingers.

Nora perched at the edge of the table, legs dangling, watching the boys with a faint smile.

Natalia leaned against the table, arms crossed loosely, taking in the scene with a quiet, amused expression.

They spoke softly, laughing lightly at Alex's over-the-top commentary on Zayn's "training techniques" and sharing thoughts about the city, the park, and snippets of mundane life they'd been missing.

Meanwhile, on the court, Zayn bounced the ball, testing its weight, tossing a few quick shots that hit the rim and clanged out. Shawn circled him silently, watching, while Alex flitted around like a whirlwind, taunting, faking moves, and occasionally letting out loud, exaggerated sighs of frustration or triumph.

Zayn grinned, dribbling and pivoting with ease. "Alright, two-on-one. Don't underestimate me just because I'm one person."

Shawn merely raised a brow. "Challenge accepted."

The game began in earnest. Zayn's movements were precise, controlled, almost effortless, but the combined chaos of Shawn's strategy and Alex's unpredictable antics made each point a mini-battle.

The ball bounced off rims, rolled across the asphalt, and occasionally sent Alex tumbling in mock agony, prompting laughter from the girls and even a brief chuckle from Shawn.

Time drifted by. Each person found their rhythm: the girls sharing stories, teasing the boys, and enjoying the warm light on their skin; the boys locked into a playful, competitive haze, energy cycling in bursts of chaos and focus.

Valerie's laughter rang softly through the park, Alex's dramatics drew exaggerated sighs, Shawn's rare smiles were caught in the fading sun, and Zayn's pride in his skill mingled with the joy of just being here, not on a field with pressure, but with newfound companions.

Eventually, the sun sank, painting the park in deep gold and dark orange. Shadows stretched long across the swings and basketball court, mingling with the soft greens of the grass.

The girls hopped off the swings, stretched their legs, and wandered toward the picnic tables again.

The boys followed shortly after, a little winded, laughing quietly as they recounted highlights and "near victories" of the game.

They settled together on the benches near the tables, catching their breath, sipping water, and letting the sky darken gradually above them. The faint hum of the city in the distance was barely noticeable here, replaced by the rustle of leaves and the creak of the swings moving gently in the evening breeze.

It was quiet enough that even subtle details could be noticed. A trash can slightly out of place, a shadow flickering near the edge of the trees, small things that might have gone unnoticed if not for the calm contrast of the golden-hour stillness.

The group left the park together, walking along the paved path that led toward Natalia's apartment. The air was cool but comfortable, carrying the faint scent of grass and the distant hum of the city. Golden light still lingered in the sky, painting the streets and buildings with long, warm shadows.

Alex was the first to talk, balancing the plush cat on his shoulder like a makeshift mascot. "You know, if anyone were watching us, they'd think this is some kind of elite tactical exercise. Swings: check. Basketball court: check. Emotional support: check."

Nora laughed softly. "Elite tactical exercise… or a mild exercise in procrastination?"

Valerie shrugged, her arms wrapped around her sketchbook. "Honestly, I don't care which. This is nice. Quiet. Slow. We should do more days like this."

Shawn's smirk was faint but real. "I think we just discovered a new type of school, outdoors, with snacks, and no homework."

Zayn dribbled a basketball idly as they walked past, letting it bounce off the pavement with soft thuds. "I could get used to this," he murmured.

"Being outside, sun fading, it's calming."

Natalia smiled at the group, walking slightly ahead, her hair catching the last streaks of sunlight. "Let's just enjoy it while it lasts. Nights like this don't come around often."

They continued chatting quietly, teasing Alex for his dramatics, debating whether a particularly crooked bench looked like a throne, and discussing the merits of using swings as a "strategic vantage point." Laughter carried through the evening air, blending with the rustle of leaves and the distant sound of traffic.

Then a sharp, high-pitched yell pierced the calm, a girl's voice echoing from the darkened edge of a nearby forest, accompanied by loud barks of a dog.

Valerie tilted her head, listening intently. "Uh… did anyone else hear that?"

Nora glanced over her shoulder toward the shadows. "Probably just someone messing around. Kids with a stray dog? Who knows. Doesn't sound like trouble."

"Yeah," Alex added, raising his hands in mock surrender. "See? Tactical anomaly resolved. Nothing to worry about. The universe is still boring."

Shawn didn't comment, but his eyes flicked toward the treeline, sharp and calculating. Zayn tightened his grip on the ball he'd been dribbling, eyebrows furrowed, though he didn't speak.

After a few moments, the group shook off the sudden tension, assuming the yell was just a playful passerby.

Conversation slowly resumed, Nora joking about their park "training drills,"

Alex lamenting the lack of a scoreboard for their swing-vantage point analysis, and Valerie humming softly under her breath as they moved along.

Then, a few minutes later, the wail of a police siren pierced the air, low at first, then rising sharply as a patrol car sped down the main road. The vehicle suddenly turned into the darkened corner that led toward the forest, headlights cutting a stark path through the shadows, illuminating trees and underbrush before disappearing from view.

The group slowed immediately, the sound catching everyone off guard. Silence fell over them, heavier now, the comfort of the golden-hour walk replaced by a quiet, urgent awareness.

The pavement underfoot felt uneven, the city's usual hum replaced by a low, anxious pulse in their chests. Alex muttered something about "tactical reconnaissance," but no one heard him; all eyes were on the car, tracing its path as it turned sharply down a narrow side street toward the forested area.

Shawn brushed past the group, moving purposefully towards the direction the siren was coming from.

Nobody hesitated, they followed behind him eagerly.

They jogged now, the sound of their footsteps swallowed by the distance between them and the car, though every once in a while, the siren pulsed again, slicing through the night.

The trees loomed ahead, its shadows thick and tangled.

The group's laughter from earlier felt impossibly far away, replaced by a sharp awareness of every sound, the rustle of leaves, the distant siren, and the low hum of the city just beyond.

As they neared the edge of the forest, the glow of emergency lights illuminated a clearing ahead.

A small crowd had gathered, clustered around a cordoned-off area. Their hearts beat faster when they got closer, the chatter of voices replaced by stunned murmurs."What... what happened?" Nora whispered, stepping closer.

Alex, unusually silent, edged forward, his playful bravado stripped away.

They moved cautiously through the outskirts of the gathering, the smell of damp earth and faint metallic tang filling the air.

Then, as they reached the perimeter, the full sight hit them: a girl, motionless, sprawled on the ground, her features pale in the harsh light of flashlights. Beside her, a small dog lay still, fur matted and lifeless.

Valerie gasped, hands covering her mouth. "Oh no..."

Shawn's jaw tightened, eyes scanning the crowd, the forest, everything beyond. "Stay back," he murmured, voice low but firm. "Don't get too close."

Nora's hand rested lightly on Zayn's shoulder. "We're not here to interfere. We just observe. Carefully."

The group lingered at the edge of the circle, the weight of what they'd stumbled upon pressing down on them. The golden-hour warmth was gone, replaced by the harsh, artificial glare of police lights, the scent of something burned or spilled in the air, and the tense whispers of onlookers.

Even Alex, who had spent the evening teasing and joking, found no words, just a tight clench of fists and a set jaw. The day's calm, the golden sunset, the laughter, all evaporated. They were back in the real world, a world that could shatter in a single instant.

Chapter 42

Valerie and Natalia drifted slightly back, moving along the street with quiet, deliberate steps. They didn't speak much, each wrapped in their own thoughts, trying to calm the tightening anxiety in their chests. Every sound, a distant bark, a rustle of leaves, tugged at nerves they didn't realize had been on edge all along.

"Just breathe," Natalia murmured softly, glancing at the darkened tree lines around them. "We've made it this far. Let's not let the tension ruin the rest of the evening."

Valerie nodded, gripping her sketchbook a little tighter. "Yeah it's just that something's lingering, you know? Like eyes on us, even if we can't see them clearly."

A few steps ahead, Shawn and Zayn stood in silence. Their usual easy composure was gone, replaced by a taut, coiled readiness.

They took one last glance and turned to leave but as they turned, their eyes locked onto something in the distant, dark trees.

Shawn quickly glanced at Zayn, whose eyes were also locked at what they saw.

A figure, partially hidden in the dark woodland nearby, watching them with deliberate stillness.

Zayn's chest constricted. The world seemed to shift, the ground beneath him imperceptibly dropping out. His stomach flipped as if gravity had inverted for a heartbeat. Shawn froze mid-step, eyes locked on the figure. Every instinct screamed danger.

The figure didn't move at first, only observed. And then the faintest motion: a hand, raised slowly, deliberately, a wave aimed directly at them.

Their hearts dropped further. The casual wave was unnervingly personal, as if it was taunting.

Without a word, Shawn and Zayn's legs coiled, their bodies ready to launch forward, instincts sharpened to a razor's edge.

Nora acted faster, stopping them in their tracks. She stepped firmly between them and the tree line, her hands raised.

"Don't even think about it. There are cops and people. You move and it'll look suspicious. Think."

The two groaned, frustration evident in every movement, their eyes still locked on the shadowy figure that lingered just out of reach. Shawn's jaw clenched; Zayn's shoulders tightened. They wanted to act, to chase, to confront, but they held, at least for now.

The figure waved again, casual and deliberate, before sinking slightly back into the shadows, disappearing. The presence was unmistakable now, the night carrying a pulse of unspoken awareness.

Nora exhaled, rubbing her temple. "You two have to learn subtlety," she muttered, eyes flicking to the treeline.

Shawn's expression hardened, but he nodded, waiting, scanning the darkness. Zayn's grip on the ball relaxed slightly, though his gaze never left the figure.

Valerie stayed close to Natalia, whispering, "This is different. Something's definitely not right."

The group lingered, each lost in their own heightened awareness, the hush of the night pressing against them. They could hear the faint hum of the distant city, the whisper of leaves in the trees, and the occasional distant siren. Everything felt sharper, slower, more fragile.

Finally, Shawn exhaled slowly, his gaze still fixed on the shadows. Zayn mirrored him, reluctant to let their attention waver. Even with the police nearby, the figure's presence reminded them that the world could intrude anywhere, at any moment, and that tonight was far from over.

The message was clear: they had been seen, and whatever game had begun, it had only just started.

Nora stepped closer to the boys, whispering, "Eyes forward. Stay together."

The walk back from the scene was quiet at first, the night wrapping around them like a heavy, velvet curtain.

Streetlights flickered on above, casting long, uneven shadows across the pavement.

Alex muttered a few sarcastic comments about "perfect tactical reconnaissance," but even his humor felt thin, forced. The glow from the distant city was soft, and for a moment, it almost seemed like they could leave the horrors of the night behind.

Then Shawn froze mid-step.

He didn't need to see it to know.

They were being watched.

Zayn noticed him stop and, instinctively, turned toward him to ask what was wrong, and his eyes also locked onto the figure.

Closer this time. Just at the edge of the woodlands, partially hidden by shadows and underbrush, standing completely still as if waiting for them.

Zayn's chest tightened. He barely breathed, every nerve screaming. His eyes narrowed, scanning the tree line along the sidewalk, trying to take in every detail. "There," he hissed, jaw tightening.

The figure stepped partially out of the shadows, just enough to be seen, their posture casual but deliberate. A slow, deliberate wave, again, taunting them.

Shawn's pulse hammered. Zayn's stomach turned over. In a heartbeat, fury and adrenaline coiled tight in their chests.

The urge to strike, to close the distance, to make the unknown accountable, was almost unbearable.

Before anyone could stop them, Zayn moved, a sudden blur, sprinting toward the figure. Shawn followed immediately, every step powered by a mix of instinct and indignation.

"No!" Nora's voice cracked over the night air, panicked. Her hands shot out, but it was already too late.

Alex froze, wide-eyed, clutching the plush cat as though it might anchor him. He guided Natalia and Valerie a few steps back, eyes wide with concern as the boys vanished into the forest, swallowed by shadows.

"Damn it!" Nora muttered, running to catch up.

She had to reign them in, but her own legs ached in the sudden sprint.

The chase had begun.

The forest was a maze of dark trunks and tangled underbrush. Moonlight filtered in jagged streaks, casting ghostly highlights across damp leaves and gnarled roots. Shawn moved like a panther, silent, precise; Zayn followed in perfect sync, each step controlled, every muscle coiled and ready. The figure was fast, impossibly so, slipping through gaps in the undergrowth, melting into shadow at every turn.

Shawn growled, throwing himself through a cluster of low branches, narrowly missing a snag that would have slowed him.

Zayn's sneakers skidded on the slippery leaves, but he recovered instantly, eyes fixed on the disappearing figure.

Nora's voice broke through again, sharper this time. "Stop!"

The words hit, but neither Shawn nor Zayn slowed. They skidded to a halt for a fraction of a second, jaws clenched, hearts hammering. They exchanged a look, frustration, desire, the need to act, before locking eyes again on the figure, who had paused briefly atop a small rise.

The figure lifted a hand, mockingly, almost amused by their restraint. It was infuriating.

Shawn's hands balled into fists. Zayn gritted his teeth, adrenaline surged through them, hot and blinding. They had been seen, and the instinct to reclaim control, to strike, to assert dominance over this unknown threat, was raw and immediate.

The figure melted deeper into the trees, taunting with movement, leading them along twisted paths of mud and roots. Every step felt dangerous, every shadow a potential trap.

Shawn lunged toward the figure but missed by mere inches.

Zayn pivoted, trying to cut off the escape.

Branches tore at sleeves, roots snagged boots, leaves plastered wet against their faces. The forest seemed alive, working with the figure, funneling them toward some invisible plan.

And then, at the edge of the wooded area, they saw them.

More figures. Not just one. A cluster, half-hidden, moving with the shadows.

Shawn froze mid-step, heart hammering. Zayn's breath caught.

They were about to be circled, trapped in a slow-motion cage crafted by their unseen enemy. Rage boiled, but panic flickered at the edges.

"Shawn! Zayn!" Nora's voice rang from the far side, calm but commanding. She was already in position, appearing from a narrow path that cut across the enemy's flank. "This way! Move!"

Instinct and training kicked in. Shawn pivoted sharply, following her direction. Zayn mirrored him, breaking away from the cluster of shadowy figures.

The boys were gone, swallowed by the protective canopy Nora had cleared for them.

The adrenaline did not fade. Hearts raced, lungs burned, but they were alive, at least for the moment. The figures in the shadows melted back into the forest, patient and deliberate, leaving nothing but rustling leaves and the echo of their presence.

Shawn exhaled sharply, glaring at the trees as if he could punish them with his gaze.

Zayn's hands were cut and bleeding from hitting branches out of his way.

Nora stepped between them, hand on each of their shoulders, grounding them. "Enough," she said, firm. "We see them. That's all we need for now. You don't charge headlong into shadows."

Shawn groaned, panting, frustration etched across his face, but he obeyed.

Zayn's shoulders slumped slightly, trying to stabilize his breathing, but his gaze never left the treeline.

Alex, Valerie, and Natalia hurried back toward them, worry written across their faces.

"Are you okay?" Natalia asked, noticing Zayn's hands.

"Yeah," Zayn said, still scanning, still tense. "For now."

Shawn muttered, "For now."

And then, almost inaudibly: "They'll come again."

The night had shifted. The chase, the taunt, the cluster of figures, everything was no longer abstract danger.

It was real. Close. Personal.

And it was just the beginning.

They regrouped, catching their breath, but the weight of what had just happened pressed down on them.

The forest loomed silently behind, waiting.

The city hummed faintly ahead, oblivious.

And above it all, the stars seemed cold and distant, watching as the first true battle of the night's hunt quietly concluded, for now.

Chapter 43

The streets were quiet, washed in the pale orange of streetlights. Their footsteps echoed, small and measured. No one wanted to make noise they couldn't take back. Adrenaline had loosed its hold, but tension sat in their bones like a stubborn weight.

Shawn led, hands in pockets, jaw set. Alex kept glancing over his shoulder, expecting movement that never quite came. Natalia's fingers brushed Valerie's now and then, a small, wordless anchor in the dark. Nora carried her phone loosely in one hand, thumb grazing the screen as if steadying herself.

They stepped into a late-night cafe that smelled of burnt sugar and old coffee. Low jazz murmured from a dusty speaker. The baristas moved in practiced, sleepy circles.

The group took the far corner booth, backs to the wall, eyes taking the door when it creaked. Silence sat on them for a long minute, and then a small sound cut it: Nora's phone buzzing. She looked down.

Aliya flashed across the screen.

Her throat tightened. They hadn't spoken in a while, not since everything went wrong.

She stepped away from the table, staring at her vibrating phone.

She hesitated for a second, thumb hovering over *accept*, before swiping.

"Hey…" Nora's voice came out softer than she meant it to.

For a moment, all she heard was breathing on the other end, the kind of pause that only exists between people who know each other too well.

Then Aliya exhaled.

"You finally picked up."

There was no accusation in her tone, just tired warmth, like someone holding back tears and trying to sound casual.

Nora smiled faintly despite everything.

"Yeah, sorry. It's been–"

"I know," Aliya interrupted gently. "I've been watching the news, Nora. Meadowcrest, the school, the cops. I thought you were…"

Her voice caught.

Nora pressed her forehead against her hand, turning slightly away from the group.

"I'm alive," she said quietly. "Barely. But yeah, I'm here."

"You sound tired," Aliya said softly.

"You sound like my conscience," Nora replied with a laugh.

"Then listen to her for once," Aliya teased back. "Get out of that mess, Nora. Please. Come back when you can."

The words settled over her like a blanket, warm, heavy, impossible.

"Once this is over," Nora murmured. "When it's safe."

"It never really gets safe," Aliya sighed. "But it gets quieter. You just have to hold on till then."

For a moment, neither spoke. Just breathing, just silence, just connection, that invisible thread between them, stretched across cities but unbroken.

Nora closed her eyes and took in a deep breath, letting it out slowly. "Once all of this is over, we can get back to our normal lives."

"Just come back in one piece," Aliya said quietly. "And don't forget to bring Layla."

Nora smiled again, a tired, aching kind of smile that didn't reach her eyes.

"Will do."

When the call ended, Nora stood still for a few seconds, holding the phone against her chest before walking back to the table. She set it down, fingers lingering over the smooth surface, eyes distant for a moment, as if letting the warmth from Aliya's voice seep in and anchor her.

Valerie rubbed her temples, letting out a soft sigh.

"I just want one night," she murmured, tracing a finger along the side of the table.

"One night without running, without feeling like something's always watching us."

The table went still. Alex nodded. The weight of her words settled, heavy and unspoken.

Zayn leaned back, closing his eyes, trying to breathe past the tension. A memory flickered through his mind, a moment from one of his tournaments in the past, Damian's voice, calm but cutting through the chaos.

"You don't win by just charging in. You calculate. Let them think they'll steal the ball, then pivot, fake them, charge. Make them slip first, then strike."

His eyes shot open and he sat back up.

He smiled and muttered, *"Thank you, Damian."*

Zayn's jaw tightened.

"We've been running their game," he said quietly.

The others looked at him, confused.

"Panicking. Moving first. Letting them catch us by surprise. But what if we flipped it? What if we moved first?"

Shawn tilted his head, considering. "Bait them?"

"Exactly," Zayn said, eyes sharp now, focused.

"Make them think they're winning, surprise them, then break them."

Nora's eyes narrowed, the spark of strategy replacing the weariness. "Then we stop letting them pull the strings," she said.

Alex leaned forward, half-smirk, but tension undercutting it. "Switching sides in their little game, huh?"

Natalia smiled. "I like that."

Shawn leaned back slightly, eyes scanning the group.

"Listen," he said, voice calm but firm.

"We regroup tomorrow at my place. We'll have space, gear, and a plan. Tonight's been messy, but we can't let it drag us down."

There was a pause, the weight of his words settling over everyone. It wasn't an order; it was confidence. The kind of confidence that made the others nod without needing to argue.

Natalia rubbed her arms, then glanced at the girls. "We'll go back to my place for tonight. We need rest if we're thinking straight tomorrow."

"Fine by me," Valerie said, exhaling softly, a trace of relief flickering across her face. "Sleep. Food. Maybe actually sit without the fear of being watched."

Shawn and Zayn exchanged a glance, no words had to be said.

"I'll stay with Shawn," Zayn said, steady but casual.

"I'd hate to deal with Alex's endless commentary all night."

Alex leaned back, unimpressed.

"You say that like you're fun company."

"Fun enough to keep you safe," Zayn shot back, smiling.

Nora rolled her eyes. "You two act like sleepovers are tactical missions."

Shawn smirked, eyes flicking between them. "Given our situation, they kinda are."

That earned a few tired chuckles.

The group split naturally, each pair or solo heading toward their temporary safe spots. The night air felt heavier as they walked, shadows stretching across quiet streets.

There was a shared sense of purpose settling in.

Chapter 44

Shawn's apartment matched the morning: minimalist, dark-toned, polished floors and black leather furniture. The faint aroma of coffee lingered, mingling with traces of old leather and faintly burned popcorn remnants of late-night gaming sessions.

The city outside hummed in low tones: distant cars, a siren far off, the steady drip of rain against metal. Inside, the world felt suspended. Muted gray light seeped through half-closed blinds, stretching long shadows across the dark walls. A couch, a low table, a punching bag by the window, and a skateboard leaned against the wall. One dim lamp painted the corners amber. Everything else was black, gray, or steel.

Zayn stood by the window, hoodie loose, watching condensation streak down the glass. Shawn moved like someone who'd been awake for hours; focused, silent, pouring coffee into two mismatched mugs.

"You ever not look like a movie villain?" Zayn asked, breaking the quiet.

Shawn glanced over. "You're talking to a guy cooking eggs in the dark."

"That's exactly my point."

Shawn smirked faintly, and the quiet between them felt comfortable, not tense.

Their phones buzzed on the counter, the group chat lighting up.

Shawn: "We're up. Come when ready. Address below."
Nora: "Got it."
Natalia: "Leaving after breakfast."
Alex: "Gearing up."

Zayn leaned back. "Think they'll actually show before noon?"

Shawn took a slow sip of coffee. "Hope not. I need quiet before chaos."

By ten, the apartment had grown brighter, though the clouds outside kept everything cold. Zayn scrolled through his phone while Shawn hovered over his laptop, maps open, locations pinned in red, the city grid pulsing faintly on-screen.

"You really don't sleep, huh?" Zayn muttered.

Shawn didn't look up. "I do. When things stop mattering."

"Guess we're both insomniacs then."

The door buzzed. Zayn exhaled and swung it open.

Natalia came in first: neat, collected, hair tied up despite the drizzle. Valerie followed, carrying two backpacks.

Then Nora, quiet, eyes scanning everything as if cataloging it.

Last came Alex, hood up, headphones around his neck, laptop bag slung over one shoulder.

"Nice place," Alex said. "Could use a plant. Or human emotion."

"Could use silence," Shawn replied.

Alex dropped his bag anyway. "Noted."

They gathered around the table. Mugs, cables, papers, and the faint reflection of gray daylight. Alex flipped open his laptop, screens glowing bluish.

"Wi-Fi?" he asked.

"'Don'tTouchThis,'" Shawn said.

"Password?"

"'TouchThis.'"

Alex blinked. "Creative."

Zayn chuckled. "That's what happens when he names things at three in the morning."

The group laughed softly, the tension from the past night easing a little.

Alex's fingers danced over the keyboard. "Pulling street cam feeds near Meadowcrest. If anyone sneezed near that school last night, I'll find it."

Nora raised an eyebrow. "Legal?"

"Let's not define things," Alex said without looking up.

Shawn leaned against the counter, arms crossed. "If it helps us, I don't care what it is."

Hours bled together in the gray glow. Rain ticked against the window. Natalia and Nora spread papers across the table, tracing lines, comparing timelines. Zayn leaned back, tossing a stress ball. Shawn paced slowly, shadow sliding along the walls, always alert. Alex typed fast, relentless, unlike the gentle drizzle outside.

Then he froze. "Check this out."

Everyone leaned in.

Alex's fingers moved rapidly across the keyboard, the clicks of keys punctuating the low hum of the apartment. "Alright," he said, breaking the silence. "I'm pulling up street cams around that old building, the one behind the woodlands we barely escaped from."

The group tensed, leaning closer as the screen shifted, but Alex's expression faltered slightly.

"Huh. No cams. Nothing covering it. They really shut down the front and the lot."

Shawn's brow furrowed. "Of course there's no working cameras in such a shady place."

Nora traced the outline of the building on the screen. "Wait. Look at that."

All eyes turned. Through the quiet hum of the mid-morning city, the warehouse appeared: gray, unassuming, tucked behind overgrown hedges, with a chain-link fence that barely hid it. Shadows stretched along the lot, but nothing flagged as unusual.

Alex zoomed in, scanning every angle. "No cameras, no signs. Nothing screaming 'illegal operation.' They move smart, clean. But you can't hide the basics."

Shawn's gaze sharpened. "Like what?"

The faint whir of surveillance drones outside the city felt distant; here, in the apartment, the real observation was in their hands.

From the feeds, a series of white vans moved in and out steadily. Each bore decals from various small companies, delivery services, cleaning crews, odd contractors. Nothing blatantly suspicious, but the timing and rhythm were unmistakable.

Nora's brow furrowed. "They've disguised everything, each van looks completely normal, but it's all just a cover."

Alex added, having pulled the feeds from the past few days, "And the pattern's consistent. Same arrivals, same departures, every single day. Someone's running this like clockwork."

Valerie sipped slowly, letting the quiet fill the room. "It's like shadow traffic. Easy to miss if you're not looking."

Zayn smirked. "So the warehouse isn't really hidden. It's there, but it's invisible because no one's paying attention. Clever."

Shawn folded his arms, scanning the feed again.

"We're not rushing in. We watch. Note the patterns. Let them slip.

That's our lead."

Alex marked entries and exits in real time. "Babysitting a criminal conveyor belt now."

Zayn laughed softly. "Babysitting a criminal conveyor belt. Classic."

They kept their eyes on the feeds, sipping coffee, tracing movements, letting the mundane rhythm of vans and trucks give them insight. By midday, they had a pattern, a clue of what was going on.

* * *

Alex was cross-referencing the van timestamps when one of the side feeds jerked into motion. It wasn't pointing towards the warehouse completely, but just barely enough to catch a van. The unmarked white van that had been slipping in and out all week pulled up early, too early, backing into the lot like it had a purpose that morning.

"Pause it," Zayn said.

He hit keys so fast the others leaned forward before the frame even stopped. The van door swung open and two men in plain jackets pulled something bulky out, wrapped in a tarp, low and awkward. They carried it like they were hauling batteries or equipment, but the way they shifted their shoulders and the speed of their steps made the movement look wrong: furtive, rushed.

Nora's voice went flat. "What is that?"

Alex scrubbed back a few seconds. The men guided the bundle through the warehouse door and shut it. Then one of them paused near the entrance, glanced up toward a second story window. The figure's head turned in the exact direction of the camera.

"For someone who covers their sites," Natalia said slowly, "they don't want that on film."

The man looked right into the lens for a beat. Not random. Not careless. He cupped his hands, shading his face, as if checking something in the reflection, and then waved, just a quick, deliberate motion toward the street.

Valerie's chair scraped as she stood. "Someone's signalling."

Alex zoomed until pixels smeared. A triangular decal caught the light on the van's rear quarter.

Shawn's jaw tightened. "They've moved something inside. Could be equipment. Could be shipments. Could be people."

Valerie swallowed. "Could be people?"

"I think we should make a move." Shawn said.

Alex quickly spoke, "It's barely mid-day, if we move then we bring attention."

"If we wait until tomorrow then that person could be dead," Zayn shot back.

"You don't wait on that," Shawn said. He moved to the window, peering down the block as if the city might hand him a different answer. "If there's any chance they've got someone in there, we don't sit and count vans."

Alex leaned forward, calm but sharp. "And what? You walk in there, mid-day, no plan? You'd hand them our faces before we even know what's inside."

Nora's voice was steady. "We wait for the window where we can control the angles. Night gives us cover, it gives us patience."

Alex turned the screen toward them.

"Whatever they're hiding, it starts *after* dark."

Nora nodded, quietly steady. "So we wait. Let them think today's routine is safe. Then we go when it's our turn to watch."

For a moment, Shawn just stared at the screen, jaw tight. Then

Zayn's voice cut through, quieter this time.

"Control isn't weakness, man. It's how we win."

"You wanna get to the bottom of this? Me too. We need patience."

That finally landed. Shawn exhaled, tension draining from his shoulders.

"Fine. Tonight, then. We do it right."

Chapter 45

They folded the day's small wins into something that looked like a plan. The dark apartment felt quieter, less like a room and more like a command center: phones, scrap notes, and the laptop glow. No map taped to the wall, no printed grids; everything lived on screens and in the heads around the table. Little things stacked into a shape: a partial plate, the recurring delivery window, the van that favored the south entrance. It wasn't triumph, but it was enough.

By late afternoon, the gray light softened. Shawn sat with his hands folded, watching Alex work. Zayn cleaned out his phone case and checked battery packs. Natalia moved through the checklist with steady, quick motions. Nora rehearsed short answers in her head. Valerie packed a first aid kit and tightened the strap on her backpack. Alex moved between feeds and tools with that odd calm only he had.

"Tonight's the night," Shawn said finally. Not dramatic. Just a statement.

Natalia's voice cut across the room, blunt and precise. "No fighting. We get footage, we bring it to the police. That is the plan." Her tone shut down anything sentimental.

Valerie set the first aid kit on the table and met Shawn's eyes. "Evidence first. If this is about saving people, we show what's happening. No one dies because we rushed in."

Shawn let his mouth pull into a half-smile that didn't reach his eyes. "I can do camera work. I can be quiet."

Zayn didn't say anything. He slid a small utility knife into his pocket and met Shawn's look with an even one: part agreement, part caution.

Alex's pile looked dramatic at first: two cheap tripods, a pair of LED bike taillights, several battery packs, a coil of painter's tape, a roll of black zip ties, and one ridiculous little mirror he pulled out of thin air like a magician. He laid them out like props.

Nora snorted. "You packed half of a hardware store."

"Resources," Alex corrected, not missing a beat.

"Resources for what, a camping trip?" Zayn teased, and a laugh broke the room's edge.

"Minimal," Alex said, pulling out a drone with a camera.

"I won't be with y'all," he said, grin faint but sincere.

"I'll camp in the cafe on the corner of that street near the park, the same one we crashed at last night. I'll be the eyes, with this thing I've got bird's eye view over everything," he said, waving the drone.

"Smart, try not to look suspicious this time," Nora said with a smirk.

"No promises," Alex replied.

As dusk pressed toward evening, they sat around the table for one last deliberate minute.

No dramatics.

No polishing the plan into something it wasn't.

Just a line of six faces lit by laptop blue and low lamp amber: focused, tired, ready.

Shawn set his backpack on the floor, fingers lingering on the zipper. He looked at each of them, slow. "We get the tape. We do not get seen. If anything goes sideways, we pull."

Natalia's nod was small, final.

Valerie's hand brushed the first aid kit.

Nora's jaw tightened.

Zayn's hand rested on his phone, thumb already over the record button.

Alex looked up from his laptop with that half-smirk that meant he was nervous in the way he was most used to: nerdy, oddly confident. He leaned back slightly, keeping his eyes on the screen for a moment, then slid a few small 360 cameras across the table toward Natalia and Nora. "I'll keep us aware with these little guys," he said. "Place them where you can, mostly on trees in the woods. We need coverage in the areas without CCTV. Keep them low, keep them hidden. If anything moves, I'll call it."

Nora picked one up, examining it quickly, while Natalia tucked another into her bag. Valerie glanced at the cameras, then nodded, already thinking ahead. Zayn stayed by Alex, watching the screens, thumb hovering near the record button.

"Spread them out, don't cluster," Alex added. "Make sure we see every angle. Phones strapped, cameras planted. That's it for now."

Zayn gave him a look and couldn't help it: "Keep it minimal, Gandalf. Not everything needs reinventing."

They stayed, not wanting to leave yet. The night would come; the plan was in their hands. For now, the moment before motion stretched long and dangerous and full of the sort of hush that meant something irreversible was about to begin.

No one spoke at first. The hum of the fridge, the ticking of a clock: small, ordinary sounds that made the silence heavier.

Nora finally said what they were all thinking, her voice low.

"If this works, we end it. If it doesn't…"

Her words faded before finishing.

Zayn filled the gap. "Then at least we tried. Better than watching from screens while people vanish."

Natalia leaned back, folding her arms tightly.

"Still feels different when it's you stepping in, not someone else."

Valerie nodded slowly. "We've all been dealing with this for a while. Tonight's where we find out if we can handle it."

Alex looked up from his screen, faint grin gone, replaced by something quieter. "Either way, it's going to change everything, isn't it?"

Shawn's gaze swept the room: every face, every quiet heartbeat written in the air. "Yeah," he said. "There's no going back after tonight."

The group fell silent again: not in fear, but in that strange unity that comes right before a storm.

Nora looked around at each of them, "Can't even remember what day it is. This whole situation has changed my life."

"I like this break from school, as much as I love academics, I don't plan on going back anytime soon," Natalia added.

"We definitely deserve a week off from school after we become the heroes that save the town," Shawn added.

Everyone laughed.

It felt nice to share a human moment before heading out to tackle the unknown.

Chapter 46

Evening draped itself over the city like a thin veil.

Shawn led the way out of his apartment building, the familiar click of the lock fading behind them.

The streets were quiet. Empty enough to feel private, yet alive enough to remind them that the city never truly slept. Sidewalks glimmered faintly under the soft glow of streetlights, the lamps throwing long, clean shadows across brick and concrete.

They moved in a loose line, bags snug against their backs, hoods drawn up. The air was crisp and cool enough to make them pull collars higher, but not cold.

A gentle breeze traced the edges of rooftops and alleyways, stirring the scattered leaves that had long since given up on summer.

Buildings shifted around them like a quiet crowd. The cafes and boutiques they passed gleamed with soft, warm light behind polished windows. Neon signs buzzed faintly, reflected in puddles of condensation on the asphalt from earlier sweeps of humidity. For a moment, the city felt almost serene, like it had paused to watch them pass.

Zayn kicked at a loose pebble, watching it skitter across the pavement. "Feels weird," he said. "Like we're ghosts walking in someone else's story."

Shawn glanced at him, expression half amused, half distant. "Maybe we are. Or maybe we just finally get to write the next chapter ourselves."

Valerie kept her gaze on the buildings, noting each possible vantage point, each shadowed corner. "Stay sharp," she said softly, more to herself than anyone else.

Natalia, ahead of them, adjusted her backpack. "We know the drill. Eyes, patience, spacing."

The cafe came into view: warm light spilling over polished tables and smooth wooden floors. Familiar enough to feel like a small anchor in the night, aesthetic in its muted elegance: cream walls, copper accents, and hanging lights that glowed like captured fireflies. This was the same place they had crashed at last night, when everything was chaos and running. Its quiet normalcy was almost jarring.

Alex lingered at the doorway, letting them enter first. The faint aroma of vanilla lattes and baked bread reached him before the door shut behind them. He slid into the back corner, laptop open, cables spread like careful tendrils over the polished tabletop. His screens blinked with camera feeds, live recordings, and the drone remote control app.

Shawn and Zayn lingered near the window, peering out into the deepening evening. The last of the sunset bled across rooftops, a thin streak of amber fading into navy sky.

"Split here," Shawn said quietly.

Natalia, Nora, and Valerie nodded, checking straps and pockets, moving into position toward the park and surrounding streets.

Alex tapped his earbud in place. "Eyes live. I'll call you all in a bit. One earbud, low mic. Keep comms brief."

Outside, the wind shifted slightly, brushing along the quiet streets and the edges of their jackets. Shadows lengthened, stretching from lampposts and corners alike. The city had gone into its night rhythm, and they were moving through it with the precision of ghosts.

By the time Alex finished settling in, Shawn and Zayn had melted into the dark streets toward the warehouse, and Natalia, Nora, and Valerie had begun their careful placement of cameras along the perimeter and woodlands. The evening had folded into night, and the city: aesthetic, quiet, patient, held its breath.

* * *

The tiny blue lights blinked when they connected, soft but alive.

"Third one's up," Nora said, brushing dirt off her jeans. Her breath came out in faint clouds, fading into the cool air. "Signal's clean."

"Cool," Natalia said, tightening the strap on her backpack. She checked the tiny screen on her phone, their video call flickered in jittery squares. "You think we should cover the other side too?"

Val, crouched beside the bench where she was organizing the rest of the cameras, looked up. "We should," she said quietly.

Nora looked toward the line of trees wrapping the park's edge. The lamplight thinned out near the roots, just faint streaks through the branches. The air had that deep, cold scent, wet bark, asphalt, faint gasoline from the road.

"Yeah... we might as well," Nora said finally. "We don't want a blind spot if someone loops around."

Val brushed a strand of hair from her face. "We can split up. It'll be faster."

Natalia frowned, chewing her lip. "You sure? It's darker past the trail. Feels like a bad idea."

"Everything we *do* lately feels like a bad idea," Val said softly, adjusting her hoodie. "Just stay on call."

214

That got a small, dry laugh out of Nora. "You sound like Shawn now."

"Let's hope not," Val muttered.

"I heard that," Shawn replied with a tone light enough to make them all smile.

The girls split, Val and Nora veering into the trees, Natalia taking the street side. Their sneakers crunched against gravel and old leaves. The lamps buzzed overhead, halos flickering as the wind shifted. Somewhere far off, a car door slammed, muffled by distance.

Nora slowed as she found a sturdy branch and ziptied a small 360 cam around it, the strap tightening against rough bark. The lens caught the dim shimmer of the park's fence. She tilted it, checking her phone, the live feed flickered, grainy, then steady.

"This good Alex?" she whispered.

"Perfect," Alex's voice came faintly through the mic.

Nora could hear the faint echo of Val's footsteps through her earpiece, crunch, pause, crunch, then silence.

On the street side, Natalia attached another camera to a fence post behind a trash can, leaning on it for balance. She exhaled hard, opening her mic. "These could get spotted so easily."

"Tell Alex not me," Nora replied. "I'm just following the know-it-all's directions."

Val chuckled quietly. "Relax. At least we have visuals for as long as they last."

"Funny," Natalia said. "How helpful."

"We need these visuals so Val doesn't go missing," Nora said.

They laughed quietly, the kind of nervous laugh that almost covered how fast their hearts were beating.

Back in the cafe, Alex sat in his usual corner, eyes darting between feeds. The place had gone quiet again, just a few stragglers at the counter. The tablet's glow lit his face, flickering as he flipped between cameras, the park, the alley, the street, the trees, the drone.

"Zayn, your cam's clean. Shawn, yours is angled down, move it a little up."

Shawn adjusted the strap on his hoodie, whispering into his earpiece, "Better?"

"Yeah," Alex said. His voice was calm, but his fingers never stopped moving.

"Girls, how we looking?"

"Street side clear," Natalia said.

"Trees clear," Nora added.

Then, a pause. Static from one end.

Natalia winced. "Ow, what was that?"

"Val just hung up?" Alex said, leaning forward, eyes scanning every other camera. "She's gone offline."

"What do you mean, gone offline?" Nora asked, voice tense.

"I mean… she left the call," Alex said, his hands already flying across the tablet. "No signal, nothing. I'm pinging the drone, wait, there."

A faint blur appeared on the drone feed, a small figure moving through the shadows along the edge of the woods. The infrared view painted her in gray, the trees a ghostly black.

"Val!" Alex whispered. The drone followed, careful, hovering low, keeping her in sight.

Her pace was normal at first, walking, maybe jogging slightly, but then something shifted.

From the darkness, hands shot out towards her. She struggled, kicking, but it seemed like she was hit and fell unconscious. Alex's drone swiveled in disbelief as her body was dragged off the path, toward the deeper woods.

"NO!" Alex shouted into the mic, fingers tapping furiously. "Shawn! Zayn! She's– she's being taken!"

Shawn and Zayn were a few blocks away, checking their alley feed. Zayn's jaw tightened. "Where? Which direction?"

Alex switched the drone feed, tracking the movement through trees, past faintly illuminated paths, toward the old warehouse perimeter. The thing dragging her moved silently, purposefully, using the shadows like armor.

Natalia's voice broke through, trembling but steady as she walked toward Nora.

"She– she just left the call, Alex. You saw her? Is she–"

"She was taken," Nora whispered, walking toward Natalia.

Natalia's eyes darted around. "That's not possible… we just heard her."

Alex's jaw tightened. "We have the footage. That's all that matters right now."

Zayn was tense, "Alex, where's the drone?"

Alex cut in instantly. "There y'all are. Okay, follow the drone to the girls. We've got enough to hand this to the cops. Let's move quickly."

Shawn didn't respond right away. He just stared down the dark stretch of road ahead of them, breathing slow, eyes unreadable.

Zayn nudged him.

"You heard him. Let's go."

Shawn nodded once, *too* calm. "Yeah."

They started back through the alley, their shoes crunching over gravel. Zayn kept his eyes darting, scanning every corner.

The tension between them was heavy, hearts beating with pumped adrenaline.

"Natalia and Nora," Zayn said through the mic, running, "keep your eyes open we're almost there– "

He stopped and turned to the noise of some leaves crunching.

"Shawn?"

No answer.

Zayn spun around. Just the echo of his own footsteps.

"Alex, Shawn disappeared."

Static buzzed through the line.

"What do you mean *disappeared*?"

"I mean he was *right behind me.*"

Somewhere ahead, deeper in the dark, a faint crunch of leaves.

Shawn's voice came through the radio, quiet, almost distant.

"They took her into the woods huh?"

"Shawn, stop. Don't do this, man," Alex said. "We're regrouping. Don't you dare–"

"I'll bring her back," he said coldly, voice firm.

Chapter 47

Shawn moved through the dark like a blade sliding between shadows. Every step over broken branches, gravel, and fallen leaves sounded amplified in his head, sharper than reality. His pulse hammered in sync with each distant echo, the wind shaking a loose sign, the faint drip of water from a rusted roof, the soft shuffle of an animal deep in the undergrowth. Everything felt amplified, urgent.

Memories clawed at him as he ran, unbidden and precise. The alleyways, the streets, the nights he'd walked that thin line between control and chaos, the smells of concrete and asphalt, the flash of fists, the silent screams swallowed by walls. Back then, fear had gripped him like iron; now, it fueled him. It sharpened him. Every nerve screamed to move, to act, to correct the wrongs he couldn't tolerate.

He dropped his hoodie, letting his hood fall low. Fingers brushed over the knife tucked into his pocket, an old habit, more reassurance than weapon. But he didn't need it yet. The thrill, the calculation, the sense of inevitable chaos were enough to sharpen him into something else, something quiet, something lethal.

Ahead, the trees thinned, and the moonlight cast long silver shadows along the path. He could see it, the faint outlines of the warehouse, the place they'd escaped from before.

The smell of damp metal and faint fuel reached him, carried by the breeze. He slowed for a moment, just enough to savor the quiet, the tension, the pulse of adrenaline that roared in his chest.

He thought of Val. Her eyes, always scanning, always curious, carrying thoughts she didn't speak aloud. The way she had smiled when he was careless once, the small laugh that lingered just a second too long. He imagined that expression now, frozen in fear or confusion.

The thought clawed at him, sharper than the utility tool at his side.

He moved faster, silent, weaving through the last stretch of trees, past old concrete ruins, listening to every movement. The memory of old streets, of past encounters, of the edge he'd walked before, pressed against his mind like a familiar itch.

Then, through the trees, he saw her.

Val. Struggling, pulled toward the shadows near the warehouse. Her small figure, half-lit by faint light from inside the lot.

The hands gripping her weren't gentle.

The figures moving her were precise, professional, but not invisible. Not to him.

His breath came fast, short, ragged, every muscle tensed.

Rage and adrenaline fused into something raw and kinetic.

His mind raced, a thousand possible ways to intervene, to strike, to take control, but he forced himself to pause.

The warehouse ahead loomed like a carcass of steel and broken glass. Rusted siding peeled in jagged strips and the chain-link fence surrounding the lot rattled faintly in the breeze. The smell of oil, damp wood, and something metallic hung thick in the air.

Through a narrow gap in the fence, Shawn could see them. Two or three men were dragging Val like predators taking prey. Two others lingered near the vans, moving crates and tools stacked haphazardly.

Val's small frame strained in the hands that held her. She twisted, kicked, threw her weight against them, and for a moment, she slipped free. Her arms flailed and she stumbled toward a shadowed corner of the lot. Relief flickered across Shawn's mind, fleeting and sharp, until he saw them intercept her. They dragged her back and pinned her to the ground.

A soft grunt, a scraping sound of concrete beneath her hands, a shudder through her body.

She was hurting.

She was struggling.

She was fighting, but not enough to escape.

Something *snapped* inside him.

The world blurred around him. Edges softened, colors muted. All he could see was her. All he could feel was the white-hot anger coiling in his chest like fire. His fists clenched, jaw tight. Every breath, every heartbeat, every shadowed corner of the lot became a drumbeat of imminent violence.

He took a careful step forward, letting the shadows swallow him. Gravel crunched faintly underfoot, betraying him to no one but the night.

Val struggled again, twisting under the weight of her captors. Her hands scraped the concrete, her face twisted in pain and panic.

A small cry escaped her lips. Shawn's chest tightened so hard he could barely inhale. His blood went warm, rushing to his head, his hands shaking the least bit, he stopped thinking.

The men nearest her glanced toward the shadows, distracted for a heartbeat. Long enough. Shawn's body coiled, muscles ready to explode.

He did not calculate, he did not hesitate.

Rage, adrenaline, and pure protective instinct fused into motion.

A van door clanged in the distance. Other men near the parked vehicles glanced up, but stealth didn't matter anymore.

Val was pinned. She was struggling. She was hurt. That was all Shawn needed.

He found a hole in the chain-link fence and charged.

The wind howled in his ears. The night stretched and contracted around him. The chain-link fence and broken glass blurred. Gravel spat against his sneakers as he gained speed. Every step was fueled by fury. Every heartbeat screamed move, strike, *save* her.

The warehouse and the men became secondary, shadows and motion in the periphery of his vision. There was only one thing he could see. Val. She was not leaving this place like that.

Shawn surged forward, a storm breaking loose on the quiet night. The world seemed to hold its breath.

His legs pumped hard, every stride a drumbeat of rage and desperation. Gravel crunched underfoot, loose stones scattering as he barreled down the narrow path toward the warehouse perimeter. Shadows stretched long under the dim moonlight, flickering across chain-link fences and the jagged edges of broken concrete.

His chest heaved, lungs burning, but adrenaline pushed him faster. Ahead, the men holding Val moved carelessly, confident in their numbers, confident in the night.

Val struggled, her small frame writhing under their grips.

Her soft, muffled cries pierced the darkness, igniting a white-hot flare of rage in Shawn.

He narrowed his eyes, sight locking onto them. The world around him blurred: the fence, the gravel, the distant warehouse lights, until all that existed was the group pinning Val and the space between them.

Shawn surged forward, pumping his arms, shoulders low, momentum unstoppable. His jacket hanging off of his shoulders as he blitzed through the wind. Each footfall sent vibrations through the gravel; each heartbeat screamed for action.

The air seemed to thicken with the tension of the moment, the smell of dust and cold metal filling his nostrils.

A man glanced up just in time to see Shawn crashing through the shadows.

Shawn collided with the first attacker like a battering ram, shoulder slamming into the man's torso with bone-jarring force. Gravel spat in every direction, the other men looked up as the man stumbled back, breath knocked out of him.

Three remained. One swung wildly, arm closing in on his head.

Shawn ducked instinctively, feeling the air whistle past his ear, and countered with a sharp hook to the man's ribs. The man staggered, wind knocked out of him, clutching his side and gasping.

The third man charged at him, feet pounding against concrete, fists raised. Shawn sidestepped at the last second, twisting and sliding a leg out like a sweep from a martial arts move.

The man hit the ground hard, arms flailing, a grunt escaping as gravel bit into his palms.

There was one man left, he let go of Val, who painfully stumbled away as the man who held her down charged Shawn.

For a brief heartbeat she looked up. Shawn's gaze met hers, a silent promise in the dark.

"Run!" he barked, voice low but urgent. "Follow the drone! Fast!"

Val's eyes flicked to the hovering drone above, its small light cutting through the shadows like a beacon. She centered her balance and started sprinting toward the path the drone illuminated.

Shawn moved to cover her, fists smashing, shoulders ramming, knocking back anyone who tried to intercept.

The man recovering from the sweep scrambled to his feet. Shawn met him with a shoulder into the chest, shoving him back violently, then hooked an arm around the next charge, using his momentum to roll the attacker onto the gravel. Stones flew, dust kicked up, the night alive with sound and motion.

Val gained distance, feet pounding the dirt, heart racing, guided by the drone's faint glow. Shawn spun, intercepting a swing from the last man, ducking low, countering with a sharp jab that sent him sprawling. Each move was brutal but precise, fueled by fury, instinct, and the singular focus of protecting her.

Shawn's chest heaved, muscles trembling, but he didn't pause. Every glance toward Val as she ran, every grunt, every strike, every block was about her, for her. The night seemed to contract around him, shadows stretching and bending as if to mirror his rage.

"Go! Go!" he shouted again, covering her retreat while the drone led her down a safer path, zig-zagging through the darkness, away from the warehouse, away from the remaining men. Shawn was a blur of motion, every strike, every shove, every dodge a testament to the raw force of his anger.

Chapter 48

Val's legs burned, lungs screaming, but adrenaline carried her through the tangle of roots and fallen leaves. Every step she took crunched sharply in the quiet of the forest, her sneakers barely touching the damp soil before pushing off again. The small drone hovered above, casting its pale, mechanical glow ahead like a guiding star. Shadows twisted around her, but the path remained clear.

Her hands were scraped, her side stung where one of the men had grabbed her roughly, but she didn't slow. One glance back and she caught a glimpse of movement in the dark shadows: Shawn, a storm barreling behind her, fists smashing, bodies tumbling, chaos following in his wake. Relief surged for a moment before concern stabbed through her. She had to keep moving. *For him.*

A clearing opened up ahead. Streetlamps flickered faintly in the distance, a sign of the road leading to safety. And there, at the edge of the clearing, stood Zayn. He held a flashlight low, scanning the treeline, eyes sharp, and beside him, Natalia and Nora crouched briefly behind a low wall, breath ragged but steady.

"Hey!" Val's voice carried, panting but controlled.

Zayn noticed but didn't move from his position until he was certain she was clear of the trees. "Here, come this way!"

Val rushed over and skidded to a stop, catching her breath for a second, then sprinted the last few feet into the circle of light. Nora grabbed her arm gently, pulling her behind a low wall, keeping her crouched and hidden just enough from the outer edges of the forest.

Nora sounded relieved. "You okay? You're safe now."

Val's chest heaved. "I... yeah. I'm fine," she said, though her voice trembled. Her fingers grazed the scrapes on her arms as she steadied herself.

The girls huddled close, checking Val quickly. Natalia's eyes flicked to the road, making sure there were no surprises. Nora pulled out the first aid kit in a backpack to treat Val's wounds.

Meanwhile in the cafe nearby, Alex's fingers flew across his tablet, pulling up multiple feeds in a neat collage: drone overhead, park entrances, alleyways, the street leading to the warehouse. "I'm calling the cops now," he said. "Got all the footage we needed. They're on their way. Just stay put."

Val leaned back against the wall, knees drawn up, finally letting herself breathe. The adrenaline still thudded in her veins, but here, with the others, she felt a fragile sense of safety.

Zayn's eyes darted briefly toward the treeline. "Everyone clear?" The girls nodded, brushing dirt off their pants, shaking from the tension.

Then he turned abruptly, eyes narrowing. "Shawn's still out there."

Alex's brow furrowed. "You're going too?"

"Yeah," Zayn said, jaw tight. "I can't let him fight alone."

Alex's hands hovered over the tablet controls, adjusting the drone's height. "Wait let me get the drone on him... got him. He's... moving like a bullet. Zayn, be careful, he's not thinking like us."

Zayn nodded, taking a deep breath. He crouched low, scanning the darkened path ahead. "I have to get to him." He gestured to the girls. "Stay here, stay in the light, stay together. The cops will arrive any second. I'll move fast."

Without waiting for a response, Zayn bolted down the path that led back toward the warehouse. His sneakers skidded over loose gravel and damp leaves, arms pumping. He followed the faint trail Shawn had left, footprints in dirt, broken branches, displaced leaves, a path illuminated faintly by the moonlight overhead.

The forest thickened again as Zayn ran, the glow from the street fading behind him. Branches whipped against his jacket, and his breath came heavy in the cool night air. The faint hum of the drone overhead flickered through the gaps in the canopy, its small light cutting through the dark like a pulse.

His feet moved on instinct: sharp cuts, tight pivots, the same rhythm he'd built on the court back when he used to train with the team. Back when every sprint, every fake, every drop of sweat meant something. Tonight, it all came back, only this time the game was survival.

Then he heard it, impact. Fists connecting. The dull thud of bodies hitting gravel. Shouts muffled by distance.

Zayn slowed, crouching low, eyes narrowing as he reached the edge of the warehouse lot.

Through the gaps in the trees, the scene unfolded in fragments of motion and sound, Shawn in the center of chaos.

His movements were raw, fast, and unrelenting. One man swung at him; Shawn ducked under the arc and drove his shoulder forward, slamming the attacker into the side of a van.

The metal groaned from the force.

Another charged, and Shawn spun, fist meeting jaw, the impact echoing sharp across the night. He moved like he was born in this storm, no wasted energy, no hesitation, just survival and fury combined into something dangerous and clean.

Zayn's eyes widened as he slowed for a fraction, taking in the scene. *He's still standing... holding them off like that? He's something else. It's like watching a storm move through the dark.*

He took a deep breath as he began to move in, fists clenched.

Zayn stayed low, eyes darting across the lot, scanning for anyone out of place. That's when he saw it, one of the men breaking off from the chaos, moving behind a stack of crates, crouched low, a crowbar glinting faintly in his grip. He was circling, creeping up behind Shawn's blind spot.

Zayn didn't think. He tightened his jaw, adjusted his stance, and moved in.

Each step was silent over the dirt, sneakers brushing through the dry weeds at the lot's edge. The crowbar-wielding man was closing in, five feet, maybe less, raising the weapon high.

Shawn caught the movement too late, his focus locked on the man in front of him.

Zayn lunged from the side, catching the crowbar mid-swing. The impact jarred his arm, but he twisted, forcing the weapon sideways. The man grunted, caught off guard, and Zayn used the momentum to drive his elbow into the guy's ribs. The crowbar clattered to the ground.

The attacker stumbled, clutching his side, but before Zayn could recover, Shawn turned sharply at the noise. His eyes locked on Zayn for a split second, pupils blown wide, face streaked with sweat and dirt, chest heaving.

"There he is, the ace basketball player," he praised, panting.

Zayn smirked, "Can't let you take all the credit."

He turned as his eyes narrowed at the men about to attack. "I'm just as *pissed* as you."

As the disarmed man tried to crawl back toward his weapon, Shawn stepped in and drove a hard kick into his torso, sending him sprawling. A sickening crack rang out, followed by his yell echoing across the lot.

For the first time, they stood side by side, framed by the flickering warehouse lights, breathing hard, surrounded by the aftermath of Shawn's rage.

Another man staggered to his feet, groaning, wiping blood from a split lip. He swung hard, fists flying, but Zayn intercepted, grabbing the attacker's arm and using his momentum to slam him into the gravel. The man curled up, done for the count.

Alex's voice buzzed through the earpiece, equally impressed and sarcastic.

"Zayn… seriously, that was smooth. Side-step, elbow, roll, you secretly auditioning for a ninja movie? Also, tell Shawn he looks like a confused bear flailing in a thunderstorm."

Shawn grunted, swinging wildly at another attacker. Zayn rolled his eyes, ducking under a low swing and using the guy's momentum to shove him into a crate. "Thanks for the tip, Alex. I'll let him know once he stops smashing everything in sight."

Alex chuckled. "Please do. Also, bonus points if you somehow teach him to punch and not redecorate the warehouse. I'm worried he's gonna knock a support beam down."

Zayn ducked another swing, elbowing a man in the ribs and sending him sprawling. "Shawn, stay on your side of the furniture!" he called, a grin breaking through despite the chaos.

Shawn smirked briefly, chest heaving, and jabbed forward. "You worry too much."

Alex laughed. "I'm just here enjoying the choreography. Honestly, if I weren't tracking you with the drone, I'd swear this was a live stream called 'Watch the Ace Handle the Warehouse Apocalypse.'"

The next attacker lunged from the side, and Zayn met him with a sharp sweep, sending him sprawling into the gravel. "See, Shawn?"

Zayn shouted, barely dodging a swinging metal pipe. "This is how you do it efficiently!"

Shawn grunted in agreement, spinning to intercept another rush. "I work differently," he said, a wry edge in his voice.

Alex cracked a joke only Zayn could hear: "Beautiful. One guy's out cold, the other's redecorating the concrete lawn. Zayn, you're making this look easy. Shawn... well, he's Shawn."

Zayn chuckled quietly, stepping up to pin the last attacker flat. "Creative's one word for him," he said softly, watching Shawn continue his relentless assault, entirely unaware of Alex's commentary.

Chapter 49

The night was punctuated with grunts, heavy breathing, and the dull thud of bodies hitting gravel. Then, faintly at first, sirens cut through the chaos, red and blue lights flickering through the trees.

The attackers froze, eyes wide, hesitation ripping through their ranks. Zayn exchanged a brief glance with Shawn, both reading the same message: help had arrived.

Shawn's chest heaved, sweat streaking dirt and blood across his skin. He squared off for one last sweep, knocking back the final aggressor with a crushing shoulder, then let himself pause for just a heartbeat. Zayn dropped into a low stance, eyes scanning the lot, ready to protect, fists still tight.

The sirens grew louder, closer. Relief mingled with exhaustion as both men slowed, muscles trembling but ready, waiting for the cops to flood the lot and finally end the night.

One of the last attackers swung a wild punch. Shawn sidestepped, grabbing the man's wrist and twisting, sending him sprawling into the gravel.

The man spat, gritting his teeth.

Zayn ducked under a low swing from the other, hooking him around the waist and slamming him beside his partner. "Don't be a bad boy," Zayn said, voice low, almost amused despite the pounding adrenaline.

Shawn jabbed a shoulder into the first attacker's side, then put him into a submission. "Next time, try harder," he growled.

The second man scrambled again, swinging a fist blindly. Zayn caught it mid-air, twisted, and slammed it down against his back, keeping him pinned. Both attackers groaned, pinned under the combined strategy and strength of the two boys.

"You guys... insane," one wheezed, struggling under Shawn's grip.

Shawn smirked faintly, letting his voice carry with calm menace. "You tried. That's... what matters."

Zayn leaned close, pressing an elbow to the other man's shoulder. "However, effort itself isn't surviving this."

The sirens grew closer, red and blue cutting through the trees. Both boys held the attackers down, muscles sore but steady. The men kicked and cursed, but it was useless.

Shawn glanced at Zayn. "Think they'll stay down for the cops?"

Zayn grinned, tightening his hold. "They better."

And as the first squad cars rolled into the lot, the boys kept the last two pinned, finally letting the night's chaos settle.

From the treeline, headlights split the darkness, and multiple squad cars rolled in, engines growling. Officers poured out, weapons drawn, flashlights slicing through the chaos. Two officers moved quickly toward the boys, gesturing to hold steady, while others fanned out to surround the warehouse and the remaining attackers.

Suddenly, a car door opened, and Alex stepped out first, tablet in hand, followed by the girls. Val, Natalia, and Nora squinted against the strobe of police lights, eyes wide but relieved. "You made it," Zayn muttered under his breath, barely giving them a nod before returning to hold the attackers down.

"Hands where we can see them!" shouted a cop, training a flashlight on the pinned men. Shawn and Zayn didn't move, just tightened their grips until the officers were close. The attackers tried to wriggle, but the boys' combined strength left them flat against the gravel.

Two officers approached the boys, crouching slightly to keep their voices low. "You can let go. We'll take it from here," one said. Zayn and Shawn finally released their hold, stepping back, chest heaving, eyes still alert. The officers guided the teens a few steps away, making space to cuff the criminals.

Alex smirked, keeping his tablet up to record and track the surroundings. "I hope the footage comes with a 'Best Duo Performance' award," he muttered, earning a grin from Val. "You two really cleared the lot," he added quietly, pride lacing his tone.

One of the senior cops approached the teens, flashlight in hand, eyes widening as he took in their flushed, dirt-streaked faces. "So, *you* three were out there?" he asked, disbelief in his voice. "Alone?"

Val swallowed, shrugging lightly. "Not exactly alone," she said, glancing toward Zayn and Shawn, who were still catching their breath.

The officer raised an eyebrow. "You mean... *these two?*" He gestured toward the boys, who were still streaked with sweat and dust, knuckles bruised. "They were taking on... how many?"

Zayn straightened slightly, smirk tugging at his lips despite exhaustion. "However many we had to stop," he said.

Alex stepped forward, holding up his tablet. "Got the whole thing on video. I think your dispatcher might want to see this." He tapped through the feeds, the drone footage showing the chaos and the fight in clear detail.

Some officers leaned closer, jaws dropping as they watched Shawn and Zayn's relentless defense in real time.

Natalia nudged Val lightly. "Guess we're not the only ones impressed," she whispered, a small smile tugging at her lips.

One of the younger cops muttered, shaking his head. "I've been on the force for six to seven years... and I've never seen anything like this. Kids holding their own like that, taking down armed adults? Unreal."

Another cop, clearly more seasoned, finally spoke. "Alright. We'll need statements, IDs, the whole thing, but first, let's get you all checked out. You look like hell."

Shawn and Zayn exchanged a brief glance, exhaustion and adrenaline still lingering, before allowing themselves a slow exhale.

For the first time all night, the tension eased just slightly, replaced with a quiet awareness that the immediate danger was over, and the cops finally were in control.

Alex let out a low whistle. "Not gonna lie... I almost feel bad for them. Almost."

Val smirked, shaking her head. "Almost," she agreed, watching the boys lean on each other, bruised but victorious.

The night air was still thick with the remnants of chaos, but for the first time, there was the sense of order returning, a fragile, hard-earned calm.

Chapter 50

The flashing lights washed over the lot in restless waves of red and blue. The air smelled like rain and asphalt, heavy with the aftertaste of adrenaline.

Zayn sat on the curb, shoulders slumped. His hands still trembled faintly, the sting of bruises and gravel biting through the heat of his skin.

Beside him, Shawn stayed silent, elbows resting on his knees, eyes fixed on the dark stretch of trees beyond the flashing lights. The calm after a fight never felt like peace, just silence that hadn't decided what came next.

Across the lot, Alex stood near a pair of officers, tablet clutched like a prized trophy.

"The drone wasn't technically meant for recon," he said, talking fast, gesturing like he was pitching a movie.

"But it's got stabilized gimbals, night vision, and live feed storage. So, yeah. Real-time visuals. You can see the whole fight from above."

The older cop squinted at the screen, impressed despite himself. "You kids planned this?"

Alex shrugged, trying for casual but clearly buzzing with leftover adrenaline. "More like... adapted. Things got bad, we made it work."

The younger officer exhaled, chuckling, "Kid's running a whole surveillance unit out of a backpack."

Nearby, Val sat on the edge of an ambulance, her hoodie pulled tight as a medic cleaned a cut along her cheek. She kept glancing toward Zayn and Shawn between questions, her expression a mixture of relief and disbelief. "They were just, fighting nonstop," she murmured, half to herself.

The medic smiled faintly, dabbing antiseptic. "Looks like they're wired tougher than they look."

Shawn caught her glance across the flashing lights and gave a small nod, barely a smile, more like silent reassurance.

She smiled back, the first real one of the night.

"You two!" called another medic, jogging toward the boys. "You need to get checked, too. Those bruises don't look light."

Shawn straightened slowly, shaking his head. "We're fine."

"Fine's not a medical term," the medic countered, crouching to check his arm anyway.

Zayn gave a tired half-grin. "Then we're... medically fine."

The medic sighed, realizing it wasn't worth arguing, and stood. "Suit yourselves. I'll be here when you decide you're not."

A few feet away, Nora and Natalia leaned against a patrol car, exhaustion mixing with curiosity as they watched Alex still talking a mile a minute.

"He's explaining frame rates," Natalia muttered, shaking her head. "To cops."

Nora chuckled softly, folding her arms. "Give him five more minutes, he's either getting recruited or arrested."

They both laughed quietly: half relief, half disbelief that they were all still standing.

Behind them, more officers were taping off the area, corralling the last of the cuffed attackers into squad cars. The chaos had softened into order, commands shouted, radios crackling, evidence bags being filled.

One officer, clearly a senior detective by the calm in his voice, approached the group.

"Alright, everyone. We're splitting you up for statements. Just standard procedure." He pointed toward the ambulance area. "Medics'll clear you first, then we'll get your sides of what happened."

Val nodded, still catching her breath. Nora and Natalia exchanged a glance and stood straighter.

Zayn rose from the curb, stretching his sore arm with a faint grimace. Shawn pushed himself up beside him, rolling his shoulders, jaw tight but silent.

The detective looked between the two of them. "You two did the heavy lifting, huh?"

Neither answered right away. Zayn finally said, "We just… didn't have a choice."

The officer studied them for a moment, then gave a slow nod. "Well… good thing you didn't freeze up. Could've gone bad real fast."

Alex rejoined them just then, tucking his tablet under his arm. "Told them the footage's clean," he said, a little too proud. "They said they'll take it as evidence."

"Shocking," Nora teased. "Bet they also said you talk too much."

"Oh hush," Alex shot back. "They were fascinated."

"Fascinated is a strong word," Natalia said, smirking.

Val chuckled softly, shaking her head as the medic finally stepped away.

Zayn glanced between them all, the tired faces, the mess of flashing lights, the sound of radios and sirens slowly fading.

The detective waved them toward the side of the lot. "Alright, let's get statements before it gets too late. The sooner you talk, the sooner you can go home."

Home.

The word hit heavier than it should've.

After everything that had happened, it didn't feel like the night was done, it felt like something deeper had just shifted.

The asphalt crunched under their shoes as the group followed the detective toward the flood of light near the cruisers. The sirens had gone quiet now, just the low hum of radios and the occasional click of a pen on a clipboard.

A folding table had been set up beside a squad car, papers clipped beneath a desk lamp that buzzed faintly. A few officers stood waiting, coffee steaming in paper cups, their tired eyes darting between the teens.

"Names, ages, what you saw," one said, motioning to a line of chairs. "We'll make this quick."

Alex spoke first, spinning his tablet once before placing it on the table. "You'll want the footage for context," he began.

"Start with your name," the officer interrupted flatly.

Alex sighed. "Alex, seventeen. And yeah, context incoming." He slid the tablet forward. The officer raised an eyebrow but let him talk.

Meanwhile, Val leaned against a patrol car, holding her side. The medic's bandage peeked from beneath her sleeve. She kept glancing toward Shawn, who stood off to the side, waiting their turn.

Shawn leaned against the hood of another police car, eyes down, jaw tight. Every time a camera flash popped for evidence, he tensed, like he was still wired for a fight. Zayn stood beside him, arms crossed, silent but steady.

"Think they'll believe all of it?" Shawn muttered.

Zayn shrugged, half-smiling. "We've got video, bruises, and hundreds of papers. If they don't, that's on them."

Shawn's gaze lingered on the squad cars where the cuffed attackers sat slumped in the back seats. "Still feels off. Like it's not over."

"It's not," Zayn said quietly. "But for now, it's enough."

Natalia and Nora were called next. They sat together, trading subtle smiles like they needed to remind each other it was real, that they'd made it out.

Nora, voice soft but steady, explained how they'd tracked the attackers through Alex's drone feed. Natalia filled in the rest, how Shawn and Zayn had refused to run.

One of the officers paused her notes. "You're saying they stayed behind to protect you?"

Nora shrugged. "No. They stayed because they're both morons."

The officer exchanged a look with her partner, who muttered something about "bravery or insanity."

Val was next. She hesitated before sitting down, fingers fidgeting with the blanket draped over her shoulders. "They didn't go looking for trouble," she said quickly. "They reacted. Fast. I don't think I would've walked out without them."

The officer just nodded, writing it all down.

Then it was Zayn and Shawn's turn.

Zayn stepped forward first, every movement deliberate, as if holding his own energy in check. "Zayn, nineteen," he said. "They took our friend, we took her back and stopped them. That's it."

"Stop who?" the detective asked, flipping a page on his notepad.

"The people behind the disappearances," Zayn said. "The ones who were here tonight."

Shawn stayed standing, answering from beside him. "They were armed. Organized. We didn't think backup would make it in time."

The detective studied them both, then sighed. "You boys realize how reckless this was, right?"

Zayn nodded once. "Yeah."

"And you'd still do it again?"

Zayn's eyes didn't waver. "If it meant keeping them safe? Yeah."

Shawn exhaled through his nose, a small grin breaking through the weariness. "Guess we're guilty of doing the right thing wrong."

The detective didn't smile, but his tone softened. "You're lucky you made it through. Most don't when they play hero."

Zayn met his gaze. "We weren't trying to be heroes. Just... stop the wrong people from winning."

For a moment, the detective said nothing. Then he nodded slowly. "Alright. Statements are good enough for now. We appreciate your efforts and research, we'll look into this."

As they nodded and stepped away from the table, the group regrouped near the edge of the lot. The flashing lights had dimmed, the energy draining from the night.

For a long moment, none of them spoke. The air felt heavy again, the kind that settled in after chaos, the silence that made everything real.

Nora sat down on the curb, resting her arms on her knees. "It's weird," she said quietly. "You'd think after something like that, you'd feel relieved."

Val glanced at her. "You don't?"

Nora shook her head. "No. Just... hollow. Like we got through it, but it's not really over." Her eyes drifted to the dark stretch of forest beyond the lot. "Layla would've said the same thing."

Zayn's head lifted slightly. "You still think about her a lot?"

"Every day," Nora said softly. "She was the one who believed something was wrong before anyone else did. She'd been watching things happen before it got serious. Then she just–"

Her voice cracked. She took a breath.

"She just vanished. And the cops said it was a runaway case."

Zayn exhaled slowly. "Mira was the same. Everyone said she just got tired of school, left town. But she wouldn't have. She used to text me every morning, like clockwork. And when I was away…" He stopped, rubbing the back of his neck. "She was gone, taken."

He stared at the warehouse lights fading in the distance. "It's not over. It's not just us. It's not just tonight. It's about them. Mira. Layla. All of them."

Val's eyes softened. "You think they're still out there?"

Zayn didn't answer right away. "I don't know," he admitted. "But whatever this secret organization is, they didn't start tonight, and they didn't end tonight either."

Shawn cracked his knuckles absently, eyes distant. "Then we find whoever's left. For them."

Zayn looked up, "Mira used to say people vanish twice. Once when they're gone, and again when everyone stops talking about them."

Nora's gaze locked with his. "Then we don't stop."

The group fell silent again, the weight of it sitting between them like a vow neither of them had to say aloud.

The wind shifted through the lot, carrying the faint scent of rain and asphalt. Somewhere beyond the trees, the last echo of sirens faded.

And for the first time in hours, they all just… stood there, bruised, quiet, and together.

Chapter 51

The night had thinned into silence.

Flashing lights faded behind them, leaving only the hum of street lamps and the crunch of gravel beneath worn-out shoes.

No one said much at first. The cold air did enough talking.

Shawn had his hands tucked into his hoodie pocket, walking ahead, hood up. Zayn kept pace beside him.

A few steps behind, Alex dragged his feet, his tablet now shoved in his backpack. "You know," he muttered, voice rough from exhaustion, "I think I hit my daily word limit back there with the cops."

Nora snorted. "You have a word limit?"

"That's hard to believe," Natalia added. "They're probably filing a separate report just for your monologue."

Even Shawn's lips twitched. "You'll live."

They turned down a quiet street lined with closed shops. The neon sign of a gas station flickered weakly in the distance.

"Please tell me that place is open," Val said, rubbing her arms.

Alex squinted. "If it's not, we riot."

The bell above the glass door jingled as they stepped inside, the sudden warmth hitting like a blanket. The place was empty, just the bored clerk behind the counter and the faint buzz of a fridge light.

They split up automatically.

Nora grabbed a pack of Oreos.

Val went straight for a bottle of water and a chocolate bar.

Alex wandered the aisles, reading snack labels like he was decoding them.

Zayn picked two energy drinks, tossed one toward Shawn.

Shawn caught it without looking. "You paying?"

Zayn shrugged. "If I don't, Alex will start a presentation about inflation."

Alex waved a hand dismissively. "I'd *love* to explain to you why sugar intake correlates directly with late-night survival probability."

Nora groaned. "We survived before your lecture. Somehow."

At the counter, the clerk scanned their stuff, half-asleep. "Rough night?"

"Something like that," Shawn muttered.

"Must've been one hell of a party."

Zayn gave a faint grin. "You could say that."

Outside, they sat along the curb, under the flicker of the gas station sign. Cars passed in the distance, their headlights stretching shadows across the pavement.

Natalia leaned her head on Val's shoulder. "I can't believe we actually did all that."

"Yeah," Nora said softly. "It feels fake. Like we blink and we're back in school tomorrow."

"I suggest we skip." Alex groaned.

For a while, no one spoke. They just sat there, bruised, quiet, chewing on snacks like it was some unspoken ritual.

Zayn stared at the cracked pavement, the half-melted ice around a drain. "Feels weird, huh?"

Shawn glanced over. "What does?"

"Being free. After all that."

Shawn took a long sip of his drink. "Freedom's just the break between storms."

Zayn huffed out a tired laugh. "You sound like Alex."

That shut them both up.

Val nudged Shawn with her elbow. "Hey, thanks. For... you know. Tonight."

He looked into her eyes for a second then looked down.

"I've got you."

Nora tilted her head, looking at Zayn. "Do you ever think we'll find Mira and Layla?"

Zayn's grip on the drink tightened slightly. "Every day. That's why I set out in the first place."

Shawn spoke up dryly. "We'll do all of it again if it means finding and saving every missing person."

Alex also spoke, while chewing. "This was just the beginning."

The group shared a faint smile, the kind that's part relief, part exhaustion, part fear, and part something they didn't have words for yet.

When they finally stood, it was past midnight. The streets were almost empty, just the hum of streetlights and the echo of their steps.

They walked until the road split, one way toward Shawn's place, the other toward Natalia's.

"Boys that way," Natalia said, motioning. "Girls this way."

Zayn waved. "Try not to overthink it tonight."

"Try not to brood about it either," Nora shot back.

Zayn smiled. "No promises."

Shawn smirked faintly. "Fair enough."

Alex gave a dramatic bow. "I'll take my leave, then. Class dismissed."

Val rolled her eyes but couldn't stop a grin. "You'd never let us live this down."

They exchanged quiet goodnights, the kind that didn't need hugs, just understanding.

Then they drifted off in separate directions, under the same thin layer of stars, their footsteps fading into the kind of silence that only comes after survival.

***

The streets were quiet, empty except for the faint glow of streetlights reflecting off damp asphalt. Shawn led the way, Zayn close behind, both shoulders sagging under the weight of exhaustion and the night's adrenaline.

"My knees hate me," Zayn muttered, flexing one calf.

"Mine filed a formal complaint an hour ago," Shawn replied, smiling.

The two walked on, the night pressing around them, soft and still, the only sounds were their footsteps and the occasional hum of a distant car. Alex followed behind, tapping away on his tablet.

Across the city, a few blocks away, the girls were on their own path, heading toward Natalia's apartment. Val leaned against Natalia as they walked, still catching her breath. "I can't believe we survived," she said quietly.

Natalia nudged her shoulder. "We didn't really have a choice. But hey, it's over for tonight."

Nora laughed softly, kicking a small stone down the sidewalk. "I keep expecting someone else to jump out, but nope. Just the night, finally."

A few minutes later, both groups reached their destinations. The guys climbed the stairs to Shawn's apartment, dropping bags and jackets with a satisfying thump, flopping onto the couch in a tangled heap of limbs and blankets.

Shawn, sprawled across the couch, glanced at Zayn. "Tomorrow, we're probably going to feel this for a week."

Zayn groaned, rolling over to face the ceiling. "Yeah, worth it, though, and Alex, please no yap."

Alex grinned as he dropped down on a beanbag. "Don't worry, I'm too tired."

Zayn nudged Shawn, smirking faintly. "He's exhausted, but somehow still thinks he ran a whole military campaign."

Shawn chuckled, eyes half-closed. "At least he's harmless when tired."

Meanwhile, at Natalia's, the girls had shuffled inside, dropping backpacks onto the floor. Val slumped onto the couch, tugging the blanket around her shoulders. "I don't think I've ever been that scared," she admitted quietly, glancing down at her hands.

Nora flopped next to her, exhaling slowly. "Yeah... watching him switch like that, it was insane. Shawn... he just went completely off when he realized you were taken. I mean, we knew he was intense, but that? That was next level."

Val shivered slightly, hugging the blanket closer. "I felt it too. Every second felt like... like the world was closing in. I didn't know if I was going to make it out."

Natalia leaned against the arm of the couch, shaking her head. "He's... protective, yeah. But that, 'I don't care who gets in my way' version of him? Scary. In a good way, maybe, but still..."

She trailed off, eyes distant.

Nora laughed softly, but it was nervous. "I mean... I've seen him smirk, fight, whatever. But that moment... he was a different person. And it worked. You're alive, Val. That's all that counts."

Val let out a shaky laugh, the tension in her chest easing slightly. "Yeah... I guess. But still... wow. I don't ever want to see him like that again. Or at least not directed at me."

Nora smiled, nudging her gently. "Don't worry. He'll scare anyone who tries. You just survived the hurricane. We all played a part tonight, and we all did well."

Val sank back into the couch, letting out a long, shaky breath. "It still feels unreal... like we were in some movie or something."

Nora chuckled softly, draping an arm across the back of the couch. "Yeah, but real life movies usually don't come with bruises and screaming. They're fake."

Natalia smiled faintly, glancing out the window at the quiet street. "Quiet streets... exhausted lungs... at least we made it through. That counts for something."

The three of them sat in a comfortable silence, the hum of the city beyond the windows filling the space, letting the adrenaline finally fade.

The girls fell into a quieter rhythm, the city outside soft and still, the adrenaline slowly leaving their bodies.

Relief and exhaustion intertwined, leaving them with the heavy warmth of having made it through, shaken but unbroken.

Chapter 52

The apartment was quiet, except for the hum of the fridge and the faint traffic bleeding through the blinds. A single shaft of morning light cut across the living room, touching the dust floating in lazy spirals.

Zayn woke first. His neck ached, his shoulder felt like it had been through a blender, and every bruise from last night screamed at once.

He shifted slightly, wincing, the old carpet imprinting faint lines on his arm. He'd crashed on the floor with just a hoodie for a pillow, somewhere between half-dead and half-conscious.

For a few seconds, he didn't move. He just breathed, slow, shallow, listening.

Alex was out cold, curled into the beanbag like a house cat that had survived a war.

Shawn had knocked out on the couch, one arm hanging off, hoodie hood half-covering his face, completely gone.

Zayn stared at them for a moment, a tired smile tugging at his mouth. They'd really done it.

Last night, chaos and adrenaline had carried them through something insane, something no one would ever understand.

Now, seeing them asleep in the aftermath, he realized how young they still were. Fighters, yeah. But still kids in hoodies and sneakers who just wanted to make it through.

He quietly reached for his phone, snapping a photo.

The sound didn't go off, but Shawn twitched slightly.

Zayn froze, then exhaled when he didn't move again.

He sent the photo into the group chat.

Zayn: "the warriors, fallen in battle"

A minute later, Nora replied.

Nora: "hold up"

Then another photo popped up:

Natalia half-asleep against the couch arm, Val sprawled like a starfish, blanket halfway off, and Nora's hand holding up a peace sign in the corner.

Nora: "the battlefield extends"

Zayn: "the lil ones are wiped fr"

Nora: "eldest privilege: insomnia and back pain."

Zayn: "we suffer so they can dream"

Nora: "prophets of sleeplessness"

Zayn snorted quietly, shaking his head. He stretched his sore shoulder, checking a faint bruise near his collarbone. Worth it. Every bit of it.

Behind him, Shawn groaned like a zombie rising from the dead.

"Bro, tell me you didn't just take pictures of us."

Zayn didn't turn. "I absolutely did."

Shawn peeked at his phone, squinting at the group chat. "You're dead to me."

Natalia: "wait we're on camera??"

Val: "i look like a fossil."

Shawn leaned his head back. "He's still out, huh?"

249

Zayn grinned. "King of doing the least but sleeping the most."
A small buzz echoed as Natalia sent another message.

Natalia: "school day check??"
Val: "mentally unavailable."
Shawn: "my soul called in sick."

They all laughed, even through the chat, the kind of laugh that came from exhaustion, relief, and disbelief that they were still here.

By the time Alex finally stirred awake, blinking like he'd forgotten what century it was, the rest had already decided their fate.

"Morning, sunshine," Shawn muttered. "Hope you're ready to skip."
Alex groaned. "Skip what?"
"Reality."
It took an hour before everyone had properly gotten up, showered, borrowed clothes, and eaten what little food Shawn's fridge could provide.

"Bro," Zayn mumbled, watching him pour cereal into a mug. "That's... not a bowl."
"Resourcefulness," Shawn said, dead serious. "It's a survival trait."
Zayn shook his head, stretching his sore arms. "You need help."
"From who?" Shawn gestured at Alex, who was face-down in the beanbag again.
"The corpse?"

Meanwhile, across town, Nora had started a video call in the group. Her voice was half-yawn, half-laugh.
"Okay, roll call, who's alive?"
Zayn answered first. "Barely."

Val: "Spiritually, no."
Natalia: "Nora is eating cereal out the box."
Shawn: "I'm considering never standing again."
Alex's camera popped up in the call, "I was dreaming of waffles."

The call dissolved into tired laughter, soft, glitchy, real.

For a few minutes, they just talked about nothing. Who had the worst bruises, who stole the best blanket, how Shawn's fridge only had mustard and Gatorade.

"Bro, how do you even live like this?" Natalia asked through the call, half laughing.

"Mustard and Gatorade is *not* a balanced diet."

"False," Shawn said. "It's called *variety*."

"Yeah," Val said, yawning. "Variety of suffering."

Alex, still down on the beanbag, finally spoke up.

"Someone door-dash this man bread or something."

Zayn laughed quietly. "Nah, let him starve. Builds character."

"Character's overrated," Shawn shot back.

The call broke into that kind of half-awake laughter where everyone talks over each other, messy, tired, human.

It was weirdly peaceful.

No alarms.

No plans.

Just comments, slander, and complaints overlapping through speakers, the kind of calm that didn't feel real after the chaos they'd seen.

"Y'all realize this is the first time we've slept this good in a while, or it's just me." Val said.

"Feels illegal," Nora replied.

"Feels earned," Zayn said.

Shawn leaned back in his chair, sipping Gatorade straight from the bottle.

"So… anyone actually going to school?"

Natalia groaned. "Why ruin a good thing?"

"Skipping confirmed," Alex said, pretending to type something. "I'll submit our group resignation letters to the education system."

Shawn smirked. "Make mine emotional."

"I'll include tears," Alex said.

Nora hummed softly through the call. "You guys really can just skip, huh?"

Shawn looked up. "What, you can't?"

She hesitated, then laughed. "As free as it seems, college doesn't stop for trauma."

Zayn smiled faintly, "Neither does life."

The tone shifted, just slightly. Enough for everyone to feel it.

Val stretched and spoke up, her voice buzzing through the phone. "So… what now?"

"Breakfast?" Shawn said.

"No," Natalia replied. "We already ate sadness and mustard."

Zayn chuckled. "Yeah, save the fridge before it files a complaint."

Val spoke again, quieter this time. "I meant like… after all this."

She paused, "What happens *now*?"

Zayn rubbed his arm absently, eyes tracing the sunlight crawling up the wall. "Guess we'll find out."

Shawn tried to break the mood.

"We could just all move in here, y'know. Live off mustard, die happy."

"Pass," Nora said instantly.

"Actually," Zayn added, "that sounds peaceful."

Alex: "Until the fridge revolts."

They all laughed again, and for a second, it almost felt normal.

But as the morning stretched, Zayn caught himself glancing at the clock. The hours kept slipping by too fast.

Part of him wanted to freeze it, this small, dumb, ordinary peace that came after a storm.

Because deep down, he knew they couldn't hold it forever.

Chapter 53

The video call energy died out, everyone half-lounging in their respective spaces, voices lazy and yawning. Then, out of nowhere, Nora's voice cut through.

"Guys! Stop whatever you're doing and check the local news!"

Everyone froze for a second. Zayn squinted at his phone, Shawn groaned dramatically, and even Alex lifted his head from the beanbag, eyes brightening.

The headline was simple:

"Anonymous Teens Prevent Escalation in Overnight Incident"

The anchor's voice rattled off:

"Two local teenagers, identities undisclosed, successfully intervened in a dangerous confrontation downtown last night. Drone footage shows precise, coordinated movements that prevented potential injury or property damage. The teens' bravery has been widely praised, though they remain anonymous."

A short clip flashed across the screen. Shadows moved fluidly in the dim light, the figures ducking and countering the four aggressors, Alex's drone work made it cinematic, even with faces blurred.

Alex shot up, grinning impossibly wide. "That's *my footage*! And they think it's heroic! Best. Day. Ever."

Shawn laughed, leaning back. "They have no idea what actually went down, huh?"

Zayn rubbed his shoulder, wincing. "Nope. Two kids. Four guys. Chaos contained. And the city is clueless about everything else... including the disappearances."

Val spoke through the speakers on the call, "It's kind of funny... the world applauds the moment but ignores the bigger picture."

Nora snorted. "Yeah, because connecting the dots is hard and apparently dangerous."

Alex held up a thumbs-up to the camera. "I *told* you, cinematic justice. Unseen heroes, global applause.

Shawn smiled. "Ghosts in plain sight... I like it."

Zayn let out a small chuckle. "Makes the aches from last night feel a little more worth it."

For a few minutes, they allowed themselves the pride, the quiet thrill of being recognized, and the rare comfort of anonymity.

The call didn't end right away. If anything, it softened.

The adrenaline fizzled into something gentler, something warm.

The girls lounged back on their couch, tangled in blankets; the boys sprawled across Shawn's living room, all of them in their own little post-chaos nests.

Zayn shifted on the floor, stretching out one leg with a quiet groan. "Wild," he said, half-smiling. "Imagine trying to explain that night to anyone."

Nora snorted. "They'd think we hallucinated it."

"Or scripted it," Alex added from the beanbag, his voice muffled by the fabric. "Honestly, that drone footage made us look way cooler than we were."

"You mean cooler than *you* were," Shawn corrected, grinning lazily at him. "I carried."

"You tripped," Zayn reminded him.

"Strategic maneuver," Shawn said, deadpan.

Val laughed softly. "You guys are always at it."

"But we did it," Natalia added, voice warm now. "We actually did."

A small beat. Not solemn, just the kind that lets the truth land.

"Yeah," Zayn said. "Kinda proud of us."

The others agreed in their own ways, a nod, a hum, a quiet grin caught on a shaky connection.

They reminisce in the way only people who lived through something together can: lightly, but with a thread of meaning under every joke. They knew exactly how close last night had come to going wrong. They also knew how right it felt to have each other's backs.

Nora shifted the camera to show Valerie poking at a bruise on her knee. "Battle scars," Val declared.

Zayn mirrored her, lifting his sleeve to reveal a faint mark on his shoulder. "Badge of honor," he said.

"Emotional damage too," Alex added.

"Award-winning emotional damage," Shawn corrected.

The group dissolved into tired laughter, the kind that hits softer than earlier jokes, the kind that comes after acknowledging something rare.

Eventually, the jokes faded, leaving them in a comfortable hush.

"You know," Valerie said, "as insane as it was... I'm kinda glad it happened."

Alex blinked. "Bro, don't say it like we summoned chaos."

"No, I mean– " she yawned, hiding her face under the blanket. "We'll remember this. Years from now. The night we... whatever-you-want-to-call-this. We did something that mattered."

Shawn leaned back against the couch cushion. "Yeah," he said. "We'll roast each other about it forever."

"And claim we won," Alex added.

"We did win yet," Zayn said. "We all made it home. That counts."

It wasn't dramatic. It wasn't heavy.

It was solid, grounding.

A calm after the storm that felt like a reward.

Zayn cracked a small grin. "So... actually, now what? Y'all down to go out later?"

Nora stretched on her couch across the town, a blanket tangled around her legs. "Yeah. But where? Somewhere fun. Somewhere we can forget all this... for a bit."

"Exactly," Alex said from the beanbag at Shawn's, finally upright enough to hold his phone steady. "Let's celebrate surviving. No homework, no chaos, just... something good."

Shawn leaned back on the couch, sipping his Gatorade. "I'm in. Mustard-free zone preferred."

Val giggled, curling into her pillows. "Deal. Somewhere fun. Somewhere loud. Somewhere that feels like a reward."

Natalia nodded. "Yeah. Somewhere we don't have to be responsible for... anything."

Zayn grinned. "Alright. How about the carnival? It just so happens to be tonight too. Rides, games, lights... total chaos, totally ours. Evening vibe, just as the sun's going down."

Nora's eyes lit up. "I'm in. Cotton candy first. Then I'm claiming a giant stuffed animal if I win a game."

Alex smirked. "You all know I'm taking the ring toss championship. Step aside."

Shawn shook his head. "Don't get cocky, Beanbag King. You've already had your highlight reel today."

The groups laughed, teasing each other across screens, the kind of easy, comfortable banter that comes from shared experience.

Midday sunlight spilled across their rooms, warm and lazy, shadows stretching on floors and walls.

They spent the next hour lounging, joking about last night, pointing out lingering bruises, arguing over who really carried the team, and occasionally drifting into comfortable silence.

The call lingered like that, not urgent, just a soft thread connecting them.

Finally, Zayn stretched again. "Okay, so plan: we meet at the carnival a little after sunset. Give everyone time to rest, grab snacks, whatever. Sound good?"

"Perfect," Nora said. "Countdown to fun night officially started."

"Agreed," Val chimed in, half-yawning. "I'll be ready."

Alex flopped back onto the beanbag, dramatic sigh and all. "Fine. I'll survive the anticipation."

Shawn grinned. "Just don't be late. Don't ruin the lights for the rest of us."

The call wound down naturally, faces lingering in the screens for a moment, soft smiles across distances. Midday sunlight bathed both houses, warm and bright, carrying a quiet, easy feeling of safety and relief.

They'd survived chaos. They were okay.

And now, a night of lights, games, laughter, and cotton candy awaited.

Chapter 54

The sunlight stretched across the city, soft and golden, but thinning as the afternoon edged toward evening. Across town, Shawn's apartment hummed with low, comfortable chaos.

Alex crouched on the edge of the beanbag, holding a shirt up to his chest, turning side to side in front of the mirror. "Okay... maybe this works," he muttered.

"Works for what?" Shawn asked, tossing a hoodie over the back of a chair.

"Not looking like a disaster," Alex said. "I can't just throw on whatever. It has to... work."

Zayn snorted, pulling a T-shirt from Shawn's pile and shaking it dramatically. "Bro, it's not like anyone's judging us. It's a carnival, not a fashion runway."

"Exactly why I'm perfecting it," Alex replied, tucking a hem just so.

Shawn leaned against the doorway, smirking. "You're exhausting."

The three of them started their own slow chaos. Zayn draped a flannel over his shoulders, pretending to be a superhero cape.

Shawn grabbed a hat and plopped it on Zayn's head, tipping it forward until Zayn made a mock glare and shoved him back.

Shawn stumbled, caught himself on the sofa, and laughed. Alex, adjusting a scarf, nudged Shawn's arm in retaliation, prompting a half-hearted shove that sent the scarf fluttering across the room.

They wrestled lightly over shoes, shoved each other off balance while trying on jackets, and shouted jokes over who looked more ridiculous.

"Beanbag King strikes again," Zayn teased as Alex flopped backward onto the beanbag with a dramatic sigh.

"Shut up," Alex said, smoothing the scarf, "you look like a lost raccoon."

"Lost raccoon with style," Zayn countered, grinning.

"Style is subjective," Shawn said, throwing up his hands as he grabbed a T-shirt to examine. "I think I just discovered Alex's obsession with details is contagious."

They laughed, tussled, and nudged each other gently, each small shove or poke carrying familiarity, comfort, and the rhythm of friendship. Every motion, a hand steadying a crooked sleeve, a playful elbow to tease a reaction, felt intimate without being serious, marking the moments as one of those small but felt memories.

Across town, the girls were in their own world. Natalia's living room smelled faintly of shampoo, fabric softener, and lingering takeout. She held up a shirt from her recent shopping haul, spinning slowly.

"Okay… too much?" she asked, tilting her head.

"Nope," Valerie said, brushing a lock of hair back and adjusting Natalia's collar. "Let me fix your collar."

Nora tried on a jacket over her dress, laughing at how oversized it felt. Natalia tugged the sleeves into place, Val teasing her about looking like a movie character. They fussed over hair, swapped accessories, and debated which outfit fit the evening vibe best.

Every adjustment, a hand smoothing a collar, a hair clip set straight, a bracelet positioned just so, became a gesture of care, the kind of intimacy only close friends share.

Outside, the sky shifted. Afternoon gold softened into pale pinks and oranges, clouds like cotton teased across the horizon. A gentle breeze curled through open windows, carrying warmth tinged with the smell of asphalt and late-blooming flowers from nearby gardens. The air felt alive: soft against skin, stirring hair and fabric, a subtle promise of evening energy that wrapped the city in quiet motion.

By mid-afternoon, the groups called each other again to finalize plans. "Okay, so… carnival?" Zayn said, voice low, tired but excited.

"Yeah," Natalia replied. "Just during sunset, give everyone a chance to rest and snack."

"Perfect," Nora said, tugging her blanket tighter around her legs. "Countdown officially started."

Alex adjusted his jacket one last time. "Fine. I'll survive the anticipation."

Shawn smirked. "Just don't be late. Don't ruin the lights for the rest of us."

The call wound down naturally, lingering smiles across screens, then each group gathered their things, stepping out into the streets. The city was soft with afternoon light, streets warm beneath their feet, the wind teasing scarves and hair.

For the boys, the walk was playful. Shawn nudged Zayn over a cracked sidewalk tile; Alex grabbed Shawn's shoulder to steady him, and they laughed as Zayn tripped lightly over the uneven curb. The smell of late-afternoon traffic mixed with grass from small parks, blending into the city's unique scent. They talked in bursts, joking about outfits, hairstyles, and who would inevitably ruin the first carnival photo.

The girls' walk was slower, lighter. They pointed at clouds shifting across the pink sky, debated snacks, complimented each other on hair and outfits. Every laugh carried across the sidewalks, a gentle reminder that these streets, and this moment, were theirs, together.

And then, the carnival came into view.

Lights sparkled across rides, each one spinning and swaying as if alive. Music blended from distant rides, stalls, and speakers, pop notes, chimes, and laughter weaving together. Popcorn, cotton candy, and fried dough filled the breeze. Kids screamed on carousels, teenagers ran between stalls, parents walked behind toddlers, and the scent of warm sugar and fried food teased at every step.

Zayn slowed instinctively, eyes wide. "Even smells like fun," he muttered.

Shawn laughed, nudging him. "Get ready, man, it's just the beginning."

Alex adjusted a sleeve, noticing how lights reflected on fabric and hair. Every detail mattered, every glow felt precise.

The girls paused as well. Natalia's eyes widened, the golden-pink light hitting her face. "This... this is perfect," she said softly.

Minutes later, the two groups merged, playful shoves and jokes exchanged, instant camaraderie bridging the distance.

"Plushie first!" Val shouted, grabbing Shawn's arm and running.

"Ring toss!" Alex corrected, tugging Zayn toward the nearest table.

"Cotton candy!" Nora countered, dragging Natalia toward a sweet stand.

"And Ferris wheel rides!" Natalia added, spinning in a circle with a laugh as she was dragged by Nora.

They moved together, weaving between teenagers, parents, and children, the carnival alive in color, scent, sound, and motion.

The sun dipped further, clouds painted deep oranges and pinks, a gentle wind teasing scarves and hair. Laughter, nudges, shoves, and playful complaints layered over the sensory chaos, every detail anchored in this moment, every step a memory in motion. The breeze complimented the dropping temperature, as the orange-pink sky complimented the setting sun.

They wandered deeper into the carnival, shoulders brushing, hands occasionally bumping in playful nudges, the air thick with sugar and laughter. Shawn pointed out a game he swore he could beat in one try, Alex countered with a strategy so precise it earned an eye-roll from Zayn, and the girls debated which ride to hit first, each suggestion punctuated by giggles and mock protests.

The lights grew brighter as the sun sank lower, painting the edges of their faces with gold and pink, turning every glance, every smile into something *cinematic*.

Music pulsed through the crowd, a heartbeat that carried them forward, threading their laughter and chatter through the rhythm of the fair.

They paused at the entrance to the Ferris wheel, looking up at the towering lit-up ride spinning slowly against the darkening sky.

The world stretched out behind them, twinkling lights, miniature roller coasters, stalls glowing like little suns, and for a moment, it felt like everything they had survived had led them here, to this small universe of chaos and joy.

Zayn leaned back slightly, taking a deep breath. "Man... we earned this."

"Absolutely," Val said, reaching for cotton candy already in her hand.

"Totally," Alex added, adjusting his jacket one last time as if to mark the moment.

The group lingered in that soft pause, letting the lights, the smells, the distant screams of the rides, and the warm laughter of strangers blend with their own joy. Every face, every glance, every touch felt alive, tethering them to the moment like a photograph in motion.

And as the first stars appeared in the evening sky, mingling with the carnival glow, they moved forward together, a single, unruly cluster of friends, alive with energy, ready to chase games, rides, and laughter into the night.

It was the kind of evening that promised memories they would carry forever.

Chapter 55

The Ferris wheel towered above them, glowing like a beacon, each gondola lit with tiny, flickering bulbs. The group paused at its base, letting the height, the colors, and the scents of the carnival sink in. Laughter, music, and the distant screams of rides blended into a pulse that matched their own energy, a heartbeat of the city alive at dusk.

Zayn tilted his head back, eyes wide. "I can't believe we're actually here."

Shawn nudged him in the ribs. "Welcome to the reward phase, man. You earned it. Sort of."

Alex adjusted the hem of his jacket, glancing at the Ferris wheel's reflection in the shiny metal railings. "I'm not sure 'sort of' counts," he said.

"Details matter. Everything matters." He paused, scanning the crowd. Neon lights danced across the sidewalk puddles left from a brief afternoon sprinkle, casting little rainbows on worn sneakers and spinning cotton candy sticks.

The girls had already grabbed a sweet stand, bags of cotton candy in hand. Natalia spun slowly, letting the candy unwind, sticky sugar dust catching in her hair. "This... this smells exactly like childhood," she said softly. Valerie laughed, nudging her shoulder. "You mean, your childhood was neon-lit sugar chaos?"

"Exactly!" Natalia grinned. "I'm soaking it in."

Nora tugged at Natalia's hand. "We should start small. Ring toss first. Claim our victories." She bounced slightly on the balls of her feet.

Meanwhile, the boys wandered toward a cluster of midway games. Zayn squinted at the ring toss booth. "I swear, I can win the big one," he said, half confident, half mocking himself.

Alex scanned the layout like a strategist, eyes narrowing. "No, no. You're going about it wrong. The rings bounce. You need to approach at a thirty-degree angle, not a straight toss. Trust me."

Shawn rolled his eyes but grinned. "Okay, Beanbag King, let's see this perfect strategy in action." He handed Zayn a ring.

Zayn crouched, winding up dramatically, exaggerating every motion, then flicked the ring forward. It clanged against the prize rack. Shawn muttered something under his breath, shaking his head. "Not bad. Not perfect. Try again."

The second toss landed slightly better, nearly catching the bottle top. Zayn smirked, nudging Alex. "See? Sometimes confidence beats perfect technique."

Shawn nudged back. "Don't tell him that," he said, eyebrows raised. "He'll take it way too seriously."

Behind them, the girls laughed at a small plushie crane machine. Nora pressed the joystick with exaggerated precision, fingers curling around the control. The claw descended slowly, gripped a medium-sized unicorn, and promptly dropped it halfway back up. Valerie groaned. "Traitor claw," she said, slapping the side. Natalia laughed, tugging at her friend's sleeve. "Next try. You got this."

"Dramatic tension," Nora muttered like a game-show host, twisting the joystick again. The claw made a perfect pick-up, then wobbled over the prize slot. With a soft plunk, it landed safely. "Victory!" she shouted, waving her prize.

Back at the ring toss, Shawn tried his own hand, wobbling in mock seriousness. "This one's for pride," he announced. The ring landed cleanly around a bottle, and he pumped a fist. "Ha! Dominance achieved."

The group meandered through stalls, inhaling the smells of fried dough, buttery popcorn, and sugary spun cotton. Kids ran past them with sticky hands, neon balloons bouncing behind them. Street performers juggled glowing pins, occasionally tossing one toward the crowd, prompting gasps and cheers.

Nora spun in a circle, letting the breeze catch her hair. "This is… unreal," she whispered, eyes wide. "We really did it, you know? Made it through last night… everything."

Valerie nudged her shoulder. "And now we get to celebrate. With sugar and lights and… chaos."

Shawn wandered over, catching sight of the towering roller coaster at the edge of the carnival. Its rails glinted under the neon lights, cars snapping around loops with screams trailing behind them. "Oh… this is mine," he said, brushing past the boys to get a closer look. "Next ride, I dominate."

Alex and Zayn stopped, eyes tracing the structure. "That's… huge," Alex said, voice low, impressed despite himself.

"Yeah," Zayn added, feeling the rush of adrenaline even from the ground. "We're doing this. All of us."

After a few minutes of joking, wandering other stalls, and each of them sneaking a quick mini-game or snack, they regrouped in front of the coaster. The ride attendant raised an eyebrow at their cluster, clearly amused by their coordinated chaos. "All together?" she asked.

"Absolutely," Shawn said, grinning.

Eventually, the group converged at the coaster entrance, loading into the rocket-shaped cars with shouts of mock intimidation and last-minute strategy tips.

They broke into pairs, six people into three carts, then they started moving.

The climb was slow, the rails creaking, the neon lights stretching below them. Hands brushed occasionally, causing small bursts of laughter, and Shawn made a dramatic show of gripping the restraint too tight.

As they rolled out the entrance tunnel, the first plunge came into view, anxious screams erupted from people across the entire coaster line, both genuine and theatrical.

The Ferris wheel had set them down, and now the roller coaster loomed above, its twisting tracks glinting in the carnival lights.

The cars ground up the first steep hill, click-click-click, each clank sending a jolt through their chests.

Shawn leaned forward, teeth clenched in a grin. "Alright... whoever screams first owes everyone else a cotton candy."

"Deal," Zayn muttered, gripping the bar until his knuckles went white. "No way I'm losing."

Alex tugged at his jacket nervously. "Focus... breathe... focus... nope, impossible. I'm officially panicking."

Nora clutched the bar, peeking through her fingers. "I hate that I'm excited and terrified at the same time," she muttered.

Valerie nudged her. "That's called fun. Sort of."

Natalia squealed softly, eyes wide. "Wait, it's... it's so high! Look at the lights! Tiny humans below!"

"Shut up! Don't make it worse!" Zayn groaned, leaning back against his harness.

Shawn elbowed him lightly. "Come on, man. Strategic panic. Makes you feel clever while terrified."

Alex pressed a hand to his forehead. "Strategic panic... yes. That's the term. We're being smart. Totally."

Nora peeked again. "Guys... seriously. If we survive this, I'm never complaining about walking up stairs again."

Valerie laughed, tightening her grip. "You'll be fine. Totally fine. Maybe slightly traumatized, but fine."

The cars crested the peak. A hush fell for a moment, hearts hammering in synchrony with the click-click-click.

Time seemed to stretch. Every faint squeak of the harness, every whisper of wind against metal, sounded amplified. Zayn's stomach lurched; he swallowed hard and tried to force a grin. "Okay... okay... maybe we're fine. Totally fine."

Alex's hands trembled slightly as he gripped the bar. "Focus... focus... we are not dying. This is just... a very steep, slightly aggressive, adrenaline-fueled gravity experiment."

Natalia's nails dug into the safety bar. "I... I think I forgot how to breathe," she whispered, jaw tight.

Nora's breath hitched, misting the metal in front of her. "Why did I agree to this?!" she muttered, half in panic, half in thrill.

Valerie's fingers clenched the edges of her seat. "If we all survive, I'm taking the first cotton candy I see," she said, trying to sound casual but failing to hide the tension in her voice.

Shawn leaned forward, chest pounding, grin stretched tight across his face. "Alright, team, this is the big one. Here comes the– " He paused dramatically, teeth clenched, eyes wide. "Moment of truth."

The track teetered on the edge. A single, slow click resonated as the car paused fractionally longer than physics seemed to allow. The world below was a quilt of glowing lights, spinning rides, and tiny moving shapes, beautiful and terrifying all at once.

Zayn's stomach did a somersault. "I hate this. I hate it. I– I love it."

Alex's jacket flapped violently in the sudden breeze. "I can feel gravity plotting against us. It's… it's personal."

Nora squeaked, gripping Val's arm. "It's… happening…"

A beat. Another click. The world seemed to hold its breath. The lights blurred slightly as adrenaline focused their vision, hearts hammering like drumbeats in a silent room.

Then, the first drop hit.

The coaster plunged, twisting and turning with fluid, terrifying grace. From above, the cars darted along the gleaming tracks, tiny bundles of motion against the blur of neon lights. The crowd below looked like scattered confetti, unaware of the chaos above. The carnival glowed in a riot of colors: spinning swings, flickering booths, and strings of lights twining through the air, all dwarfed by the towering coaster.

In the front car, Shawn leaned back, arms gripping the bar, grin impossibly wide, hair whipping in the wind. Zayn's knuckles were white, head thrown back in a mix of terror and exhilaration, while in the car behind them Alex's jacket flapped and hood caught the breeze, every twist and dip reflected in his wide-eyed panic, matched with Natalia's expression of amusement.

Behind them, the two girls clutched the restraints, faces pressed close together. Nora's camera dangled uselessly in her lap, forgotten for the moment, while Valerie's laughter was half-choked by wind. Natalia's eyes were wide, sparkling in the carnival glow, mouth opening and closing in stunned delight. Every scream, every laugh, every shouted warning to each other carried across the cars like a chorus of reckless joy.

The coaster spiraled, looping over the carousel, dipping close to the ground, racing past the ring toss and cotton candy stands. Tiny figures darted between stalls below, and the smell of sugar and popcorn reached upward, mingling with the adrenaline-thick air. The ride arced high again, silhouetting the group against the twilight sky, the Ferris wheel twinkling like a distant star.

From above, the motion was chaotic yet graceful, each dip and curve a heartbeat, each spin a pulse of life. The group's shrieks, laughter, and gasps were scattered across the cars, a tangled symphony of friends suspended in motion, alive in the neon chaos below.

When it finally slowed, the group tumbled off, breathless and laughing. "Again!" shouted Shawn, shaking out his arms. "We survived. We must celebrate with… everything else!"

Nora pulled out her digital camera, crouching slightly to snap group shots in their gondola. "Okay, everyone, look natural, or at least like chaos-ready teens," she said. Val nudged Natalia forward, Alex adjusted his jacket dramatically, Shawn made a ridiculous flex, and Zayn threw up a peace sign with exaggerated flair.

"Angle it from above a bit," Alex instructed, squinting at the screen. "Make the lights pop. Background chaos is essential."

"Stop bossing us around!" Shawn muttered, but leaned in anyway, arm brushing Zayn's shoulder, earning a playful shove.

Click. Another photo. *Click*. More laughter. Nora rotated the camera for a wider shot, catching everyone mid-smile, mid-laugh, arms tangled or pointing, cotton candy in hand.

Descending again, the group tumbled toward the next ride, candy-sticky and radiant with excitement. Neon lights reflected in their eyes, laughter echoing across the carnival. Every glance, every nudge, every inside joke threaded the evening into a living memory, cinematic in detail, infinite in small moments.

They chased more rides, played mini-games, exchanged playful insults, and paused for tiny interactions with children: cheering them on, showing silly tricks, and joking about winning prizes. By the end of the night, the carnival had become a universe entirely their own, a chaotic, glowing bubble where they could breathe, laugh, and exist freely, tethered only to each other.

Their night blazed brightly, a rare cluster of friends alive, unruly, and entirely in the moment.

And for now, that was all that mattered.

Chapter 56

The neon glow of the carnival had softened as the night deepened, lights blinking lazily across rides and booths. The group drifted toward the Ferris wheel, their steps slower now, bodies tired but still buzzing from the roller coaster and the chaotic energy of the midway.

"It's been three hours already? Woah. Final ride?" Shawn asked, stretching his arms, a grin tugging at his lips. "I vote yes. Wind down with some height, some perspective, and maybe less screaming."

"Agreed," Zayn said, rubbing his wrists where the coaster harness had left impressions. "Strategic calm. Time passed by so fast, we should end off with something calm."

Alex adjusted his jacket, smudges of cotton candy still faintly visible. "Perspective is essential. And Ferris wheel height is perfect for observation. You'll thank me later."

The group walked back to the Ferris Wheel and settled into a gondola when their turn came, the soft sway of the Ferris wheel immediately more soothing than the adrenaline spikes of the roller coaster.

The lights of the carnival stretched below them like a miniature city, rides spinning lazily, the glowing booths casting pools of color, tiny figures wandering in the warm haze of sugar and laughter.

Nora pulled her digital camera from her bag, smiling as she set it up. "One last set of photos. Something calmer... something to remember this night without nearly breaking our hearts."

Valerie leaned back, hair catching the faint breeze. "I'll take calm over terrified any day. This is nice."

Natalia rested her head against the gondola wall, candy sugar still on her fingers. "It's... perfect. The lights, the sounds, the chaos that's finally soft now. I could stay here forever."

Shawn elbowed Zayn playfully. "Even you're quiet. That's how you know it's good."

The wheel crested slowly, giving them a wide view of the city beyond the carnival. Streetlights stretched in neat rows, car headlights blinked like fireflies, and the river shimmered faintly in the distance.

For a moment, no one spoke, just the soft hum of the wheel and the faint echo of distant laughter.

As the Ferris wheel crested its peak, the gondola swayed gently, the city and carnival below shrinking into a kaleidoscope of lights. Nora angled her digital camera carefully, pressing it against the inner edge of the gondola window, framing everyone just right.

"Timer's on," she said softly, her fingers tapping a few buttons. "Alright... chaos-ready teens, hold still-ish."

The group scrambled into positions, playful nudges and exaggerated poses, Shawn grinning dramatically, Zayn giving a peace sign with flair, Alex adjusting his jacket like a strategist, Natalia spinning slightly so her candy-glossed hair caught the glow of the lights, Val rolling her eyes and showing her upside-down smile.

Click. The camera flashed once, then another soft chime announced the capture. "Boom," Nora whispered with a grin, grabbing the camera.

She pulled up the photo immediately, and they all leaned in. The frozen moment reflected the night perfectly: laughter caught mid-gasp, arms tangled, hair blown by the breeze, neon lights spilling over their faces.

"Wow," Natalia breathed. "We actually look... like a group of friends who survived chaos."

Alex squinted at the screen, tapping the image. "Details... perfect. Lighting, expressions... this will haunt us in the best way."

Zayn nudged Shawn lightly. "Not bad for a collection of panic and sugar."

Nora pressed a button to escape the photo, and the image disappeared, leaving only the soft hum of the Ferris wheel and the distant glow of carnival lights.

The group sank back into their seats, shoulders brushing, hearts still racing from the height. A quiet contentment settled over them. Natalia tucked her candy into her lap, smiling faintly. "It's nice... just being here, all of us."

Valerie nodded, leaning her head back against the gondola wall. "Yeah. No games, no rides, no chaos, just this."

Shawn let out a slow breath, grinning faintly. "Even I have to admit... this is good."

"Okay," Alex said. "We've stored enough memories, captured enough chaos. Time for sustenance."

Nora laughed, slinging the camera over her shoulder. "Agreed. I vote something greasy, cheesy, and glorious. No one's arguing."

Valerie grinned. "Dinner plans then. Let's make this night officially perfect."

Shawn stretched, smirking. "Post-carnival chaos officially closed. Let's refuel."

Zayn slung an arm over Alex's shoulder. "Strategic consumption of food. Step one in memory consolidation."

The gondola crested its final arc, the wheel slowing to a gentle stop. They stepped off together, sticky and tired, hair mussed by the wind, sugar dust clinging to sleeves and cheeks. Radiant and laughing, they moved toward the neon-lit streets, ready to trade rides for fries, laughter for soda, and chaos for calm conversation.

The carnival lights blinked and twinkled behind them, a fading constellation of chaos and color, and the sounds of rides and laughter felt both distant and intimate, echoing in their ears long after the immediate frenzy had ended.

They moved together through the now-quieter paths, feet crunching over scattered paper wrappers and stray popcorn. The neon glow of signs reflected faintly on wet asphalt patches, while a cool night breeze carried the lingering sweetness of fried dough and spun sugar.

Children's distant laughter faded into the background, replaced by the soft hum of streetlights and the occasional murmur of late-night traffic. Each step was slower now, measured, a gentle comedown from the whirlwind of the evening.

Natalia adjusted her hair, shivering slightly as the wind teased her hair.

Zayn nudged Alex lightly. "We survived," he said with a grin.

"Barely. And I'm claiming first dibs on dessert later."

Shawn elbowed him, smirking. "Step one: survive rides. Step two: survive food decisions. This is chaos, too, man."

The group fell into an easy rhythm, walking shoulder to shoulder, laughter softening into quiet conversation, teasing one another about screams, prize wins, and silly selfies.

Nora fiddled with her camera strap, glancing back once at the carnival, capturing a final flicker of neon light in her mind before the glow began to fade into the night. Valerie hummed a little tune, matching the cadence of their steps, while Alex noted the way the city looked different now, calmer, softer, the chaos replaced by gentle outlines of streets and buildings.

Ahead, the warm glow of the small food place they had all agreed on came into view. Its windows spilled amber light across the sidewalk, promising greasy, cheesy comfort and a chance to talk through the night's adventures. The scent of fried food mingled faintly with the cool air, a quiet contrast to the sugar-laden chaos they were leaving behind.

The carnival receded fully now, lights and screams blending into memory. But the group walked on together, a small cluster of friends tethered by laughter, adrenaline, and shared chaos, ready to trade rides for fries, stories for soda, and spinning lights for the cozy warmth of a booth waiting just ahead.

The night had stretched long, but it felt infinite in its way, one perfect, unruly, unforgettable evening.

The group walked slowly down the emptying carnival paths, the bright lights fading behind them. The air had cooled, carrying the faint tang of popcorn oil and spun sugar that lingered like a ghost of the night's chaos. Puddles from the earlier sprinkle reflected the neon signs, catching flashes of color as the occasional breeze rippled across them. The quiet made each footstep feel deliberate, measured, a contrast to the chaotic clicks and screams of earlier rides.

"Look at those footprints," Natalia said, kneeling slightly to point at the wet pavement. "All our little paths, like… evidence of the chaos we caused."

Valerie chuckled, brushing a strand of hair from her face. "Evidence, huh? I'd say proof of survival."

Shawn kicked a stray paper wrapper ahead of him. "Proof of absolute chaos, if you ask me." He paused, looking back at the dimly glowing Ferris wheel in the distance. "You know... it's wild. Every ride, every laugh, every shriek– it's all fading already. Feels like we just blinked and it's history."

Alex glanced at the reflections in the puddles, catching his own expression, tired but grinning. "History... or memory storage," he said with a smirk. "Either way, we archive moments better than most people get in a lifetime."

Zayn nudged him. "Strategic thinking, man. Even while walking away. Classic Alex."

They slowed near the edge of the carnival, where the neon lights grew sparse and the shadows stretched long across empty booths and closed stands. The sounds of rides had dwindled to faint mechanical whirs and the occasional distant laughter of stragglers leaving. A carnival tune, somewhere far off, played in soft loops, warped and echoing, almost haunting.

Nora adjusted the strap of her camera, glancing back at the glowing horizon of the midway. "It's weird... it's like the night condensed everything: adrenaline, sugar, chaos, into this... tiny capsule of time. And now we're just walking away, carrying it with us."

Valerie reached over and gave her shoulder a quick squeeze. "We've got it all. In our heads, in photos, in... well, all these small stupid inside jokes we'll never let go of."

Natalia tilted her head back, taking a deep breath. "I want to remember this smell," she said softly. "Caramel, fried dough, popcorn, a little rain... it's so small, but it's perfect."

278

Shawn grinned and made a dramatic show of sniffing the air. "I can smell sugar dust, mild panic, and victory. That's a solid scent profile."

Zayn laughed quietly. "And yet somehow we're still hungry. Logical contradiction."

Alex glanced down the street, where the warm amber glow of the diner waited. "Destination visible. Step one: Continue walking. Step two: Strategic consumption. Step Three: Optimize dessert order."

The group moved in loose formation, shoulders brushing, hands occasionally bumping. The night felt slow now, almost suspended, a gentle drift from chaos to calm. Faint echoes of carnival games lingered in the distance, the click of a dropped token, the laughter of children who had stayed too long, but it all seemed softened, distant, like watching a memory through frosted glass.

As they approached the diner, the neon signs came into full glow, warm and inviting. The smell of frying potatoes and cheese hit them, rich and comforting. Their steps quickened slightly, anticipation replacing the gentle calm of the walk.

Nora paused to look back one final time. The carnival had shrunk into a cluster of flickering lights, distant and dreamlike. She smiled faintly. "Goodbye... until next year?"

Valerie linked arms with her. "Until next adventure, wherever it is."

The group stepped through the diner doors together, the warmth washing over them like a soft, familiar blanket. The chatter of patrons, clinking of silverware, and the smell of comfort food grounded them. The night had been loud, dizzying, and chaotic, but now it settled into something quiet and perfect.

Shawn slid into the booth first with a flourish. "I declare the evening officially complete. Begin feasting."

They laughed, the last remnants of carnival chaos fading completely, leaving only warmth, friendship, and the infinite potential of long, small moments.

Chapter 57

The small-town diner was cozy; the booth hugged them close, a safe little bubble away from the night's chaos. The boys were on one side, and the girls were across them, sharing the same table.

A waitress introduced herself and handed out menus to be passed around. Alex scanned his like a general assessing enemy territory. "I'll take the ultimate grilled cheese. Extra gooey. Cheese Factor: Maximum."

Natalia smirked, already pointing to her own order. "Same. And throw in the mac-and-cheese. I'm fully committing to cheese tonight."

Shawn leaned back, grinning at Zayn. "I'll go chicken sandwich. Keep it classic. I like my meat uncomplicated."

Zayn nodded. "Solid choice. I'll match. Simplicity, efficiency, victory."

Valerie rolled her eyes at them. "Uncomplicated? I'll have the strawberry smoothie and the avocado toast. And a side of… well, whatever looks cute and tastes good."

Nora grinned. "I'll do the same. Girl-power brunch vibes at night."

The waitress jotted it down, smiling at the group's animated chatter. "Got it. Drinks?"

Alex perked up. "Milkshake. Chocolate. Thick. Strategic nutrition."

Natalia raised an eyebrow. "Alex... is everything a strategy with you?"

"Always," he said, perfectly serious.

Shawn groaned. "I'll do root beer. Zayn?"

"Root beer too. Synchronization matters."

Valerie smirked. "Strawberry smoothie."

Nora smiled at the waitress. "Pink lemonade."

The waitress closed her little notebook and confirmed the order, "perfect, I'll have those right out for y'all!"

The table erupted in light banter again.

"Grilled cheese," Natalia said, "is basically adult comfort food. If anyone tries to argue..." She raised a finger, mock-serious.

"Cheese is universal," Alex finished for her. "The world can take notes."

Shawn picked up a fry, waving it like a sword. "Chicken sandwiches. Superior. Battle-tested. Survival-approved."

Zayn mimed saluting. "Acknowledged, Colonel Fry."

Valerie rolled her eyes. "You two are ridiculous. Battle sandwiches? Really? That sounds like something in a video game."

Nora laughed, holding up her camera. "Time to document the nonsense.

Instagram, beware! Peak chaos dump."

Alex groaned. "Do not publicly shame us."

Natalia reached over and snagged a fry from Shawn's complimentary fry basket. "We're officially in the stealing phase of dinner."

Shawn gasped dramatically. "Traitors! But fine... just don't touch the chicken. That's sacred."

The group laughed, passing fries and swapping bites, teasing each other as the first plates arrived. Cheese pulled with satisfying gooeyness, chicken sandwiches looked perfectly fried, and Valerie and Nora's plates were colorful and picture-ready.

Then, every phone buzzed at once. Heads snapped up, eyes meeting across the table in confused silence.

Shawn was the first to break it. "Uh, did anyone else just get a message from someone unknown?"

Valerie's eyes widened. "Wait yeah. Mine's from an unknown number too."

Alex quickly checked his phone. "Mine as well. Okay, that's not normal."

Natalia put down her fork, frowning. "So all of us got the same kind of message?"

Nora's voice was small. "Yeah, mine too. What the hell is this?"

Zayn leaned back, staring at his phone. "That's six out of six. Every single one of us got it, and at the same time."

A heavy silence settled over the table as they all processed it. Then, one by one, they read the messages aloud, each revealing their letter: Shawn cleared his throat.

"*'The fist that breaks first answers last when strong men fall.' R.* That's mine."

Valerie's voice trembled slightly.

"*'The quiet gaze that keeps your secrets finds its final pall.' I.* Someone is sending us something."

Alex squinted at his screen. "*'The mind that cracks the system will not stop the crawl.' P.* This can't be a coincidence."

283

Natalia hesitated. *"The bright that draws a crowd will learn the cost of standing tall, then fall.'* M. It's... some kind of code?"

Nora's hands shook as she read hers. *"The gentle smile that trusts the dark will wake to silence, then fall.'* D. It's definitely a code."

Zayn finally spoke, voice tight. *"The keeper of the pack will find his pack becomes his thrall.'* E."

Alex spoke up, so if we unscramble those letters, it spells out *primed*, which basically means to stay ready for something.

The word hung in the air, heavy and deliberate.

The word hovered in their minds. Each of them felt it differently.

Shawn stared at the table, fingers tracing invisible patterns on the wood. The line about breaking first and answering last kept echoing in his head. He could almost hear it as a warning whispered from somewhere far away, directed at him and no one else.

Valerie pressed her palms together, thinking about the quiet gaze, the secrets, the final pall. What could someone know about them that they didn't know themselves? The thought made her shiver, and yet there was a strange clarity in it, a sense that understanding was only just beginning.

Alex leaned back, phone still warm in his hand. The crawl of the mind that cracks systems, the cost of standing tall, the pack becoming thrall. It was all a puzzle, a test, a map drawn in lines of poetry and letters. He felt the familiar thrill of a challenge, sharp and dangerous, but underneath it was a shadow he could not ignore.

Natalia's gaze drifted across the table, at the friends she had trusted without question. The bright that draws a crowd, the falling, the silence. In that reflection, she understood that being ready was more than just staying alert. It was about who they were together, how they would move when everything shifted.

Nora sat very still, the gentle smile trusting the dark. She thought about falling into silence, about the quiet and the dark, about what it meant to be ready. To be primed. To be awake when the rest of the world was still asleep.

Zayn's jaw tightened. The pack, the thrall, the warnings, they were not words on a screen. They were instructions, a challenge, and a promise all at once.

PRIMED. The letters formed a word, yes, but the meaning stretched far beyond that. It was a state, a readiness that demanded everything from them and left nothing behind.

The six of them looked at each other. Each of them turned the lines, the letters, the poems over and over in their mind, trying to catch every nuance, to feel the weight of what had been sent to them.

They knew that there was more behind what they uncovered, but the thought of what it could be kept them silent.

And in that silence, they realized that no matter how hard it gets from here, they have each other.

And that was enough.

www.ingramcontent.com/pod-product-compliance
Lightning Source LLC
Chambersburg PA
CBHW020305200626
46814CB00006BA/2097